Sorrows Road

A NOVEL

Ray Stefanelli

Stefanelli & Black Publishing

Order additional copies online at
www.amazon.com

Copyright © 2009 by Raymond D. Stefanelli.

All rights reserved.
No part of this publication may be used or reproduced in any manner whatsoever without the author's written permission, except in the case of brief quotations embodied in critical articles or reviews.

This book is a work of fiction. Names, characters, places, and incidents are used fictitiously or are products of the author's imagination. Any resemblance to actual events, places or persons is entirely coincidental.

ISBN-13: 978-1-4392-2915-6
ISBN-10: 1-4392-2915-5
Library of Congress Control Number: 2009901409

Designed by Vicki Black
Inset cover photo provided by iStock

Sorrows Road

ONE – Summer 1953

Roy hears the screen door slam at Uncle Jack's house fifty yards away and he sees Dorothea standing outside. He kneels down and lowers his head to scan the dirt.

Living so close, he sees Dorothea often and sometimes they talk. But he is usually cautious around girls. He has learned that you can never know exactly how they think about things. At times even his sister and mother are hard to figure out.

Bracing himself with his left arm, Roy lightly brushes his right hand across the dirt with a deliberate motion—first one way then another. The earthy smell is familiar and satisfying. He is kneeling on the west side of the long, wooden building where the words "Grocery & Meat Market" are painted.

Roy brushes his hands together and then up and down on the front of his shirt. The shirt is a summer pullover—blue with white and red stripes. It is mid-morning and until Dorothea came outside, there was no one around. Most people are at work or in their homes, going about their usual business. It is quiet and the air is still.

Rising up, Roy digs into his pocket, pulls out a small pocketknife and opens it . . . short blade straight out, long blade at a 90-degree angle. Out of the side of his eye, he sees Dorothea walking in his direction, her simple feed sack dress waving back and forth across the front of her body. He squats down and places his right knee on the ground. Holding the knife between his thumb and index finger, he jerks his hand upward to practice mumblety-peg flips. Because early morning rain softened the ground, the knife blades stick easily.

Dorothea comes to where Roy is flipping the knife. Her confident, cheerful smile catches Roy's attention. She watches him quietly with her arms hanging in front and her hands clasped together.

"Whatcha doin?" she asks in a perky voice. Her dress has wide shoulder straps and a pattern of tiny red, white and yellow flowers.

Roy looks up at her. She looks clean-washed, like she has just taken a bath. Her teeth are even and white.

"Practicing mumbly-peg," he drawls. He learned to play yesterday at Billy McAllen's house with Billy and Tommy Ritchie. He had a pocketknife, but he never knew there was a game like this. He had done well for a beginner, but it's the type of game you want to practice and get better. The loser has to use his teeth to dig out a small wooden peg driven into the dirt by the winner.

"Wanna go with me?" asks the quick, smiling voice. Her skin is creamy white in the mid-morning light, her shoulder-length hair, thick and dark.

Roy feels clumsy and flushes at the question. He stands up, wipes the dirt off the knife blades between his thumb and forefinger, and folds each blade into the handle. He is about the same height as Dorothea. He looks into her brown eyes.

"Where ya goin?" Immediately, his pulse quickens. He feels slightly awkward. He stands rigid in an attempt to conceal his uneasiness.

She turns her head slowly to see if anyone is nearby. Then cupping her hand to the side of her mouth she whispers, "I'll show you my pretty."

She smiles, turns and walks away slowly. Glancing sideways, she watches to see that he will follow. Roy hesitates briefly and then falls into step. Thoughts race through his mind. He's never heard anyone say "my pretty" before. He thinks he knows what she means. He steps more quickly—the possibilities energize him.

They walk alongside the store where light and dark ripples of passing clouds reflect on the white boards. Toward the front of the building, brightly colored signs—"Nehi," "Apple Chewing Tobacco," "Chesterfields"—are nailed high up the wall. Leaving the softer dirt near the store, they walk out to the hard-packed side road. The color of buttered sweet potatoes, the clay road runs from the store out past Dorothea's house and into the pinewoods. Rarely is a car seen on the road, since only two or three of the colored people who live beyond the tall pines have cars.

Dorothea is barefooted. Each foot touches the ground on the side and then the rest of the foot twists and touches the ground, a girlish manner of walking—very deliberate, pliable and delicate. Roy thinks she may be the same age as him or a year older. Maybe two years older, he isn't sure. He never sees her at school; doesn't know if she even goes to school.

Dorothea's father, Uncle Jack, seems smart enough, seeing how he owns so much. But then he isn't really her father. Roy overheard his mother talk about it and she said Eula Mae already had Dorothea when she married Uncle Jack. Doesn't matter though, everyone thinks of her as Uncle Jack's daughter. In fact, with her dark hair and soft features, she looks more like him than her mother.

It wouldn't surprise him if she doesn't go to school. He knows there are children who don't. He can tell by the way some adults talk that they probably didn't go to school for very long either. Dorothea's mother Eula Mae is one. Roy thinks she's very loud and rough. She says things that he has never heard in school.

Eula Mae wears loose-fitting, feed sack dresses and her brown hair is always pulled back into a ponytail. She's usually barefooted or she wears shoes with the backs crushed flat under her heels. They flap at the bottom of her feet as she walks. She dips snuff too.

Uncle Jack, who is the uncle of Roy's mother, is friendlier. With his potbelly and talkative nature, he is always pleasant and cheerful. He owns the grocery store and several other buildings at this end of town. He got so busy, he asked Roy's parents to move to Cuttsville, back in 1946, to lease the store.

"Come on," Dorothea says, jerking her head to the side. Her lips tilt up in a playful smile. Roy has intentionally lagged back a little. "We've got to cross over the road," she says. She waits for him to get closer.

Reaching the pavement, Dorothea and Roy look both ways, up and down the gray road. The asphalt road that runs in front of the store goes south to Bronson Lake and north to Paradise Lake. There isn't much traffic any more, now that there's a new highway on the other side of town that also goes to Bronson Lake. They start across. It's a quiet morning. No cars and no one out and about that they can see.

Roy is glad Dorothea is in a happier mood today. Last week he watched her from a tree in his backyard and she didn't seem happy at all. She was in back of her house, lifting clothes out of the washer, running them through the ringer and dropping them in a laundry basket. Her younger brother and sister ran after each other, grabbing onto her dress and squealing loudly. She shouted at them, "Rosie behave. Johnny quit." Of course they paid no attention.

Roy was sitting on his imaginary horse—a lower limb jutting out from the huge camphor tree. His legs dangled on either side and a length of rope was tied around the limb for reins. It was hard for him to pretend to be a tough, rambling cowboy out seeking adventure while he could see Dorothea shackled to the laundry and putting up with her brother and sister misbehaving. Other times, though, he had seen her skipping along the street swinging her arms—probably imagining herself in another place doing something more interesting than babysitting or washing clothes.

Dorothea takes large, bouncy steps to cross the warm pavement quickly. Roy moves quickly as well.

"Where we going?" Roy asks, not exactly sure what Dorothea has planned.

"Over to this other house. I'll show you." Her soft smile and flirty glances are enticing. A little mysterious as well.

"It's kind of a secret place I know about." Her arms swing back and forth. Roy is careful not to bump into her.

Across the street a long, concrete-block building stands vacant. Interior walls divide the structure into three units.

Each unit has a rectangular opening for a door and a large square opening for a display window. But there are no doors and no windows, only a cool, black emptiness. The building is one of Uncle Jack's newer projects.

A new, concrete sidewalk lies flat and clean in front of the building. To the side, where Roy and Dorothea walk, the old sidewalk is broken and warped. Sprouts of grass grow through the seams and crevices. Dorothea leads the way. Roy is a half step behind. He focuses on the side of her face and the slender arc of her neck not hidden by hair.

Dogs bark in the distance. Their sounds come from different directions, sparse and dim in the morning air.

Behind the new building, the street is lined with two-story, wood framed houses. They have wide porches and touches of fancy woodwork. The nearest house is one Uncle Jack rents. It has peeling paint and gaps of exposed gray wood, as do some of the others on the street. Roy lives in the same type of house on the other side of the store.

Oak trees line the street like stalwart giants in the flat landscape. Their bushy limbs spread out in lofty canopies high above the street and houses.

"This way," Dorothea says softly. She veers to her left. The house sits more than two feet off the ground. Thick, brick pillars support its wood beams. A short, stout woman lives here. Most evenings she sits on the front porch with her arms folded across her apron. Her empty chair is the only thing on the porch.

The shaded yard is bare and tranquil. Grass grows sparsely in small patches. The air, heavy and damp in the morning, swells with the rising temperature.

In silence, Roy and Dorothea walk toward the rear of the house. Roy looks intently at the house. "Is anyone here," he says in a hushed voice. Dorothea shrugs her shoulders and continues walking.

A large dogwood tree dominates the small backyard. Thick clumps of leaves brush against the top of the house and sunlight streaks through the leaves to create tentative puddles of light on the ground. A robin hops away from the intruders and takes flight. Beyond the tree, weeds and brush flourish for some distance.

Dorothea slows her pace. Her bare feet lightly touch the warm earth. Roy follows alongside but not quite even with her. A dull sense of risk, even danger, lurks in the back of his mind. He looks in every direction.

Toward the back of the house, Dorothea squats down to go under the porch. She puts her hands flat on the dirt to brace herself. She waddles awkwardly on bent legs, moving under the porch edge. Roy does the same, lagging a few steps behind. He surveys the dim spaces under the house. His eyes move side to side over the ground. The soil is softer and dark.

Dorothea stops and glances back at him. Her calm and playful expression makes it easy for Roy to follow. Her eyes are reassuring. She moves farther under the house. Odors of moisture, old wood and fine dust mingle in the air.

Dorothea continues her crouched walk behind the back porch steps toward a large, concrete form that extends from the house to the ground. Roy moves slowly, careful not to hit the rough beams that run over their heads. The two of them move deeper into seclusion.

As she reaches the abutment, Dorothea turns and balances herself with her hands. She sits on the ground and leans back against the concrete form. She brushes her hands against each other and then on her dress. She smiles at Roy. Even in the semi-darkness her eyes are bright and unwavering.

Roy sits also. He crosses his feet and loops his arms around his bent knees.

"Come a little closer," she says softly.

Roy puts his hands on the ground and scoots forward. Their feet almost touch. He brushes his hands on his shorts. His hand feels the hardness of the knife in his pocket.

Dorothea pulls her knees up and reaches for the hem of her dress. She pulls her dress over her knees, against her waist. She's not wearing underpants. Her legs move farther apart and she looks down to see that her "pretty" shows.

Roy stares steadily. His mind floats, he is transfixed.

TWO – Summer 1955

In June, Roy turned 12, old enough to help in the store. His father deals with all of the sales people and deliveries during the week and runs the store by himself most of the time. Of course Reuben is there to provide some help. Most days, people drift in and out, with hardly ever more than two customers at a time.

Friday afternoons and Saturdays are different. Roy's mother works the front end and cash register, while his father operates the meat department in the back part of the store. Friday and Saturday are when most people do their shopping. His mother also comes in at the end of each month when people get their government checks or monthly paychecks. Some people come in then to buy all their groceries for the next month, especially people who live in the country and make only one trip to the store each month. Everything is bought in sizeable quantities: a slab of bacon, a five- or ten-pound bag of flour, a bag of grits, a can of lard, a large bag of navy or pinto beans, five pounds of sugar, a five-pound can of coffee and a few other staples in large portions. Some raise their own chickens for eggs and meat, and some also have gardens for vegetables.

Roy stocks the shelves, bags or boxes up groceries and carries them out for people who need some assistance. Reuben also works on Saturdays, as well as a few hours each day of the week. He usually does the same jobs as Roy, unless Roy's father, "Mista Hank," has Reuben doing something else. Since they are close in age, Reuben being two or three years older, they hang around together when business is slow.

"Roy," his father calls as he walks by, "watermelons are coming today. So you and Reuben need to help unload them. While you're at it," he lowers his head to look straight at Roy, "don't forget to check them. Make sure that none are cracked or have holes in them."

"Okay," Roy answers. It's a job he doesn't mind at all.

A short time later, Roy hears the screeching of truck brakes out front, but he can't see if it's the watermelon truck. He continues stacking cans of black-eyed peas on the shelf. He folds the flaps inside the empty box and carries it into the storeroom. When he returns, the watermelon man is talking with his father. Reuben comes from the back room. Together Roy and Reuben walk toward the front door.

Roy's sister Melissa is also at the store on Saturdays. She is too young to be much help, but since no one is home she spends the day with the rest of the family at the store. She stands behind the counter with her mother as the boys walk by.

"Don't hurt yourself," Melissa says, grinning and opening her eyes wide to mock Roy.

He and Reuben push through the double screen doors and walk down the steps. As they descend, Dorothea walks toward them. She smiles broadly and says, "Hi, Roy." Her moist lips and teeth make her smile gleam.

Roy is delighted that he is the focus of such special attention. He stumbles on the bottom step and then smiles, pretending that the misstep was intentional and meant to make her laugh—which she does. Pleased with his humorous performance, Roy walks jauntily to the rear of the watermelon truck while Dorothea goes into the store.

"You boys ready to catch some melons?" The watermelon man, wearing a chambray shirt and faded overalls, lumbers down the steps behind them. He is stout. With each step he takes his body rocks from side to side.

"I reckon," Roy says, rubbing his hands together.

The man reaches for the tailgate and lifts his foot onto an angle iron step that extends down from the truck frame. Pulling himself up, he pushes and jerks on the right half of the tailgate until it comes free. His arms are stout, as well.

"You boys wanna take this?" He leans to the side, holding on with one hand.

Roy steps up, reaches for one end of the tailgate. Reuben moves beside the man's leg. Holding the side with one hand, the man lowers his end to Reuben.

With some effort the watermelon man pulls himself onto the truck bed. Roy and Reuben lean the tailgate against the side of the truck. Roy moves behind the truck, ready to carry the watermelons. In a sidelong glance, he notices Dorothea walking away from the store.

"Here yeh go." Breathing heavy from the bending, the man hands down the first watermelon, carefully setting it in Roy's outstretched hands. Then he picks up another one for Reuben. They set the melons on the shaded, concrete floor. The store's roof extends beyond the front of the building by ten feet. Four evenly spaced posts hold up the overhang. Under here the watermelons are shaded from the sun. People going in and out of the store see them lined up and ordinarily they sell quickly.

Roy and Reuben move back and forth, back and forth, their feet shuffling mechanically between the truck and the end of the porch. Their arms bent and taut, their shoulders pulled back against the weight, hoping anyone passing by sees them hard at work. Roy keeps an even pace. Since Reuben limps, he cannot move as quickly. Within fifteen minutes they have all the warm melons laid out. Sweat glistens on Reuben's dark face.

"Reuben." Roy stands by the gate ready to hand it up. Reuben picks up the other end. The watermelon man is wiping his forehead with a large red handkerchief. He stuffs it in his back pocket. Reaching down, he pulls the tailgate up into the now-empty truck bed and lays it flat. Turning and holding the other half of the tailgate, he stretches his leg down until his foot finds the bumper. Once down, he pulls his handkerchief out again and goes inside to be paid.

Roy looks at the collection of striped, oblong melons. "Let's separate these into different sizes so I can tell how to price them." In a while his father will come out and check them. He'll make sure he got what he paid for and that Roy priced them correctly.

Roy wipes sweat off his face and arms with a hand towel he brought out. "Take this inside," Roy calls to his sister who is watching from the steps. He throws the towel to her. "Ooooow!" She scrunches her nose. She stretches her arm outward, the damp towel dangling from between her thumb and finger. She opens the screen door and steps inside, still holding the limp towel as far away as she can. Roy grins.

"What about taking this one inside to the meat cooler to get it cold?" Roy hands a medium-sized melon to Reuben. The large, walk-in cooler where meat is hung stays near freezing. It won't take long for the melon to get cold. "Just ask Dad if it's okay if we eat one before it gets too busy."

Reuben is supposed to work while he's being paid to be at the store, but Roy knows his father won't mind them eating watermelon while business is slow. After lunch and into the afternoon they will be busier. Roy continues marking prices on the melons.

His dad has almost always had a colored boy working at the store. Reuben has been working nearly a year. This summer, with Roy helping, Reuben doesn't have as much to do. With Reuben's crippled foot, his dad is not very strict about how hard he works. He does come in handy for bringing things out of the warehouse or if someone needs gas or kerosene. Roy and his father stay behind the counters so they can wait on customers.

When there is sugar cane at the store, Roy and Reuben sometimes sit out front and chew on a stalk of cane. They each cut off a joint and then strip the hard covering to chew the pulp and suck in the sweet juice. They don't talk much, mostly just kid each other about things that happen at the store or push on one another to show how strong they are.

Reuben comes back outside, moving down the steps cautiously, one at a time.

"You can stack some of those small ones up in the back," Roy points and wiggles his finger to indicate where the melons should go. He has finished marking prices on the watermelons and thinks it's best to place them in the smallest amount of space possible.

"Mercy be," Reuben says, taking a step back, "sho is a mess uh watermelons."

"They look like good ones too," Roy says. He bends down and thumps his index finger against one to show his skill in interpreting the sound of ripeness.

Reuben moves another watermelon and then looks at Roy.

"Here," Roy says, picking up a melon, "we need to move these in front to the back." He carries it close to the wall and stacks it on top of some other melons. "They stick out too far, somebody'll be tripping over em." Roy picks up another melon and Reuben follows his lead.

A long bench runs part way along the wall, from the steps to where the watermelons are stacked. Roy and Reuben sit on the bench, resting and watching cars and trucks go by.

Later, after Roy's father has looked over the display, Roy brings the watermelon out from the cooler. It is cold to the touch and wet on the surface. Reuben is sitting at the end of the bench, near the melons. Roy also brings a sheet of the heavy butcher paper that his father uses to wrap meat. Laying it on the floor, Roy settles the melon on the paper and sits down beside Reuben. He bends over, and with the large knife his father allows him to use, he presses down with both hands to cut through the center of the melon.

"Um, um, get dat knife a cuttin." Reuben rubs his hands together, watching as the melon breaks open. A hollow popping sound indicates its ripeness. Inside, the watermelon glistens a luscious tint of red. The center is dotted with rows of shiny black seeds, with fewer small white ones in the middle. Roy slices off a piece, hands the knife to Reuben. They both eat eagerly, tasting the crisp pulp that bursts with juice. Leaning forward, the juice drips and seeds drop tat-a-tat-tat on the stiff, coral-colored paper.

Looking toward the gas pump, Roy sees Dorothea again on the side road. Not long ago she had a birthday and Roy's mother gave her some things like a comb and barrettes for her hair. She has her pleasant smile. She looks over at Roy and her smile grows wider as though she's ready to giggle out loud. Her arm lifts and she flips her hand backward, motioning to him.

Roy sets the melon rind down. He walks toward her, wiping his hands on his jeans. He likes the way she acts toward him; he feels they have a special bond. "What are you so happy about?" He can tell by the way she is standing with her hip cocked to one side, her wide smile and the glint in her eyes that she is excited about something.

"I'm buddin," she exclaims. She puts her face closer to ensnare Roy's full attention. "I'm buddin," she repeats.

Roy is uncertain how he should reply. He isn't even sure he knows what she means. His mouth open, he hesitates and then says, "You're buddin?"

"I'm gettin breasts. Like a woman." She moves with subtle energy, finding it hard to contain her enthusiasm. Her cheeks are rounded, her lips stretched wide. Her eyes are glaringly open as though she has a new understanding, a revelation. She stands straight and tall. She pushes her chest outward and motions tentatively with her head.

She is, sure enough. Two small mounds rise against the knit shirt she is wearing. It is not enough that Roy would have noticed had she not mentioned it. But now that he looks, with her chest out like this, he can definitely tell that she is getting breasts, small as they are.

"I'm getting to be a woman!" She expels the words, breath hissing through her teeth. Roy breathes deeply, feeling his chest swell too. He never would have expected her to just come right out with an announcement like this. He stands idle, not knowing what to expect next.

"Id-din it great?" Her arms hang down to the side of her body, stiffly, with her fists clenched. Her feet are planted, but she moves her upper body with girlish excitement.

"Uh . . . yeah." His mouth still open, the jubilation is beyond his grasp. He is speechless, unsure how to react. Standing limp and unguarded, he smiles, consciously holding the smile. He is mildly curious, but uncertain about why Dorothea wants to be a woman or exactly what this means.

"I gotta go." She flushes with pride. Quickly she turns and heads toward the road, swings her head around with a broad, coquettish smile and says, "See ya!"

Roy is not able to appreciate the elation she is feeling. Her stride is that of a dancer all keyed up to perform, ready to dazzle the waiting audience. His eyes follow her as she heads across the road. Remembering the watermelon, he meanders back to the bench. He doesn't look at Reuben because he knows he has probably been watching.

"Dat yo girlfriend?" Watermelon in hand, Reuben pauses and looks at him.

Roy sits on the bench. Reuben takes another slurping bite of watermelon, his eyes fixed on Roy. "No. She ain't my girlfriend. You know who that is. It's Dorothea. She's Uncle Jack's daughter."

"I know dat." Reuben continues looking, eating, wiping juice from his bottom lip with his hand. "I think she like you."

Roy shifts his weight on the bench, trying hard not to be responsive to Reuben's taunting. He bends down, picks up the knife and begins slicing into the melon. Reuben doesn't say any more. He picks up the rinds at his feet, raises up and walks to the side of the store. A couple of flies are buzzing around, landing on the uncut melon.

"You done already?" Roy looks after him, his mouth half full.

"I eat some mo when I come back." He continues ahead, limping. One leg shorter. Roy watches. He doesn't know what happened, maybe polio. Reuben's body dips with each step on his left leg.

When Reuben returns, he sits down and begins cutting another piece of watermelon. Roy sees Dorothea crossing the street again. She walks to the side of the store. Her stride is a little showy, maybe self-conscious. Her head tilts to one side. She looks at him, a subtle, alluring smile. Then quickly she averts her eyes down and away, which strikes Roy as a hint of embarrassment. He is puzzled by her actions. One minute she is bold and lively, and then the next she seems shy and withdrawn. She continues along the side road, body erect, chest out, until she's out of view.

"Dere she go." Reuben grins, thinking he might get a response. He nudges Roy with his elbow. "You sho she ain't yo girlfriend?"

Roy doesn't say anything. Reuben breaks out laughing, "Ooh-ee, laudy, laudy," and then pats Roy on the shoulder lightly, uncertain about teasing him too much. Roy shakes his head as a sign he is ignoring the gibing.

Their conversations are usually short. If Reuben talks about anyone in particular it's his mother. And one time he had something to say about Preacher. Every time Preacher comes into the store he looks around for Reuben and asks, "How's Reuben doin?" Once when Reuben wasn't looking, Preacher came up to him and asked, "Reuben, how you doin?"

Surprised, Reuben said, "Doin jus fine, thank yeh Rev'en."

Later, Reuben told Roy if he sees Preacher coming he sneaks out of sight. "He toll my momma one time she ain't sposed to be tellin peoples bout de future. He say dat ain't right. But my momma she tell Preacher she got the holy spirit deep inside her, and she don't tell people nothin de Lord don't put in her mouth."

"What'd he mean about telling the future?" Roy asked.

"She tell people what gonna happen to em in deh future. She know things don't nobody else know bout."

Roy jerks his head with a look of skepticism.

"It's fo sho she do," Reuben emphasizes. "Peoples dey comes to ask her things and she study it. And she tell em what to do and what gonna happen."

Occasionally she comes into the store and Roy watches her. She dresses nicely and seems normal to him. If Roy's mother is there she talks to Reuben's mother about Reuben, telling her how helpful he is. Reuben's mother beams at this.

Reuben also said his mother believed she was going to have twelve sons. "She name me Reuben. Den she have another boy and he die right den. And den de next was born awready dead. After dat she say God tell her she ain't needin no mo chilren, Reuben all she need."

They sit on the bench, content with their fill of watermelon. A car pulls in front of the store, another pulls in at the side and parks. "Looks like we're gonna get busy," Roy says. He picks up the remnants of the watermelon, bundling the paper around the leftovers. Holding the package a distance in front to avoid spillage, he walks to the side of the store. He allows juice and some seeds to run off the edge of the paper and onto the grass. Reuben follows with a rind in hand. They walk toward the trash barrel near the back of the store.

THREE

A light chilling rain is falling as Roy leaves school. At noon he was able to see that it was becoming a damp and dreary November day. He walks to the end of the block looking for Melissa. He doesn't see her, so he continues toward home. Two blocks later he sees her and a friend a short distance ahead.

Roy decides to stop in the store for something to eat before going home. When he enters, his mother and father are standing close together talking quietly. They act surprised to see him. "Where's Melissa?" his mother asks.

"She went on to the house." He can tell by their stance that something unusual or secretive is taking place. "What's going on?"

They continue to look at him in silence for a few seconds, but it seems longer. "Uncle Jack died," his mother says. Her face is stern. His mother and father wait for the message to sink in.

It sounds scary. Dead? Uncle Jack is dead? Roy stares at his mother; bewildered, he can only wait for clarification.

"He went to Parksdale to pick up some equipment," his father says. He steps closer to Roy and places his hand on his shoulder. "On the way back he had a heart attack. Luckily he was able to pull off the road."

"Gosh," Roy says, "he wasn't even old." No one could have expected such a thing to happen. Uncle Jack was always so busy doing things and building things that it's hard to believe that things would be different now.

Two days later, the day of the visitation, Roy's family walks into the big white house behind the new and still-vacant building. Uncle Jack is laid out in a shiny casket in the front room. The house is now unoccupied, since the woman who was living here has moved away. Roy looks from a distance at the silent face with its closed eyes. His uncle is wearing a dark blue suit, lying flat in the casket with white satin lining all around the inside and a satin pillow with ruffled edging under his head. Hands lying together on his stomach like pieces of marble. His face, cold and hard, is powdered and much paler than normal. The cheeks tinted to look rosy. Roy has never seen a dead person before.

Roy listens to the people talking in muffled voices. Most are saying the same things: "Yeh just can't never tell." "He just worked hisself to death." "When your time comes, there ain't nothin you can do." Roy knows that people die, but it is something that he's not familiar with and something people rarely talk about. He doesn't want to try to comprehend it. The room is warm. He hopes he will not have to stay too long.

At the funeral the next day, Roy sees Dorothea at a distance. He rarely sees her anymore. Being in school every day, he doesn't make it to the store until Friday afternoons and on Saturdays, which are always busy.

Dorothea sits near the closed casket beside her younger brother and sister and her mother. Eula Mae's eyes are down, her hands clasped. Her appearance makes it difficult to tell her age, but she is probably not yet 30 years old. She had Dorothea when she was very young. After marrying Uncle Jack they had Rosemary and John. Eula Mae's face is plain and solemn; she doesn't wear makeup. In hard light, the lines and dark circles around her eyes made her look older.

"You have to feel sorry for her," Roy's mother says after the funeral, "three children and no husband to help her."

"Well, she's got enough money to do okay," his father says, "if she doesn't do something foolish and waste it."

In the spring, about six months after Uncle Jack's funeral, Eula Mae marries another man. His name is Ned. Tall and thin, his upper body is an inverted curve. His skin is dark and leathery from working outdoors in the sun. His hair, wavy brown with crests of blonde, is slicked back with oil.

"She sure didn't waste no time finding another man," Roy's father says. "Reckon she'll be living high on the hog with Jack's money." He packs tobacco in his pipe. "For a while, anyway."

These feelings subside after a few weeks. Roy's mother determines that with Eula Mae having three children to care for, maybe her having a husband isn't such a bad idea. They are friendly enough toward Ned when he comes into the store.

Ned has a relaxed, easy-going way about him. He tells Roy's father that he works for the state doing highway work. From time to time, Roy has seen men working out in desolate areas along highways, cutting grass or repairing roads. He can only imagine that it is hard, monotonous work.

When Ned is with Eula Mae he doesn't have much to say, she usually does most of the talking. Eula Mae has inherited all the buildings that Uncle Jack had, including the store, five or six houses and the new building across the street. This would seem to provide her some security, but at the same time, someone has to keep them rented and in good repair. Most of the houses are old.

Roy's father bought a newer house and the family moved just before Uncle Jack died. His father had been renting the house next to the store. The new house is about half a mile away in a more attractive neighborhood. It has a big yard with thick St. Augustine grass and two large pecan trees in back. On either side of the front door are two tall spruce trees and beyond those are hedges with the tops trimmed flat and even. The house also has a large screened porch in front, a nice place to sit in the evening.

The grocery business continues to be good. It gives the family more money than most regular jobs Roy's father could work at. In fact, it's not easy to find a good-paying job in a small town like Cuttsville. Farms surround the town right up to its very edges and most people depend on farming plus a job to get by. The people with businesses in town, like a furniture store or a drug store, generally live better than most other folks.

Roy's father had intended to talk with Uncle Jack about the store lease. Before he died, Jack said he might consider selling the store, but told Hank he could lease it as long as he wanted. Of course with him gone things might be different now. The lease expires at the end of the year, and with Christmas drawing near, Hank is beginning to get a little anxious about it.

One day when he is talking with Eula Mae, he asks her in a very direct manner, "Can we talk about the lease? I want to extend it and get something in writing."

"Well, Pa's uh helpin me with all them things, so I can't say nothin by myself. You want to come out to Pa's house on Sunday afternoon? Reckon we could talk about it then, see what we can figger out."

Hank is surprised by the answer, but doesn't give it much thought. By getting together this way, he believes they will at least get things settled.

Eula Mae's parents live a ways out of town, so on Sunday Roy asks if he can come along. He always likes riding out in the country. "You can come," his father tells him, "but you'll have to stay in the truck or come inside and stay quiet."

When his father turns off Route 40 onto the hard-packed dirt road, Roy notices the painted sign on a post reading Sorrows Road. "Dad," he says, "did you know this is called Sorrows Road?" He turns his head to look at the backside of the sign.

"I guess that's right. Funny, I knew a guy one time named Soro." He turns the wheel to miss a dip. "Dominic Soro . . . he was a pistol." His father is moving his head quickly, looking for the next turn.

"This girl at school was saying something about it." Roy looks at his father. "But when she walked away, I couldn't hear what she was saying."

His father doesn't reply.

Roy continues looking toward his father, but he isn't paying attention to him. He can tell he's thinking about other things. Maybe he's worried about the store.

His father turns right onto another dirt road that is so narrow it would be difficult for two cars to pass. Roy has never been out this way before. There are tall pine trees on both sides of the road, with thick brush growing between the trees. As they approach the Crawley's house he is surprised at how small it is. Its wood exterior is unpainted and weathered to a soft gray. The tin roof is also gray except in a couple of spots where it is scarred with rust.

The grocery truck pulls into the Crawley's yard and several brown chickens scatter, fluttering their wings. Roy notices a small boy sitting on the steps of another house about fifty yards away. He remembers that Eula Mae's younger brother D.W. lives near their parents. As they step from the truck, the chickens continue jumping and clucking, moving away in their neck-jerking retreat.

Two wooden steps lead up to the front door. Inside, the house is sparse. The front room looks as though it is used for cooking, eating and everything but sleeping. On one side is an open fireplace with two, smoldering black logs sitting atop a pile of ashes. Roy looks at the windows on either side of the fireplace, coated with a hazy residue, making it difficult to see through.

After a perfunctory greeting, Eula Mae, her father and Hank sit at the table near the center of the room. D.W. stands a few feet away, leaning against the wall, one foot propped up on a wooden chair. Roy looks at him from time to time, curious about his unkempt hair, the piece of straw hanging from the side of his mouth.

At Eula Mae's direction, Roy sits on a short stool close to where her mother sits in a rocking chair. Mrs. Crawley's hair is a muted white and combed straight back. She has the same hard features and wiry frame as Eula Mae, although her aged skin is loose and wrinkled. Roy is careful not to stare, but he thinks she does not have teeth. Her upper lip is sunken in with thin vertical lines and fine hairs. Her bottom lip bulges out over a pinch of snuff that is wedged against her gum. She smiled at Roy when he sat down, but she hasn't spoken since they came in.

His elbows on his knees, Roy looks around the room at nothing in particular. Mrs. Crawley raises her right hand to her mouth, making a "V" with her forefinger and middle finger. She throws her head forward, spitting, sending brown liquid flying into the fireplace ashes. Roy has never seen anyone do this inside a house before; he is amazed by her accuracy.

He tries to sneak glances in her direction in a way that she won't notice, so she won't be offended. He doesn't want to be conspicuous. He doesn't want to be a distraction. It's cold. Roy has no interest in the conversation at the table, but he notices his father's face is redder than usual, his body tense. They seem to be arguing or at least disagreeing. He hears Eula Mae repeat several times, "Me and Ned been thinkin about the store."

"Sure beats working fer someone else," Mr. Crawley says.

"Ain't that a fact," D.W. comments, but no one acknowledges him.

Roy's father is obviously upset, even Mrs. Crawley stops rocking and looks toward the table.

"When Jack and me talked about this . . ." His father stands up, pushing the chair back with his leg.

"Hank, you got to realize Jack ain't in this no more," Eula Mae interrupts. "It's mine to do as I see fit."

"You done mighty well with the store, Hank," Mr. Crawley says in an amiable way to calm the tension. "We's just askin for some time to think on it, that's all." D.W. pulls his foot off the chair and stands straight. Not knowing what to do with his bony hands he finally loops his thumbs onto the back pockets of his jeans.

"Well, I guess you'll do what you want," Roy's father says with some finality. His jaw tight and eyes narrowed, he turns his head, "Come on, Roy."

The ride back is somber. His father looks straight ahead, teeth clenched. Roy looks out the side window. Most houses along the dirt road are set far apart, separated by pine woods and open fields.

Once they reach the highway into Cuttsville, Roy decides to ask, "Didn't things go too well?" He's embarrassed that his voice is not bolder.

His father breathes deeply and pushes his lips together and out. Staring ahead his expression softens. "No. Didn't go like I thought it should."

"We gonna keep the store?"

"Don't know just yet." He wags his head side to side in disbelief. "We'll see, we'll see."

Roy looks at his father. Tries to read his facial expression. It's calm, reflective. He can tell he is thinking things over, trying to see ahead, see how things might turn out.

Back at home Roy's mother asks the same question as they walk into the kitchen. "How'd things go?" Roy passes through the kitchen and into the living room. Picks up the "Reader's Digest" as he sits down, but keeps his ears open. He hears his father's voice. "I think Eula Mae's got this damn fool notion she and Ned can run it."

"Oh . . . my goodness," she draws out her words, surprised by the news. Having known Eula Mae for some time, she shakes her head, "I don't see how they can expect to make a go of it."

He hears his father pace back and forth. "In addition to the time you have to put in, how the hell are they going to learn to order and price things? I don't know what they're thinking."

"And what if they start giving credit," his mother says, "because people are going to expect it. They may end up over their heads in no time."

Roy has seen the box his father has with watches, rings and necklaces. He has two or three pistols and a couple of shotguns; all things people have given to him with the promise to pay what they owe.

The sun on the truck riding back into town made Roy a little drowsy. He puts the magazine down and heads outside for fresh air.

On Monday, Roy has no homework, so his mother tells him to ride his bike to the store to see if his father needs any help. She also asks him to bring home a gallon of milk and four or five of the Rome Beauty apples that were delivered last week. While at the store, Roy sees Dorothea again when she comes in for a can of Peach snuff. "This for you?" he asks, jokingly.

"No. It's Ma's," she says giving him an icy stare.

Roy feels shunned by her coolness; he has no response. He makes change and hands it to her.

Her eyes lowered, she says, "Bye," and turns and walks away.

"Bye." Roy's eyes follow her. She seems to have changed, acting more distant and less friendly than in the past.

Later that week Eula Mae announces to Hank that she and Ned want to run the store themselves. Roy learns that his father will get a rental house about a block from the store for the equipment and inventory. He doesn't really understand all the details of the deal. He knows his father doesn't have any choice.

At the end of the year, everything is as relaxed and normal as usual. Roy's father doesn't seem to be worried. "The business is changing, maybe it's a good time to get out," he says. Another time Roy hears him tell his mother, "Well, we have money in the bank, and when I need to find work, I'll find something. First though, I'm going to do some fishing." And that seems to be the final word.

Not going to the store anymore seems strange at first. Roy's father goes fishing a couple of days a week. At times, he also works for a friend who owns a liquor store a few miles west of Cuttsville.

Within a year's time, what Roy's father had predicted came true. After running the store for eight or nine months, Eula Mae and Ned close it. It might be that they were ineffective in running the business. Or it could be the recent opening of a new, larger store located closer to town that is attracting a lot of attention—what people are calling a "supermarket." Whatever the reason, lack of ability or competition, they close the doors.

Roy's father is now convinced he got out of the grocery business at the right time. To his surprise, however, a few months after Eula Mae and Ned close the store, Mr. Crawley and D.W. reopen it. From what Hank hears, they continue to stock groceries and also add other items like feeds and tools.

This doesn't have any affect on Roy's family. They have become accustom to their new life without the store. His father works more at the liquor store and he and his friend are making plans to open a bar and juke joint with music and dancing in a vacant building near the liquor store.

On a warm Saturday, Roy and two friends decide to ride their bicycles to Bronson Lake. They stop at the store to buy cold drinks they can drink while they ride. Roy is curious, wanting to take a look inside the store again.

He notices that the block building Uncle Jack had built is now painted white and one section is rented. There is a rectangular, plastic sign high on the corner of the building announcing automobile parts. It seems that this end of town may continue to have some life. Not exactly thriving, but at least surviving.

When they enter the store, D.W. is behind the counter reading a comic book. He never has a friendly look about him. Lanky and angular like the rest of the family, he has squinty eyes and thin lips that are not given to smiling. "What you doin down here?" He looks up at Roy, but doesn't move.

It seems almost confrontational. He is taller than Roy and his friends. He swaggers toward the counter, eyes steadily on Roy.

"Just riding bikes. Wanted to get some drinks."

"Yeah," he drawls it out with his mouth forming a smirk. He sets his comic book to the side. "What kind?" He leans forward, both arms stiffly braced against the counter top. They give their choices: two Pepsis and a Nehi orange.

D.W. brings their drinks and picks up the coins they lay on the counter. He returns with their change and plunks it down on the counter.

"Thanks," Roy says, picks up the change and the trio heads for the door. D.W.'s cold stare follows them out.

Once outside, Ronald says, "That guy is an asshole." Roy doesn't answer. Both friends know this was once his father's store. He felt intimidated, yet he hardly knows D.W., having only seen him a few times. He was expecting a better reception.

Roy never goes back to the store. No reason to. He is glad he doesn't have to work there anymore. It gives him more free time for sports and spending more time with friends. He never mentions the incident with D.W. to his father or mother. They would not understand D.W.'s attitude any more than he does.

FOUR – August 1958

Dorothea has been at Patsy's house for three weeks since Eula Mae ran her out of the house. Accused her of flirting with Ned, which Dorothea thought was plain foolishness, her being just sixteen. It scared her. To think her own mother could be so hateful and turn against her like that. Of course Eula Mae's been a holy terror, a bitter woman since she lost the store.

Patsy said with Dorothea so pretty and shapely, maybe Eula Mae thought Ned was the one making eyes. Hadn't of been for Patsy, Dorothea doesn't know where she would have gone.

Since D.W. is at the store every day and goes fishing or hunting on Sundays, he's hardly around. She and Patsy have a wonderful time together, enjoying each other's company, talking about girl things. Dorothea can't think of anyone that's ever been so good to her, except maybe Poppa when he was alive.

"Don't worry none about it," Patsy says to calm her fears, "I asked D.W. did he mind about you staying here, and he said it didn't matter to him." Patsy puts her arm around Dorothea's shoulder and rubs her hand across her back. "And James Earl is taking a real liking to you."

"James Earl is such a sweet boy. He's just like his ma." Dorothea blushes at speaking out with such tender feelings.

"Besides I need someone to talk to myself." Patsy lifts Dorothea's chin and looks into her bashful eyes. "When James Earl starts school, won't be no one around to talk to except Ma Crawley!" she giggles, puts her hand to her mouth to hold back the laughter.

Dorothea loves how Patsy is so good and understanding; she's more like a big sister or best friend than an aunt. On the following Sunday she begins to feel even more a part of the family when D.W. asks if she wants to go fishing with him and James Earl.

"You reckon it'll be okay?" she asks Patsy, her eyes wide open. "I ain't never been fishin."

"Don't worry none," D.W. blurts out before Patsy can answer, "all you do is hold a fishin pole over the water." He raises his brow and grins to indicate just how simple it will be.

"Looky here," James Earl comes through the front door like a gust of wind. Holds out a can of worms to show his mother.

"Eeehhuuu," Patsy turns her head. "See why I don't like fishing. Dorothea you let James Earl put them worms on the hook for you."

"Ah, they ain't nothin to be scared of." James Earl holds a long night crawler up to show Dorothea. She wrinkles her nose and backs away.

D.W. takes brown bottles of beer out of the refrigerator, places them into a small box. Dorothea has noticed that he keeps a supply of beer and always takes a couple with him when he is going somewhere.

"Y'all don't stay gone too long," Patsy says to no one in particular.

D.W. passes bye, giving her a sidelong glance. "James Earl, where's your durn hat, boy? I toll you to put a hat on your head."

James Earl runs to his room and returns with a tattered ball cap on his head. Patsy grabs his arm and then holding him, kisses his cheek. "You be careful around that water, you hear me," she says sternly.

"Yes'm," James Earl tries to pull away. D.W. is already out to the truck.

"And you stay with Dorothea and help her learn to fish, okay?"

"Yes'm." He hurries to the front door.

"Lordy, iffen I catch a fish I won't know what to do." Dorothea throws her hands into the air. She almost stumbles over her own feet, following quickly behind James Earl.

Not much is said until they arrive at a small farmhouse about a mile away.

"James Earl, go on and see if your buddy, Lamar, can go fishin with you."

James Earl looks up at this father. "Go on," D.W. says.

Dorothea opens the door and steps out so James Earl can go to the house. She steps back up to sit on the edge of the seat.

After knocking, James Earl talks with a small woman at the door. Soon a boy with blondish-white hair also comes to the door. They talk briefly and James Earl returns.

"She says Lamar can't go cause his pa ain't home." His voice goes softer and his head tilts down, "She says I can stay here and play, if you want."

"Sure, you can do that. You stay and play with Lamar. We'll pick you up later." He starts the truck. "Go ahead and close the door Dorothea."

Dorothea quickly pulls the door shut and then watches James Earl stuff his hands into his pockets and slowly saunter back toward the house. She feels strange to be left alone with just D.W. She was looking forward to spending the afternoon fishing with James Earl; she wasn't expecting it to be this way.

"Roll that window down," D.W. says in a casual tone, "it's gettin kinda hot in here." She does as he asks without looking his way. Feels the warm breeze come in. "Go ahead and open us a beer."

Dorothea looks at him in confusion. "I ain't twenty-one."

"Don't matter," he says matter-of-factly, "you a growed up woman ain't you?" And before she can answer: "You sure do look like a growed up woman." He takes a quick look at her and then turns his eyes back to the road.

"I ain't never drank no beer before," Dorothea says, still bewildered by the prospect of actually drinking alcohol. "Does Patsy drink beer?"

"Patsy don't do nothin wild, like drinking beer. You don't wanna be thata way. You wanna try things out, see how things is. Go on, open up two of them beers."

His voice has a commanding tone. She leans over to pull two bottles out of the box on the floorboard.

"Church key's in the glove box."

Her head turns to look at him again. "Wha . . . What's that? What's a church key?"

"The opener." He grins. "Whooee," he yells as he swerves the truck, trying to hit a frantic rabbit darting across the road. "Dammit, missed em."

Dorothea holds onto the beer tightly, still unsure of what is happening.

"You gonna sit there holding them beers or you gonna open them?"

Dorothea opens the glove box and her hand jolts back as she sees a shiny long-barrel pistol lying in the glove box.

Seeing her reaction, D.W. says, "Oh, don't pay no attention to that. It ain't loaded. Just find the opener."

She pulls out the bottle opener and flips the lids off of both bottles, letting them fall to the floor. She hands one of the bottles to D.W.

He guzzles a quarter of the bottle. "Ahhh, that's mighty tasty." He holds his bottle out toward Dorothea. "Drink up."

She smiles a weak smile and puts the bottle to her lips. Taking a mouthful, she swallows and quivers as the strong liquid goes down. She feels it coming up her nose. Puts her hand over her mouth and pinches her nose, coughs but holds back the beer with her hand. "Lordy," she says, bending forward.

"Don't choke." D.W. laughs. Turns his bottle end up and chugs down more beer.

She has never quite known what to think about D.W. One time her friend Becky told her that people said D.W. was as loose as a snapped guy wire. She wasn't sure what that meant, but the way Becky said it made it sound like D.W. was crazy. Now Dorothea is surprised at how nice he is being, and treating her like she is already grown up.

She takes another drink and likes the way the coolness feels in her throat. "Bitter," she says, her face grimacing. She is not so tense now; beginning to relax a little.

"You'll get used to it," D.W. claims in a carefree manner. He turns the wheel sharply and the truck heads down a less-traveled road, mostly two worn ruts with grass growing in the middle. The truck rocks with the unevenness of the road. "This here's a good spot. Fish bite pretty good," D.W. laughs, "iffen you're lucky." Tight grip on the steering wheel, he raises the bottle and gulps down the rest of his beer. Dorothea watches and takes a drink of her beer as well.

"Durn, I think this beer's making me woozy. What the world would Patsy think if I was to get drunk?" Dorothea sits straighter, trying to take this turn of events in stride. She uses her left arm to brace herself.

Both sides of the road are heavily wooded—pine, scrub oak, some sweet gum and plenty of brush. The air is heating to another August scorcher, heavy with summer humidity even though it has not rained in several days.

"It ain't gonna make you drunk." He throws the empty bottle out the window. It makes a hollow clunking sound, but doesn't break. "Open me another."

She puts her bottle between her legs so she can use one hand to brace against the dashboard and the other to reach for the beer. D.W. watches her while keeping one eye on the narrow road. She opens the bottle and hands it to him.

As he lifts the bottle to drink, the road leads into an opening. Dorothea can see the edge of the lake to the right. She takes another drink of the beer, hoping it's near the bottom because she doesn't think she can drink much more.

The truck stops. D.W. turns the key off and opens his door. "Here we are, home of the big'uns. You ever seen a big'un Dorothea?" He smiles and steps on the running board.

"I don't rightly know," Dorothea says as she opens her door and steps down. She holds onto the door momentarily to steady herself.

D.W. takes the fishing poles out of the back of the truck. Turns his beer up and nearly finishes it. "Get them other beers and the church key outta there."

He walks by her and drops an old blanket on the ground. "Spread that blanket out and set the beer on it," he calls over his shoulder.

She squats down to spread the blanket, keeping her legs close together. The shorts she has on come nearly to her knees, but they have wide legs. She finally manages to spread out the blanket and then sets the box of beer on it. D.W. is hooking a worm on one of the fishing poles.

"Come on over here," he calls. He holds the pole by the end and swings the line out over the water. "Now all you do is stand here and hold on to it. When you feel the line a jigglin, that'll be a fish hittin the worm and you jerk it right up."

Dorothea takes the end of the pole in both hands.

"Take your shoes off and you can stand in the water," D.W. says. "Iffen you want."

She pushes one foot against the other, slipping her shoes off and moves closer to the water. Within a few minutes D.W. returns and hands her another beer. "I can't feel nothin movin yet," she says.

"You have to be patient." He places his hand on her shoulder. "Just watch the water, drink your beer and relax. That's what fishin's all about, relaxin and takin it easy." He stands so close it makes her nervous. She continues watching the line in the water, waiting for a fish to grab the hook.

D.W. moves away. Dorothea tries to find things of interest. She looks around the lake as far as she can see, but everything is quiet. She shifts her weight from one foot to the other, takes a sip of her beer and steps closer to the water to wet her feet. She tries to slap at a mosquito that bites her arm, but she can't because of the beer bottle, so she just rubs the cool bottle on her arm. As time elapses, she thinks maybe fishing is not so great. Maybe there's something she doesn't understand. She pulls the line up and sees that the worm is still there, although it is limp and bluish in color. She drops the line in a different direction hoping there are fish waiting nearby.

She begins to feel light-headed. She wonders how much longer she has to stand here before something happens. Her vision is blurring and she feels drowsy. She moves the line to her right and in seconds sees the line jerk. Excited, she pulls the front of the fishing pole up quickly and it waves wildly in the air. There is no fish and no worm.

She turns, wondering where D.W. is, and sees him sitting on the blanket watching her. She turns back around, sensing that he has been staring at her.

"Bring that pole here and I'll put another worm on for you," he calls.

Dorothea picks up the can of worms and walks to the blanket. She hands the can to D.W. "If you was to fish, maybe you could catch something."

"Aw, you're doin just fine." He holds the hook and digs into the can for a worm. "I want me a boat like I seen. That's when I'm gonna do me some fishin. I need me a boat and a new truck. I'm gettin tired of that ole jalopy."

"You gonna buy em for yourself?"

D.W. is looking close at the fishhook trying to see it well enough to put the worm on. He turns the hook one way then another. Dorothea watches, thinking he must be getting drunk.

"Once I figger out how to get the money I'll do it. Yeoww!" He jerks his thumb back away from the hook.

"You and grandpa can make money in the store can't you?"

"Yeah, maybe in a hundred years." He releases the hook and the ends of the worm wiggle wildly.

"Ma said Mr. Hank made money in the store. Least that's what she said," Dorothea poses this timidly, hoping she is being helpful.

"Yeah, well some people is just luckier than others." D.W. looks up at her with the right side of his mouth drawn up. He does it on purpose, like a smirk.

Dorothea turns to walk back to the water. "Oh well, here I go," she says.

"Oh well," D.W. echoes.

Dorothea can tell, without seeing him that his eyes are on her as she walks away. She swings the fishing line out in the water. She hopes he will soon get tired of just sitting there drinking beer and decide it is time to go back home. She wishes James Earl was here; he would be some company for her and they could make it fun. She doesn't like being here with just D.W. and she doesn't like being stuck with no way out.

"Where'd you put that damn church key, Dorothea," he yells.

"It was right there in the box, last I seen," she replies, swinging her head around.

"It sure as hell ain't here now. Put that pole down and come find it. I'm needin me another beer."

Laying the pole on the ground, she walks to the blanket and kneels down to look in the box.

D.W. lifts up so he is also on his knees, undoes his belt and quickly unzips and pushes his pants down in one swift motion. Then he grabs her arm.

Dorothea freezes. Reacts by trying to pull free, but he forcefully pulls her sideways so that she topples backward to the blanket. " What . . . What are you doing D.W.?" Her voice is choked and frightened; her eyes wide with alarm.

"I told you, you need to try some things, Dorothea." Reaching over he grabs her other arm and pins her down. He leans over her. "Ain't no use in trying to get away, you gonna learn about being a woman today." His hand undoes the button and pulls at her shorts. They come away easily even though she jerks her legs in protest. She shakes with anticipation, alarmed by her nakedness. He leans and jams his legs between hers, and then lowers himself, trapping her underneath his body.

She is disoriented and starts to scream, but he clamps his hand over her mouth. What will he do to her? She thinks of the pistol in the glove box. Will he kill her? She tries to push against him.

His attack is merciless. He bellows and grunts, writhing, pushing hard against her. She feels searing pain and gasps in shock.

He is obsessed, his body shaking and plunging like an animal. She is suffocated, losing consciousness, dizziness overcoming her. She twists and pushes. Frantic, she tries to displace him, gasping for air. His body, his strength is overpowering. She is sweating profusely, helplessly pinned beneath as he hammers against her. Tears flow down the sides of her face, blurring her vision, distorting her equilibrium.

Groaning and squeezing her arms tighter, he rages against her.

Paralyzed by fear and shame, her senses are inflamed. Her head throbs; bubbling, boiling, gushes of tears and fluids swell and spill. Her mind is on the verge of snapping like a flash of lightning and madness gaining control. Her senses are clogged and numb, she awaits darkness and a deep sleep under the earth, crushed by its weight.

Her body is battered. Her dignity and sense of life's goodness have been brutalized beyond anything she has ever known or imagined. He rolls off of her. She shivers with panic. Trembling, she turns to the side grabbing the blanket to cover her shame, crying deeply, her body convulsing uncontrollably.

She lies on the blanket sobbing and shaking, bewildered at why he would do this to her. She hears him rattle beer bottles and senses that he is moving away. Is the gun in the glove box really empty? Could she get to it before he does?

She sits up, reaches for her shorts and yanks them on. She pulls the edge of the blanket and wipes away fluids from her face and nose.

Suddenly, a crashing sound comes from the brush. Dorothea jumps to her knees, afraid to move in any direction. D.W. drops the fishing pole and moves quickly toward her, crouching low, his eyes scanning the woods for movement. He passes by without looking at her, quietly pulls the truck door open and reaches in. With the pistol in front, he walks toward the brush.

Crouching low, Dorothea moves to the front of the truck for protection. Her heart pounds frantically. Breathing clogged with fluids, her chest heaves as she gasps for air. Peeking out from behind the truck she is certain that a wild animal will come charging at her or that D.W. will emerge from the woods clawed and bloody, firing his pistol at her repeatedly. She is paralyzed with fear, her head throbbing with pain and disgust.

She hears thrashing in the brush and sees D.W. backing towards the truck. "Get in," he tells her. He gets the fishing pole, throws it in the back of the truck. Moving hurriedly, he picks up the box with two clinking bottles and hands it to Dorothea through the window. He grabs the blanket, rolls it into a ball and tosses it in the back.

D.W. watches the woods closely as they ride slowly out to Sorrows Road, his right hand holding the gun at his side. On Sorrows Road he continues searching, the truck barely moving. After a mile or more, he turns around. He doesn't speak to her on the way to pick up James Earl.

She wonders if someone saw. What if they did? What if word gets around about her . . . with her uncle . . . on a blanket, at the lake? What if Pasty finds out? Dorothea puts her right hand to her face, her fingers gripping tightly over her nose and mouth, stifling a surging scream, stabilizing her head—which wants to shake loose.

She struggles to hold back tears; she can't control the sniveling. Her life is shattered. Maybe it's like Granny said, that she is too prideful, that she shows-out too much. Granny warned her about being showy in front of boys.

"Hand me a beer, dammit." His voice rattles her. "Open it," he commands. Timidly, she holds the beer out not looking in his direction, her hand shaking.

D.W. drinks the beer in slow gulps. Dorothea hovers close to the door, hoping only to make it to the safety of the house, fearing her eyes are swollen, hoping she has straightened herself enough so Patsy won't notice anything. Her stomach begins to spasm. "Stop," she yells. She grabs her waist with one hand, the other goes to her mouth. D.W. stops the truck and as soon as the door swings open she leans out and vomits. She coughs and spits repeatedly, trying to get the taste out of her mouth. Disgusted with herself, she wants to regurgitate ferociously to expel her misery. She sees a soiled rag peeking out from under the seat; pulls it up to her face to wipe away the sour smell, forcing it against her face to help her gain control.

As the truck pulls in the drive to the farmhouse, James Earl and his friend are wrestling on the ground. The two boys look up and then James Earl walks toward the truck, brushing his hands over his jeans to knock away dust and dirt. Dorothea steps out, spits to the side and wipes her mouth on the back of her arm. James Earl climbs into the middle of the seat. His friend watches, waves to him.

"Catch any fish?" James Earl asks, partly curious, partly disappointed.

D.W. wraps his hand about James Earl's neck. "Anybody asks you about fishing today, you say we didn't catch none." The threatening tone stiffens James Earl and Dorothea. "You don't tell nobody you stayed at Lamar's house, you hear."

James Earl doesn't answer. "You hear me boy," D.W. growls in his face and tightens his grip.

"Yesir," James Earl stammers.

"You don't do as I say, boy I'll whoop the britches plumb off yeh."

FIVE

Her head rages; still will not clear after two weeks. Dorothea feels her heart becoming more callous every day. At times, she feels dopey headed and all loose and silly and doesn't really care what happens. She just thinks to herself how silly everything has become and laughs. Nothing seems to matter anymore. She reasons that God is making her dopey headed so she won't lose her senses and cry herself into craziness.

Billy doesn't say much at all. Just lets her wander about and do as she wishes. She feels safe with him.

She had only talked to him once before that day they met on Sorrows Road. He came to Joann Kemp's birthday party and was standing off to the side by himself. She picked up a piece of cake and walked to where he was leaning against the doorframe and held out the plate to him. Billy declined the offer—said he never did like desserts—but they began a conversation. Dorothea realized later that she probably had asked him a million questions.

It was lucky he came along. After what had happened she knew she couldn't stay at Patsy's any longer. Not sure what to do. Even considered taking a knife from the kitchen to kill D.W. or herself. Decided she couldn't do either and took off walking. Didn't say a word, went outside and just kept going. Figured when she reached Sorrows Road she'd just walk until she found somewhere to stop. She had no idea where, just wanted to put some distance between her and the danger and fear she felt.

She often cries at the thought of leaving Patsy, such a sweet friend. She walks around dizzy, stumbling, her head hurting. She feels deep shame at what she has done to Patsy. Doesn't know how she could have stopped him, but keeps thinking she should have found a way. It wasn't right. Why didn't more strength come to her? She hates herself as much as she hates D.W.

From talking to Billy before, she knew that he lived on the farm and that his ma and pa lived over in Banely. Billy stayed at the farmhouse and watched over things. She was just stumbling along the edge of the road, looking down, fighting back tears, fighting back the loss of control that gripped her. If Billy hadn't hollered at her, she wouldn't have even noticed him driving by.

After getting in the truck, she just blurted out, "Billy," her face was distraught, her eyes desperate, "can I stay at the farmhouse with you?"

Surprised Billy. He jerked away like the words would bite. He didn't know what to say. "Wha . . . Wha . . . Whata yeh mean?"

She had nowhere to go; figured she had to ask. "Please," she pleaded. She would have begged and begged until he said yes.

He looked scared; still hunched close to his door, looking at her. "I . . . I reckon." He quickly looked back at the road after momentarily forgetting that he was driving.

She felt a great relief. "I won't be no trouble, I guarantee. And I'll do whatever you ask." She turned her head away, looking toward the floor at her feet. Maybe she said the wrong thing. She looked at Billy again. He was looking straight ahead at the road. He ain't nearly as big as D.W., and he's younger, she thought. She felt it would be okay.

Didn't know what might come of it, but felt good about riding down the road with Billy. It was all new. It wasn't from the past and, whatever came of it, it was a new direction. She clasped her hands together in her lap. The gesture reminded her of praying, though she had not intended it. She focused on the long dirt road, trees in the distance and hazy blue sky.

Billy turned off Sorrows Road onto Sandy Bottom. They rode in silence, dust billowing behind.

Thinking that talking would make them both more comfortable, Dorothea asked, "Where is your farm, Billy?"

"Ah, it's on down after crossing over Tilliston Highway."

"You stay there all by yourself?"

"Yeah," he smiled. Dorothea could tell he was relaxing. So was she.

There was a stop sign at Tilliston Highway. It is one of the few paved roads out this way. Billy crossed the highway, shifted gears and kept going. Dorothea couldn't tell distance very well; only knew she was getting farther and farther away. They passed open land that was fenced, interspersed with large areas of woods and tall grasses that were not fenced. From the road, only a couple of houses could be seen off in the distance. Eventually, Billy slowed down and pulled into a narrow road and stopped. He got out. There was a cattle gap and a gate, scattered trees and a few low hills. A barbed wire fence ran parallel to the road and it looked like grazing land, but there were no cows or horses that Dorothea could see.

She could see what looked like a barn far in the distance, partially hidden behind large trees. Billy drove across the cattle gap; the truck shook as the tires hammered against steel rails. He stopped and got out to close the gate behind them.

When the farmhouse came into view, Dorothea saw chickens roaming about. They squawked and scattered as Billy pulled in front of the house.

"This is it." Billy opened his door and slid off the seat. Dorothea opened her door, carefully stepping down, looking for chickens, following Billy toward the house. She noticed the back of his shirt was wet from the heat.

Inside, Billy went to the Frigidaire and lifted out two bottles of beer. Held them up with his right hand, "Want one?" He reached in a drawer for an opener.

"I reckon," she answered timidly, unsure about drinking beer again. "I don't usually drink beer."

A wide grin came across Billy's face. "It ain't gonna make you drunk. Just sit down and drink slow. It's right good, specially on days like this."

He flipped the opener and the metal cap fell clinking in the sink. The next cap flipped in the air and fell to the floor. Foam bubbled up. "Here," he said, handing her one of the bottles. He raised the other bottle to his lips and took a long drink. "Ahhhhh." He smacked his lips.

Dorothea took a sip and tasted the bitterness. She hoped Billy might leave the room long enough for her to pour the beer down the drain. "Got anything to eat, Billy? Don't reckon I've had much today. My stomach's a growlin."

"Ain't nothin but crackers and peanut butter right now, but I aim to make a run to the store. Iffen you'd like chicken, I can kill a chicken. You'd have to cook it though." He moved quickly to a side room and came out holding a rifle in one hand, his beer in the other. "I can go kill a rabbit iffen you'd like."

"No, that's okay. Reckon I'll just eat some crackers and peanut butter. You gonna eat some?" She pulled a chair from the table and sat down.

Billy sat his beer on the wooden table, turned around, opened a cabinet and pulled out the peanut butter jar and crackers. Nothing else was on the shelf.

Dorothea noticed how slight he was. Very thin. Had on Levis . . . no butt at all.

"You sure you got somewheres for me to sleep." she looked at Billy, her eyes wide, lips smiling.

"Yeah." He put the crackers and peanut butter on the table and motioned quickly off to the side with his arm. "Here, there's a bed in there." He reached for the other chair. "I sleep upstairs." He paused. "My room's upstairs."

She sensed he was as nervous as she was. But she wasn't scared. Wasn't anything anyone could do now that would be worse than what had already happened.

"Got a knife, Billy? For the peanut butter."

He moved quickly to the counter and opened a drawer. Handed her a steak knife.

"Eat all them crackers you want. I'll go on and get us some more groceries." He stuffed his empty hand into his pocket. "Just make yourself at home, you know, just . . . "

"I'll be fine." She looked at him. "And I really appreciate you letting me stay." He lowered his eyes to avoid hers. "I promise I won't be no trouble," Dorothea said.

Billy turned away and then let his body swing back part way. "Sure," he said. He tilted his head back, taking a swig of his beer. He quickly glanced at Dorothea and then walked with measured steps to the screen door and outside.

Dorothea watched him walk away and then she spread peanut butter on a cracker and began eating. She heard the truck start.

Being in a totally different environment gives Dorothea a feeling of distance from what occurred with D.W. However, the incident has not left her mind. She walks around the farm feeling the bright sun on her skin, trying to think of other things, trying to break away from that belligerent memory. But it's hard not to think about it; it hangs in the air like the lingering stench of a dead animal, always there, rotting. She replays the event in her mind again and again; trying to understand what she did wrong . . . how she could have changed things to make it end up differently. She stumbles along, feeling totally defeated, humiliated and beaten, hot tears welling up in her eyes. Used like throwaway trash. Her life ruined. Her best friend gone. Some days she wonders why she should go on living.

She knows if she puts her mind to it, eventually she could kill herself. It might take some time to build up to it, but she could do it. Not before. But now, yes. Being a victim of brutality has made her more acrimonious, less softhearted. She knows she can put her mind to something and then do it.

Her innocence has been obliterated and she has become a different person. Her past is like a dream, now she's been woke up to what the world is really like and she knows she can't be weak or childish any longer.

As the days pass, Billy never says much. Goes off to the barn. Goes out in the woods with his rifle (she hears him shooting from time to time; a distant crack like a limb snapping). He acts a little strange sometimes, so she never knows what to expect.

A couple of times he drove off in the evening and she left a light on, but he didn't come back until morning. One of those times, after she had gotten up early and noticed the light was still on, she looked out the screen door and saw Billy's truck parked in front with the door open. She couldn't make out if he was in the truck or not, so she went out to look. Billy was stretched out across the seat with his head hanging off the edge of the seat. The smell hit her before she got close to the truck. He had thrown up and she could see it splashed on the running board and a murky puddle on the ground. It looked as though he'd passed out, so she let him be.

Mostly he is pleasant. She is kind of liking him, like a friend. As far as she can tell, he isn't mean or unkind. Mostly he ignores her. Which is okay, because it gives her time to herself. Little by little, she knows that she is adjusting and remaking herself. The fear is dissipating. Sunny, quiet days are invigorating and give her strength.

She misses Patsy and James Earl. The day after she moved in with Billy, she asked him to drive her over to Patsy's house to get her things.

"Dorothea, where you been?" Patsy looked angry, scornful. "I was worried sick over what happened to you."

"I knew you would be, Patsy. That's why I come back to tell you." Then she explained, "I just didn't want to be no hardship on you, and I think it's better if I start making it on my own." She could hardly bear to look at Patsy.

Patsy reached out and grabbed her arm. "Dorothea is there something you ain't telling me?" Her stare was hard. Dorothea felt it on her heart, felt her chest caving inward.

"No, there's nothing I ain't telling you," Dorothea shot back, trying not to be hateful. She couldn't break down and let this get away from her; she had to be persistent. "I like Billy and this is what I want to do." She held her own. She could feel her face radiating heat; she knew it was turning red.

Patsy let go of her grip and stepped back. Her eyes softened.

"I need to get my things." Dorothea swung her body in a gesture toward James Earl's room where she'd been sleeping.

"Okay," Patsy said softly, her eyes still focused on Dorothea, trying to penetrate, get below the surface.

Dorothea moved quickly, went into James Earl's room and put her things into a cloth sack. Hurriedly, she came out and hugged Patsy, knowing she couldn't speak because of the heaviness in her chest, her eyes holding back a flood of tears.

"You be careful now." Patsy embraced her, on the verge of trembling, no way to stop her from leaving. Dorothea slid out of her arms and darted out the door.

As Billy drove down the road he could see that Dorothea's face was flushed red and her eyes were pools of moisture, but he didn't say anything. They rode in silence for a time. The windows down and noisy, hot wind blowing through. The bumps in the road actually felt good, helped her relax, regain her composure.

"Well, I reckon you're stuck with me now." She smiled at Billy even though tears were running down her cheeks.

"Hmmm," Billy cleared his throat. "I don't mind. Reckon it'll be good having some company around." He looked ahead, wanting to sound nonchalant about the whole thing. Leaning against the door, he let his arm dangle out the window.

As the long, quiet days pass, Billy slowly begins making overtures toward Dorothea and becoming friendlier. When he brings back groceries and beer, he brings a couple of magazines for her. He shows her how to tune the radio so she can listen to music when she wants to. Tells her to make herself at home, look around all she wants.

"I ain't got nothing to hide," he says, smiling, "cept don't touch my guns." Then he laughs. "I don't want you shootin your foot off."

"You don't need to worry about that, I don't know nothin about guns."

"Well," Billy draws himself up, "Maybe I'll teach you how to shoot sometime." Then, he turns and strides toward the door and then outside.

Dorothea allows what he said to sink in. She can tell he is trying to act like a grown up man, talking about shooting guns. But if he does teach her to shoot his gun, it might be real useful. The more she thinks about it the more it excites her. She won't let Billy forget what he said. He pretty much promised he would teach her. She can visualize herself taking aim and shooting Billy's rifle. There are plenty of places out here where she can practice.

D.W. has a gun. So maybe someday soon she'll have a gun of her own.

SIX - November 1958

With Billy bringing groceries into the house, Dorothea has started cooking. She asked him to bring some bacon and sausage. It's easy to cook, there are plenty of eggs, and breakfast has always been her favorite meal.

Having seen her mother and grandmother cook, she thought once she started things would come to her. She also remembers a few things Patsy has shown her about cooking.

"All I ever done was open up cans and heat stuff up," Billy says, looking at her with a puzzled expression.

"Well, reckon I can't do no worse, lessen I burn everything up." Dorothea smiles at the thought of being a homemaker—how it's beginning to feel like a real home, nice and comfortable-like.

She keeps her eyes focused on the frying pan. "How come all these pots and pans are here? Where'd you get all them?"

"Them's from when Ma and Pa lived here. This was our house when I was growing up. This here's the only'st place I ever lived, right here in this house."

She hears Billy pull a chair away from the table. She has hamburgers cooked and she put a can of peas in another pot to warm up. She puts a hamburger on each of the two plates and brings the plates to the table. Then she spoons peas onto the plates.

"Durn, this tastes pretty good," Billy says, as he cleans his plate.

"Well, I'm glad you like it. If you want me to try cookin a chicken, I seen Patsy do it before."

"Yeah, I reckon that'd be good," he says, pushing his chair back from the table. "I'm getting a beer, want one?"

"Sure." She doesn't really like beer that much, but she wants to be good company and it's a change from water.

Rain falls light and steady, and sounds like it will probably continue on into the night. She likes the sound of the rain on the roof. It has cooled the air; the evening is pleasant with the windows up and the front door open.

Billy turns on the radio. Voices mumble faintly, there is a lot of a static and whining noise as he turns the dial. He turns up the sound, but it just makes louder crackling noises.

"Shit," he hollers at the radio and hits it with the side of his fist. He shakes his fist because it has hurt him more than the radio. Click. He turns it off, grabs a magazine off the counter, walks over to the couch and throws himself down. Urrrk! The couch scrapes on the floor.

The house is not very wide. The front part of the first floor is one large room. On the right side is the kitchen with the table, two chairs, a stove and refrigerator. On the left side, there's the couch, a blonde-wood coffee table and an ornate stand up lamp. Billy leans into the arm of the couch, looking at the magazine and drinking his beer.

Dorothea can sense that he is restless. She carries the dishes to the sink.

"Think I'll have another beer." Billy lays the magazine down and pulls against the arm of the couch. "You finished yours?"

"Lordy," Dorothea says playfully, moving away from the sink, "if I drink another, I will get stone drunk." Billy opens two beers.

Darkness has overcome what little light there was. The rain continues its soothing cadence and occasionally the low rumble of distant thunder can be heard. Dorothea turns off the main light over the table. The kitchen light is on and the lamp, which casts a mellow light across the couch. She sits on the couch next to Billy and can tell she is unsteady because of the beer. She smiles at herself.

"Billy," she says softly. He doesn't look up from his magazine. "You want to sleep with me tonight?"

He jerks his shoulders back abruptly, catches himself and holds steady so he won't appear nervous. His mind is working feverishly, but he doesn't know what to say. "Yeah, wh . . . Yeah, ah . . . Yeah . . . Iffen you want."

She leans toward him, hoping he will respond. He turns his head and their lips meet, but his kiss lacks any passion. She moves slowly and carefully, inviting his caress. Billy remains stiff and unyielding. She presses her body against him and wraps her left arm around his chest. Then she takes his hand in hers.

"You wanna go ahead and go to bed now?" She asks.

They walk together into her bedroom. She slips her dress over her head and slides under the bed covers. Billy looks but quickly averts his eyes to the task of unbuttoning his shirt. He sits on the edge of the bed and takes off his shoes and socks, and then removes his jeans.

In the morning, Dorothea is up early, making coffee, cooking sausage and thinking about last night: how Billy got on top of her, didn't try to kiss her or anything, just pushed in and out, and the bed went to squeaking—sounding like an old witch cackling on Halloween—and she was thinking the bed might crash to the floor any minute. She didn't know what to do. She managed to relax somewhat and it was beginning to feel good, but then he stopped and it was over. He left to go to his own bed.

She takes the spatula and turns the sausages. She wonders what Billy thought about it, wonders if he thought it was alright.

The odor of frying sausage fills the room. "Damn, girl, you a cookin up a storm," Billy says, as he walks from the bathroom and sits down to put on his shoes.

"Well, I just figured you'd be hungry," she says without turning toward him. She isn't sure about the tone of his voice. "You want a couple of eggs?"

"Reckon. Seeing how you done started, I might as well." He stomps his shoe on the floor to get his foot in.

Billy eats his breakfast, mostly in silence. She doesn't want to say anything, if he isn't going to talk. She looks up from her plate, but Billy is eating quickly, his mouth full.

"Reckon I better go out and see what the rain did," Billy says, after cleaning his plate. He stays gone all morning; then around noon she hears the truck start and he drives off. He doesn't return until evening.

Dorothea is sitting at the table; she has eaten. Billy sets a small box of chocolate candy in front of her. She smiles. "You hungry?"

"No, I done ate somethin." He walks to the Frigidaire for a beer. "Want a beer?"

"I reckon. Thanks for the candy."

Billy returns with the beers opened and sits at the table. He looks at Dorothea with a boyish grin. "We gonna do it again tonight?"

Her lips widen into a big smile and her cheeks become rosy spheres. She thinks she can smell whiskey on his breath, but he doesn't seem drunk at all. "I think I'd like that," she says. She continues smiling at him and he has a grin on his face as well.

After she has a second beer and Billy drinks a couple more, they go to bed early. This time it lasts longer and Dorothea, blocking out the noise of a creaking bed, wraps her arms around Billy and thrusts her hips upward in an effort to be more involved. She likes it better than last night and is sorry when it ends.

The next morning, she is up early and fixing breakfast again when Billy steps out to see what she's cooking.

"We keep doing this Billy, we're gonna have to get married," she says in a calm, matter-of-fact manner. She knows from talking with Patsy and hearing what other girls say: that if a man does that to you, then you might get pregnant and have babies. In the back of her mind she worries that D.W. may have already made her pregnant.

She has seen women with their bellies all swollen up before they have babies. She's always known about women having babies, but never really considered the details of what it would be like.

"Yeah, I reckon we do," Billy answers in a very even voice, "I'm gonna get my ma and pa over here to meet you on Saturdee. That be okay?"

"Sure." Dorothea looks at him, attempting to gauge his sincerity. "I'd like to meet em . . . If that's what you're wantin to do."

Billy walks into the bathroom and closes the door.

She's glad she asked. She never has been shy about asking questions.

She remembers that time she and Becky saw Margie Hawes at the Pentecostal church and she was holding her little baby. Becky went up to Margie and asked her what it was like when she had her baby. Margie whispered so only Dorothea and Becky could hear. "It's somethin like shittin a watermelon," she said. Then she backed up and her eyes went wide and her mouth popped open like she was as surprised as they were.

Dorothea smiles remembering how Becky just started laughing so hard she cried. Dorothea laughed more at Becky than what Margie Hawes said. She couldn't help but wonder what that would feel like—even a small watermelon. It didn't sound like something you'd want to do. But, on the other hand, plenty of women do it, so maybe it ain't as bad as all that.

She pours Billy a cup of coffee and brings it to the table as he sits down. "You gonna teach me to shoot your gun today?"

"Well, maybe a little later. I'm gonna go out looking around first off." He leans back in his chair and cautiously sips the coffee. "You want I should learn you to shoot the pistol or the rifle?"

She brings a plate with bacon and eggs to the table and sets it in front of him. "Both, I reckon."

Billy spews coffee out of his mouth and spills more on the floor as he stands up and dances backward, laughing.

"Whu . . . Heh . . . Heh . . . Heh . . . Whueee." The chair falls over backwards, knocking against the floor.

"Lord, I ain't never heard such." She laughs at Billy and moves out of the way.

Billy walks spraddle-legged to the sink, turns the faucet on and runs his hand under the water to cool it and wash the coffee off. "Whueee," he says, laughing, "you surprised me with that one . . . Holy moly . . . Which one . . . ? Heh, heh . . . Both . . . Heh, heh."

Dorothea giggles at him and his antics. She puts her hand to her mouth to stifle the laughter from bursting out and she shakes with laughing. It lifts her spirits.

Saturday is sunny and warm. Around noon, Billy's parents pull up to the house in a big, shiny white car. Dorothea doesn't know anything about cars, but she knows it's fancier than what most people have. She stands up and stares at it from the front porch. Billy stays in his chair.

Dorothea can feel Mr. Yarborough staring at her through the windshield. Mrs. Yarborough gets out with some difficulty. She smiles and calls, "Well, hi there, Billy Boy."

Billy slowly rises from his chair. "Hi, Ma," he says. He puts his hands in the front pockets of his jeans and pushes down, stretching his arms, hunching his shoulders forward.

Mrs. Yarborough walks up the steps, slowly taking one at a time, and puts her hand on the post for support. "This here is Dorothea," Billy says while motioning to the right with his head. Dorothea is smiling, arms folded across her chest, beneath her breasts.

Mrs. Yarborough looks up, finds Dorothea's face and smiles. "Hello, Dorothea," she says cheerfully. "Well, girl, you're just as pretty as a picture, ain't you.

"Damn steps need fixing, Billy," Mr. Yarborough's gruff voice booms. Unlike Billy, he's tall, red-faced and his belly sticks out.

"Yessir, I was thinkin about fixin them . . ."

"Thinkin, shit man, thinkin don't get it done. You need to quit thinkin on it and get out the damn hammer and saw."

"Dolphus," Mrs. Yarborough says, looking at her husband, "them steps can wait. You ain't said hello to Dorothea, even."

He looks at Dorothea, but doesn't say anything. Her smile is gone.

Inside the house, Dorothea asks if anyone wants iced tea.

"I'll have some," Billy says.

"Yes, let's all have some," Mrs. Yarborough says. She smiles at Dorothea and lowers herself onto the couch. She is plump and her legs seem weak.

"Where you from girl?" Mr. Yarborough bellows at Dorothea.

"Cuttsville," she answers politely.

"Your ma and pa know where you at?" he asks.

"Well, my pa died and I don't think my ma rightly cares where I'm at."

"She don't, huh?"

"What's this about you all getting married?" Mrs. Yarborough interrupts, smiling broadly at Dorothea and then Billy.

Dorothea hands Mrs. Yarborough a glass of tea, then sets a second glass on the table. She goes back to the counter and gets two more glasses. Billy has taken a chair at the table. She hands him tea and stands behind him.

"Yeah," Billy says, "we aim to get married right soon I reckon."

"What for?" Mr. Yarborough almost shouts the question.

"Dolphus!" Mrs. Yarborough's stern voice cuts the air.

Billy looks at his pa and stutters a reply, "Cause it ain't right, us just living . . ."

"Bullshit," Mr. Yarborough rumbles, "boy, you ain't got a lick a sense." He swallows a mouthful of tea and takes big steps across the floor and out the door. He pushes the screen door open so far that it flies back with a loud smack, stinging the air.

Dorothea is afraid he'll kick her out of the house. She sees he's not someone you can argue with. He sets people back on their heels, just talking to them. She can feel the fear in Billy's shoulder, under her hand.

"Don't pay no mind, Billy," his ma grunts as she struggles to raise herself. Billy stands and takes her arm to help her. "Y'all go on to the courthouse and get a license." She puts her hand on the table to steady herself, reaches up and pulls a knotted kerchief out of her brassiere. Undoing the knot, she unrolls two ten-dollar bills and hands them to Billy. "The preacher over that Mount Olive Baptist Church . . . Durn if I can remember his name . . . You know, Billy, over toward Banely, he'll marry y'all for five dollars."

"Thank you, Mrs. Yarborough," Dorothea says softly.

Mrs. Yarborough smiles and pats Billy on the arm. "You let me know when the preacher says he'll marry y'all and your pa and me will stand for yeh." She walks slowly to the door. The car horn blares.

"Don't pay him no mind," she says, looking at Dorothea with a steady and determined look. "He just don't like to see things change from the way they was." She pushes open the screen door. "He'll get used to it."

Dorothea is surprised that the visit is so brief. She doesn't know what to think about Mrs. Yarborough; seems she would have a hard time getting Mr. Yarborough to do anything he took a mind not to do. They certainly were not what she was expecting.

When the day came for the wedding, Mrs. Yarborough and Mr. Yarborough were at the church waiting when she and Billy arrived. Mr. Yarborough never said one word the whole time. After they were married, Billy's parents did not come back to the farm again for several months.

Dorothea felt strange that none of her family was at her wedding. She figured it had been three years since her poppa had died and she missed him terribly. She always felt safe when he was alive and looking after her. She would never have thought she would be alone and only sixteen and a half years old. At least being married to Billy would bring some stability back into her life. Dorothea often thinks about the unexpected, topsy-turvy turns her life has taken so quickly. She never could have dreamed things would turn out this way. Now she will have to make the best of what she has.

As for her mother, she thinks about her from time to time, but she has no regrets about living apart from her. She wishes she could have asked Patsy to come to her wedding, but she didn't want to risk anyone knowing where she was.

Married life doesn't bring any big changes. Billy teaches her how to shoot his pistol and he drinks beer most of the time. Sometimes he leaves the farm without saying anything and does not return for two or three days. Once he stayed gone for a week. He never tells Dorothea where he goes and she never asks.

He doesn't do much work on the farm. There is a flatbed truck and an old tractor in the barn that he sometimes tinkers with. Occasionally he starts one of them up and Dorothea can hear it running. There are a few scrub cows around that stay mostly in the woods and a bunch of chickens roaming everywhere—until he starts shooting them.

Billy's parents send him money every month. Dorothea doesn't know how much, but Billy always buys plenty of groceries, plenty of beer and anything else he wants.

After about six months at the farm, Dorothea begins getting sick some mornings. She thinks it may be something she is eating, but Billy doesn't get sick. Then as time passes, she realizes she must be pregnant because her stomach is beginning to pooch out and she can feel movement.

She asks Billy to drive her over to see Patsy and they go during the day when D.W. is at work. Having Patsy to talk with helps ease her fears, she knows she can trust whatever Patsy tells her. After that, Patsy begins coming to the farm every few weeks to check on Dorothea. She tells Dorothea things about being pregnant and what it will be like to have a baby. Patsy makes arrangements to take Dorothea to Parksdale, the largest nearby city, to see a doctor. She tells Dorothea that the doctor will make sure she's doing okay and then, when she has gone full-term, he will be at the hospital to deliver her baby.

SEVEN – Summer 1960

"You was a listenin to Pastor Brown, you wasn't lookin at dem girls in they fancy dresses?" Esther asks Rueben. She looks straight ahead, but can feel her lips and cheeks move upward forming a near-smile.

"I was listenin to everything Rev'en Brown say." Rueben smiles to himself knowing full well his mind was on the girls in church more than on what Reverend Brown was saying.

Rueben follows a step behind his mother, his shorter leg beginning to tire. Looking down, he notices the brown dust from the road is covering his black shoes.

"Now, don't you be tellin yo mama no stories." She likes talking as they walk, it seems to make the journey go more quickly.

"I ain't storying none." His look becomes more serious, just in case she looks back at him.

"Well, I don't mind you lookin at dem girls, dat's what young mens does."

Reuben feels he can't help himself. Whenever he is away from the house and his mother he thinks about girls plenty of times. He is only sorry he's not tall and big and strong so he can talk easily with the prettier ones and introduce them gentleman-like to his mother.

Sorrows Road

With his gimpy leg and now no job and no money, well, he pretty much expects to spend his life as a bachelor. But that doesn't bother him much because he has no intention of leaving his mother alone anyway. As his mother has always told him, "In most things, there's good to be found if you just look hard enough."

Their strides slow a little as they reach the yard and walk toward the house.

Esther walks up the three steps onto the porch and then notices the door is standing wide open. "Reuben, you done lef this here front door open. Honeychile, anybody who want, could walk right in."

"Well maybe dat's what they done. I don't member leavin no door open." Reuben has one foot on the first step, but he stands still looking at his mother and the open door. He is tired from walking all the way from church. His left leg being two or three inches shorter puts a strain on him. He wants to sit down and rest.

He puts his hand on his raised knee, as though he might hold that position for some time. "Sides, what dey wanna go in dere fo, ain't nuttin dey can steal."

"Now dat ain't so, maybe I's got stuff you don't know about. And sides dat, I don't want no raggedy sinner walkin through my house."

"Why mercy be, I thought all dem raggedy sinners was in deh church," Reuben cocks his head sideways, knowing he is being contentious.

"A bunch was. But a passel uh sinners don't make it to the church. They burn up, they step inside dat church." She smiles big at Reuben, turns and walks to the rocking chair on the porch. With her back to Reuben, she reaches up just behind the pastel cloth flowers on her straw hat and pulls out a long pin.

Turning, she sits down in the rocker. "I jus gonna sit here awhile and cool down. You ain't dat hungry jus yet, is yeh?" She holds the brim of her hat and fans back and forth, closing her eyes to enjoy the coolness.

Reuben comes the rest of the way up the steps and sits in the slat-back chair on the opposite side of the porch. Loosening his tie, he wags his head to help with the tie's undoing, undoes the buttons on the cuffs of his white shirt and rolls each cuff twice.

"Surprises me you don't wanna see if a bugler stole somethin."

"No." She stops fanning. "You's right, it'd have to be a mighty dumb bugler to come to dis house." She laughs in a very light, feminine manner. "I reckon he'd be so mad after lookin in dere, he'd go on ahead and get him a job." She laughs again.

"Dat's what I gonna have to do fo sho." Reuben leans forward, resting his elbows on his knees.

"Sweetpea, I's hope you ain't mad at this ole crazy woman fo speakin her mind. But I sure nuff dreamed about dat Mista D.W. and them snakes was jus crawlin outta him and going all over and bitin people and everybody runnin. It was a terrible sight. I ain't never seen so much evil in my dreams, lessin it was deh devil hisself." She waggles her hat back and forth, attempting to swoosh away the memory.

"I done toll you, Momma." He turns his head in her direction. "Dat ain't why he let me go. It's cause don't nobody come in dere to buy groceries. When it was Mista Hank's store, peoples come in all deh time."

"Well, I jus knowed he was full uh the evil." The hat-fan slows, then stops. Her graying hair is pulled back into a round bun. She looks into the distance. "It's my Christian duty to help people when deh devil's got holt uh them."

"He's a mighty hard man, Mista D.W. I done worked in dat store fo over six year, and it was a fine place when Mista Hank was dere. He's treats people like he should. But Mista D.W., he don't care a hoot about nobody cept hisself." Reuben's face is sour, his lips puckered.

Esther rises from the rocker. "Some folks treats they dogs better'n they do other peoples. Dat's how some folks is."

She walks to the open door and places her hand on the doorframe. "Don't you go worrin about dat job, we do jus fine. And then you probably get a job better'n workin fo dat man.

Reuben rises and follows his mother inside. The house is mostly one large room with a back wall partitioning off the kitchen on one side and the bathroom on the other. The front room is open and uncluttered; a table is near the center of the room. A grayish-colored cloth drapes over the small, round table, which is flanked by two chairs. Atop the table sits a milky-blue vase with several wildflowers bunched together. Cot-like, metal beds are near the walls on both sides of the room. Clothesline wires running from front wall to back wall hold up cotton spreads hanging mid-way to conceal the beds.

Esther walks behind the flower-pattern spread on her side and sits her hat on the narrow bed. She unbuttons her dress. Thinks about the last time she was in the store. Her dream told her for sure that the devil had gotten inside of Mista D.W. She had hoped she would be able to help him see the error of his ways.

"Mista D.W.," she said, "you don't look good." She stared directly into his eyes trying to fathom the devil's hold. "You needs to talk wit God and let him lift yo burden." Her face was calm, in a languid, questioning way.

He stood straight, lifting his hands to his hips—arms angled out. "Esther." He had a confused grin. "You take care uh yourself and let me worry about myself," he said. "I don't need no advice from the likes uh you."

When she started walking out, she looked back and said the first thing that came to her mind: "They's a stain on yo soul Mista D.W." She said it in sympathy, hoping that her words would penetrate and help him. Later she wished she hadn't said it.

As she left, she heard him tell Reuben, "Keep her outta here. That woman's plumb loony. She needs to be locked up."

"Mista D.W.," Reuben said as he shied away, leaning back, like the bigger man might take a swing at him, "she helps lots a folks when she tell em things."

Despite his attitude, Esther feels sorrow for the man. She knows that God gives her dreams so she can help people. She has done it her whole life and never regretted it once. It's a gift that God has given her and she knows it's a special blessing. That same afternoon, Mista D.W. told Reuben he would not need him to work in the store anymore.

Esther pulls her everyday dress over her head. Hears a bird near the front porch. Thinks of the beautiful red cardinal that often comes around with his less colorful mate. She welcomes the song. Sundays are usually quiet, restful days. Other than an occasional dog barking, there is a stillness and peace that allows her to be contemplative, to recall the preaching she heard at church, and the hymns too. Most Sundays she continues singing spirituals throughout the day.

Reuben sits on the edge of the bed on his side of the room, behind a gray spread, tugging at his tight shoes.

"I reckon if Mista D.W. go to church," Reuben says loudly, "he be sittin on deh lass row. Ain't you say dat's where deh sinners is?"

"Honeychile, we all has sinned and come short of the glory of God. They ain't never been a person without sins but Jesus Christ hisself. But the big sinners mostly sits in deh back. You know when Rev'en Brown is uh preaching them words from the Bible they's mighty powerful. They can pierce right through a person's heart. And by the time they's reached the back uh the church they's cooled down some and they ain't as strong. So if you's a bad sinner, you kin take in them words much better in the back uh the church."

"Reckon Mista D.W.'s so bad he don't even make it to deh back row?"

Esther ponders the question, makes a low humming sound and murmurs softly, "What do it profit a man if he gain deh whole world and he lose his own soul?"

Reuben looks up. This procedure is normal. It's her way. He knows she is thinking about his question, studying it: thinking about Bible readings, preachings, dreams, feelings in her heart, and tellings passed on by her ancestors. Only then is she prepared to give Reuben her answer.

"Truefully," she says slowly, deliberating what she's thinking, "Mista D.W. been on my mind, but I didn't know should I tell you. That dream worry me so, I done gone and had another las night. Unh, unh, unh, I don't know zactly what gonna happen."

Reuben slips on his everyday pants, stands and eagerly barefoots it to the center of the room. "What you seen this time?"

Esther emerges from behind her spread, walks to the table and sits. Looking at Reuben, she lays her arms on the table, puts her hands together with interlocking fingers.

"The wind was blowin and Mista D.W. is standin out in the tall grasses. Then I seen three, or maybe they was four, women. Dere hair is blowin. They has on long dresses what's flyin about in the wind. Mista D.W. is in the cen'er uh dis field and them womens is throwin stones at him. I don't know who they is, but they's angry and strong and them stones is hittin on Mista D.W."

Reuben's hand reaches and rests on top of the wooden chair. It helps him ground himself so he won't lose his balance, which he sometimes does if he concentrates hard on something. Esther looks at him, but her eyes are blank. She is lost in the remembering.

"And Mista D.W. can't dodge them stones and they's hurtin him bad. He got cuts and bumps and they's bleedin. He try to get outta dere, but when he runs this here bull wit big horns comes uh runnin at him and then the bull disappear into the sky and them womens is throwin mo stones."

She tilts her head, lowering her eyes. Her face showing the strain of these heavy thoughts, cheeks slack and chin drawn long.

Reuben's arm, braced against the chair, twitches. He sees the battlefield, serene except for the embattled figures. Sees the hulking bull—spotted, mostly white with black and brown splotches of color, fleshy muscles, yellow-gray horns, snorting through wet, pink nostrils with spiky hairs. Reuben shutters with fear. With his gimpy leg, what chance would he have against a bull like this? The sky is bright cerulean with warm white clouds gyrating this way and that, signaling a coming storm. The tall grass like tawny wheat, blowing in waves, first one way then another.

Mista D.W. has cuts on his face. He holds up his arms, his hands are cut. He moves but the rocks find their target every time.

Mista D.W. is totally bewildered. Reuben ain't ever seen him this way. His amber eyes are milky, cloudy, reflecting the sky. His purple mouth is partly open, stretched back in anguish. He drops down on one knee then gets up. He is worn and battered, but he doesn't cry out, his voice gone, his will gone, or simply a refusal to call out.

"Mercy be. God have pity on his soul." Reuben whispers with sympathy.

"I tried to tell em. Course he ain't gonna lissen to no ole crazy woman. Specially no woman at all. Don't reckon he lissen to nobody, jus deh devil."

Long, dark fingers splayed out on the table, Esther pushes herself up from the chair. "Reckon that's enough tellin. I needs to get uh fixin some vittles."

Reuben doesn't move. He feels pain in his temples.

Esther shuffles her shoes over the creaking wood floor, toward the kitchen. "They ain't nothin we can do no ways."

Her sad words float softly, dissipating into the still afternoon air.

EIGHT – November 1961

Patsy has gotten used to the temperament of Mr. Crawley's old International pickup. Most of the time it runs fine, even in the colder weather. It comes in handy when she needs to go to town for things they don't have at the grocery store.

The sky is bright and the weather is mild. Of course, this time of year you can't tell from one day to the next what the weather will be like. With the sun out, the inside of the cab is warm. She wants to reach across and crack the window a little, but is afraid she'll run off the road if she tries.

Patsy thinks about Dorothea and tries to remember what her baby girl looked like the last time she was out. Hard to believe she's almost two. She won't forget the day Donna was born, September 4, 1959. She went out several times to check on Dorothea and then almost every day until finally taking her to the hospital. It was a shame Dorothea couldn't depend on Billy for any help; he never seems to be anywhere around.

Of course all she knew of Billy was what Dorothea told her. Saw him sitting in his truck, saw a picture of him standing by his mother when he was about ten years old, but that was it. Awfully queer how he would go away for days, and how he would always disappear when Patsy came over. Didn't make sense.

She just hoped she was not the cause for Dorothea's predicament. She had her suspicions about what might have happened. She loved Dorothea like a sister, or maybe the daughter she never had, always energetic and full of life, always curious and asking questions. Like she told her, "There's never a dull minute when you're around." Since moving away though she has lost some of her spark. Who wouldn't, living out here alone—almost alone anyway. Having a child and of course she's older now.

Such a pretty girl. Big, dark eyes. Beautiful smile. Always attracting attention since she was fifteen or sixteen. Patsy feels envious, but not in a jealous way. She has always been plain and knows it. Doesn't like attention anyway.

She stops at the cattle gap to open the gate. As she gets closer to the house, she hears shooting. Wonders if Billy is shooting chickens again, like Dorothea says he's done before. She crosses the small wooden bridge over a creek that runs through the property, passes the stand of large trees and comes in view of the house. Dorothea is standing at the porch smiling as she drives up.

"Boy, am I glad to see you," Dorothea reaches for the door. As Patsy steps down, Dorothea throws her arms around her neck.

"How you doin sweetheart," Patsy gushes with joy the way she always does in meeting Dorothea. She sees the pistol and holster lying on the edge of the porch. "What the world! Was that you doin that shootin?"

Dorothea doesn't want to let go of her, but she does and steps back a step, holding onto Patsy's arms and then her hands. "It sure was," she says sprightly, "Billy learned me how and I'm gettin pretty good."

She tugs at Patsy's hand. "Come here, look at these cans." About thirty feet to the side, is a long, weathered log with three cans sitting on it. As they get close, Patsy sees six or seven tin cans scattered behind the log. Dorothea steps over the log to pick up one of the cans.

"Where's Donna," Patsy looks back toward the house.

"Right over there," Dorothea points with her left arm. Donna is sitting on the ground near some bushes. "Can't hardly keep up with her since she started walkin."

"Hi, Donna," Patsy waves and Donna looks up.

"Looky here," Dorothea holds the can for Patsy to see. It has a round hole in one side and a bigger tear out the other. "Billy says I'm a durn good shot."

"Where is Billy?"

"Patsy," Dorothea's face grows serious as she says, "I don't know where the heck he is. He's been gone a couple of months." Dorothea throws the can back on the ground.

"Well, girl, why didn't you let me know. You doin okay?"

"Yeah, everything's okay. I expect him to come back any day. I told you he does this from time to time." She looks at the ground, her head hanging down.

"But, a couple of months? I thought he stayed gone a couple of days."

"Well, I reckon it has been a long spell. But I don't know what I can do. I don't know where he goes or what he does. He don't tell me nothin, just leaves."

"Lord," Patsy holds Dorothea's hand tightly and looks at her downcast face. "I hope ain't nothing happened to him."

She's amazed that Dorothea is not more worried about Billy being gone.

"Naw, he's alright. He's just kinda strange in that way." She lifts her head, avoids Patsy's eyes, and looks toward the road as though Billy's truck might be coming toward the house at any minute. "I reckon he'll be back." The words trail off. Her voice doesn't have much conviction.

"Let me see that girl." Patsy quickly steps to the side of the house, walking toward Donna.

"Hey there sweety pie," her voice lifts in a sing-song tone. She squats down on her haunches to look at Donna. "How's my little girl?"

The little girl stretches her arms out toward Patsy. "My goodness, I'd say you're getting kinda messy in this here dirt," She picks her up and softly brushes her hand across Donna's dress and legs to brush away the sandy dirt.

"Goodness sake, I think this little angel likes playing in the dirt."

Dorothea rushes up to take Donna. "I'm sorry, Patsy. Let me take her in and clean her up." She takes the girl from Patsy. "I just let her wallow out here cause that's what she likes to do. I reckon I ain't being a very good mom."

"Well, it looks to me like you're doin just fine." She reaches for the little girl's leg and playfully pats it. "Looks like she eats good too."

"Oh, she's a good eater, that's for sure." Dorothea starts up the steps. "Patsy, would you bring that pistol inside for me?"

Patsy looks at the pistol. "Heck no! I ain't pickin that thing up. I don't know anything about guns." She reaches for

Donna. "Don't want to neither. Gimme that girl and I'll clean her up." She takes Donna back. "I ain't got no little girl to love on, so you're gonna have to share."

"How's James Earl?"

"He's doin just fine. Getting bigger all the time. Do you believe he's in the fifth grade already?"

"Lord a mercy, fifth grade!"

"And he's doin real good in school, and he really likes his teacher."

Dorothea lays the pistol on the table and puts her arm over Patsy's shoulder. "Well with a mommy like you, no wonder he's doin so good." She leans her head against the back of Patsy's head, breathes in her aroma. "Mmmm, your hair smells so good. What's that shampoo you're using?"

Patsy bends to let Donna stand on the floor. "Why, you know, that's the same shampoo I always use." She looks up. "Where you want me to undress her?"

"Just lay her right there by the sink. Let me get you a wash cloth." She steps quickly to the bathroom.

Putting her hand under the little girl, Patsy lifts up and slides the dingy-gray, cotton panties off. She slips Donna's dress up over her head and then ruffles it playfully in front of the girl. Donna scrunches her nose and smiles. With the sun coming through the window it is warm inside. She keeps her hands on Donna's legs. Looking up, Patsy sees the gun on the edge of the table. "You ain't been shootin any chickens have you?"

Dorothea walks into the room holding a washcloth. "No, I ain't killed nothin but cans." She smiles. "There ain't many chickens left. Billy done killed a bunch of them."

"Why you reckon he done such a thing?"

"I ain't never figured it out. He'd just sit there with his rifle and every once in a while he'd just take a notion to aim and shoot."

"That's the craziest thing I ever heard. Maybe you're better off being shed of him." Patsy turns on the tap and continues to hold onto Donna, wiggling her arms and legs. Dorothea picks up the dirty clothes and takes them into the bathroom.

"How in the world you gettin along without him being here?" Patsy raises her voice. "How you gettin groceries and stuff? You ain't got no car." She pauses, picking Donna up and letting her stand upright on the counter. "Where you gettin money to buy things with?"

Dorothea walks back out, carrying a folded towel. She sets the towel on the other side of the sink. "Mrs. Yarborough sends money every month. I hate to spend it, but it's all I got. I don't spend all of it," she quickly adds. "And there's another truck in the barn. It was hard learning to shift gears, but I can drive it when I need to."

Patsy is embarrassed at asking so many questions. Maybe she's being too nosy. Looks like Dorothea is getting along okay and learning to take care of herself.

"Should I wash her in here?"

"Yeah, that's what I do. Put this here stopper in there." She hands Patsy the sink stopper. "I'll get some clean things for her."

After Patsy is finished bathing Donna, Dorothea lays her down for an afternoon nap. Then she and Patsy sit on the front porch drinking bottles of Orange Crush.

"You be sure and let me know if you need anything. I don't like the idea you being out here all by yourself."

Dorothea thinks about it. "It can get lonely sometimes, but I reckon Billy'll be back before long."

"You got company a coming," Patsy notices the thin cloud of dust.

"Well, I don't know. I wonder, maybe it's Dwayne bringing me some groceries." Dorothea looks straight ahead.

"Who? Who is it?" Patsy asks in a surprised voice.

"Oh, he's a friend of Billy's, name's Dwayne. When he found out Billy weren't here, he said he'd help me out." She can tell that Patsy is sitting forward, her eyes focused on her. "I mean, he thought Billy was here and came out to see him. But since Billy wasn't here, he told me he'd bring some groceries. And I pay him for the groceries."

The car is a bright sky-blue color, a newer model Chevrolet. It slows down as it approaches and proceeds to move forward even more slowly.

"Well," Patsy stands, "I better be gettin out of here. Got to be back before James Earl gets home."

"Don't run off. I want you to meet Dwayne." Dorothea raises up and holds onto Patsy's arm.

They both stand near the edge of the porch as the car stops and Dwayne gets out. He has on a tie and white shirt. Tilting the seat forward, he reaches into the back of the car and comes out with two bulging sacks. He walks to the steps looking from Dorothea to Patsy and back to Dorothea. "Hi," he says and smiles.

Patsy doesn't know what to think. He's a handsome man. Must be in his late twenties. Dark hair combed back. Nice clothes. She smiles politely, her arms hanging at her sides. She notices his shined shoes. Patsy tries to contain her surprise. She's not sure if she should continue looking at Dwayne or avert her eyes elsewhere.

"Dwayne, this here is Patsy, my best friend in the whole world." Dorothea puts her arm around Patsy's shoulders.

He walks up the steps. "Patsy, I'm glad to meet you." He has a broad, friendly smile. Patsy notices his nice, even teeth. "Let me set these bags down and I'll be back."

Dorothea pulls the screen door open and he walks inside.

Patsy lifts her head and narrows her eyes, her mouth seems poised to ask questions. But Dorothea looks inside the open doorway, waiting for Dwayne to step back out. Patsy relaxes, hoping her smile looks genuine and not suspicious.

Dwayne reappears. "What y'all doin today? Just visiting?"

"Yeah, just visiting," Dorothea says.

"I need to be getting on. I was telling Dorothea, my boy James Earl's bus will be along before too much."

"Well, now don't let me run you off," Dwayne beams a smile. "I ain't staying myself. I just brought Dorothea some things like she asked me to."

"No. It ain't that. I been here for a while and I need to be getting on home." Her hands clasped in front, she takes a small side-step toward Dorothea. Her lips draw back in an awkward smile.

Before any more can be said, Patsy puts her arms around Dorothea. "It's so good to see you. Now, get you a telephone so you can call me. And come see me anytime."

"Thanks for coming over. You know I'm always glad to see you." Dorothea has her arms around Patsy's waist and she rocks from foot to foot. Patsy sways back and forth with her.

"Thanks for letting me help you with Donna." Patsy pushes back from Dorothea, holding onto her shoulders. "She is such a little angel."

Patsy turns for the steps. "It was nice meeting you Dwayne."

"And very nice meeting you, Patsy."

Patsy descends the steps, her eyes focused on each plank, her arms out to the side for balance. She walks straight to the truck; feels a tingle run up the back of her neck as she reaches for the tarnished door handle. She looks back at Dorothea. "Bye." She puts her hand to her lips and smacks, throwing a kiss.

"Should I help you unload those grocery bags?" Dwayne asks Dorothea.

"There ain't much. Wait though, let me get you the money."

Patsy hears their voices as she pulls the squeaking door inward. She starts the pickup and puts it into gear. She throws her left arm out the window and waves to Dorothea and Dwayne, who remain standing on the porch watching.

All the way home, she can think of nothing else. She pictures Dwayne's confident smile and clear gaze. She feels sure there's more to it than just groceries, even though it could be as innocent as Dorothea says.

She hates having doubts about it, not knowing what's best for Dorothea. Patsy's mind whirls, she hardly pays attention to the road.

Her thoughts turn to Billy and she tries to imagine him sitting on that same porch shooting chickens. She remembers the loud, metallic clank of shots being fired when she arrived. Her hands grip the steering wheel tightly. She visualizes the gun on the table, considers Billy's absence, and then Dwayne. She shakes her head. "Lordy," she chastises herself out loud. She shakes her head again and then allows it to droop forward and wobble side to side, weighted down by unwieldy thoughts.

NINE – October 1962

Dorothea has not seen Patsy since she came home from the hospital with Darlene, her second little girl. That was in July, nearly four months ago. She worries that Patsy might be staying away because of Dwayne and knowing Darlene was Dwayne's baby and not Billy's.

She couldn't have been Billy's baby because he had been gone for one year in July. Besides that, Dorothea knew that she and Billy hadn't had sex for months before he left.

It isn't like Patsy to not visit her sooner than now, especially after having been with her when Darlene was born. Patsy asked Dorothea why she didn't have Dwayne get her a telephone so they could call each other. Dorothea said she would talk to him about it. But she didn't. She worries that Mr. and Mrs. Yarborough might somehow find out if she gets a telephone. They have not been to the farm since last winter, and then Dorothea put on a heavy coat that concealed her pregnancy and went outside.

"Seems like Billy ain't never home when ya'll come," she said, standing on Mrs. Yarborough's side of the car.

"You tell that boy to come see his ma once in awhile," Mr. Yarborough said in his gruff voice. Dorothea stood so she didn't have to see his face.

"And how's my little baby girl?" Mrs. Yarborough smiled and patted Dorothea's hand.

"She's okay, ceptin right now she got a little bit of a cold."

"Oh, my." Mrs. Yarborough frowned.

"She's sleeping right now. She'll be okay though, it ain't much."

"Well you tell her I miss seeing that pretty little doll baby."

They drove away and seemed to accept Dorothea's explanation. She hated it when they came and she had to lie about Billy. Dorothea worries about what has happened to him, but Dwayne seems to think everything is okay. "As long as the Yarboroughs ain't worried about him, why should you?"

She feels guilty about living in Billy's house and spending his money without him being there, even though Dwayne said, "You're his wife. You got a right to be here."

When Dwayne came to the house this morning, Dorothea asked him to stay with the girls while she went to visit Patsy. He didn't come that often, but when he did he usually stayed for a couple of hours.

Dwayne had the flatbed truck running good. Put a new battery in it and said there wasn't that much wrong with it. Dorothea had practiced driving the truck around the farm and felt comfortable enough driving it to Patsy's house.

At Patsy's house no one answers her knock, so Dorothea walks over to her grandmother's and knocks on the front door. The door swings open more quickly than expected. James Earl looks up. "Dorothea," he shouts.

"Hi, James Earl." She tousles his hair playfully. Where's your mommy?"

"She went to the doctor."

"Hi, Granny." Dorothea sees her grandmother moving forward in the dark interior. Light streams through the doorway, creating a diagonal pattern across the floor.

"Girl, what you doin here? Lordy, ain't seen you in a while. You okay?"

"Yes'm, I come to see Patsy and she ain't home."

"No, she ain't, she had to go to the doctor again," her voice creaks with lack of use. "She's got something wrong and they's trying to figger it out."

Dorothea notices her grandmother is looking older and more pallid than she remembered. "Well, what in the world's wrong. Is she sick?"

"Honey, I don't rightly know what it is." Her grandmother reaches out with one hand and supports herself against the door's edge. "She just ain't doin well. She's kindly sickly and tired mostly. Whyn't you come on in, honey?"

"Nah, I can't stay." She reaches out and runs her fingers through James Earl's straw-colored hair. He stands quietly, leaning against the door. "I need to get on back to my girls. I ain't seen Patsy in a while. I sure hope there ain't nothing bad wrong."

"Patsy told us you got you another little girl. You didn't bring them babies with you?"

"No, mam, I got someone watching them for me so I could come see Patsy."

"Well, I know Patsy wishes she was here to see yeh. But you knows womens has problems wit they health sometimes, more so than men it seems. I reckon they'll figger it out in due time."

"James Earl," Dorothea says, looking down into his green eyes, "tell your mommy I was here to see her and I'll come back. Tell her I hope she gets to feeling better."

"I will," he says, with a despondent look.

"Granny, I gotta leave, but I'll be back over real soon."

"Next time you bring them babies with you, yeh hear."

"Yes'm, I'll try." Dorothea turns and walks toward the truck.

"Bye." She hears James Earl's delicate voice. She turns and waves. They stand in the doorway, their eyes following her.

Clouds of dust billow behind as the truck rattles down the narrow country road. Eyes straight ahead, Dorothea thinks about Patsy. Envisions her in bed, thermometer in mouth. She doesn't like the idea of Patsy being sick.

She tries to remember what Patsy looked like last time she saw her: Was she pale? Was she walking slower?

At Sorrows Road, she turns right. The dirt is packed hard and it's a wider road. She thinks about James Earl. Thinks about her own girls. Not far from the lake her mind turns to D.W. and her jaw muscles tighten. She feels heat in her forehead above her eyes and knows it hurts too much to think about.

Road is like a washboard, can't go very fast. She sees a man with a hat on walking in the same direction, on the other side of the road. She slows down. Doesn't want the dust to rise up and fall on his clothes. Stays far right. The man is on the left and has a slight limp. She looks out the open window and continues at slow speed. "That's Reuben!" She stops. No other cars on the road. He slowly catches up.

"Reuben, that you?" She has her arm resting on the door, staring hard at the dark face under the straw hat.

He looks up and keeps walking in the slow steady pace, looking at her. "Yes'm it's Reuben. Who you be?"

"Dorothea. Remember, Mister Jack's girl?"

"Yes'm, I members," he says and smiles broadly. "My, my, how you be, Miss Dorothea?"

"Ah, I'm okay I reckon."

"Yes'm, you looks fine." He moves his head up and down in agreement. He stands in the middle of the road, a yard from the truck.

"You live out this way, Reuben?"

"No, mam, I comes out here to see my cousin, Zekiel. You knows Zekiel, Miss Dorothea?"

"No, can't say I do." She is beginning to recognize the younger Reuben she knew as a girl, in this older, more weathered person. The hat makes a difference. His features are harder. But the broad smile exposing his white teeth is still the same.

"He be's the one what's peoples call 'goatman'. You member he always ride his bicycle?"

Dorothea smiles. How could anyone not remember goatman? He was such an unusual character. She remembers how he would perform what seemed to be a goat imitation, putting his hand to his chin and jiggling it while making a bleating sound like a goat. He followed that by kicking out one of his legs and shaking it up and down as he puckered his lips and made a sound like farting. People would laugh and he would do it again.

"Oh, yeah, I remember him. I didn't know he was your cousin." She looks down the road for other cars. "Come on and get in, I'll give you a ride up the road a ways."

"Yes'm, I appreciate it. I get on deh back here."

"Nah, get up here where we can talk."

"No'm, I best get on deh back." He starts to move.

"Reuben, come on and get up front. Ain't no one gonna know the difference."

He walks around the back of the truck and opens the passenger door. Stepping up to the running board, he has some difficulty getting up into the seat. His right hand grabs the frame by the windshield and his left claws at the seat. With an exerted effort, he finally pulls himself up on the edge of the seat. He struggles to pull the door shut, reaching far out. Slam. It closes. Stiffening his arms, he lifts and scoots further onto the seat.

"How come you come out here to see the goatman?" Dorothea asks as she lets out on the clutch.

"My ma, she say it's deh Christian thing fo me to do. Zekiel, he don't always takes care uh hisself." He talks slowly, enunciating his words carefully. "My momma and Zekiel's momma deh was sisters, and Zekiel's momma she's died, so now we's his only family."

"And he lives out this road?"

"Yes'm, he do."

She was remembering more about goatman and some of the things he would occasionally talk about. "Is that quicksand pit he always talked about, is that out here too?"

"Yes'm, Miss Dorothea." He looks at her, his face suddenly shifting from smile to perplexity, eyebrows lowered, eyes quizzical. "Why you ast about dat?"

Her foot pushes down on the clutch, the other on the brake. She looks at Reuben. "Will you show me where he lives? I want to see that pit."

"Miss Dorothea," Reuben's voice becomes shrill, "dat's a dange'us place. I ain't never been near dat quicksand. It ain't no place fo you to see."

"Come on, Reuben, just show me where it is, I ain't gonna get near it." She pulls forward, reaching for the gearshift. She looks at Reuben, her eyes waiting for an answer.

"Miss Dorothea, what's you wanna do dat fo?" He has a worried look.

"I want you to show me where goatman lives and I want to see where that quicksand pit is." Going faster now, she and Reuben bounce in the seat. The truck cab rattles and a spare tire bangs on the truck bed. "How far?" Dorothea asks.

"Miss Dorothea, I don't thinks you need uh see no quicksand." Reuben looks at her sternly, but his voice is wavering, almost pleading with her.

"That's where we're goin Reuben. You tell me when we get there."

"I reckon you set yo mind on it, Miss Dorothea." He looks ahead, resigned to the fact that she is determined. "You has to keep goin out Sorrows Road uh ways and tween some trees they's a small road. It's jus big enough to get in dere, but I don't think no trucks been it dere fo a long time."

Dorothea keeps her eyes on the road, not talking. Reuben holds onto the door with one hand and the seat with the other.

"See dem trees up here, Miss Dorothea, you go up uh ways and it's on deh leff."

She slows the truck, looking for an opening.

"Here it tis now." Reuben points with his left hand so Dorothea can see.

A space between two big trees. No road. Just a worn path. She pulls in slowly, foot on the clutch. The truck is jarred by a bump at the edge of the road. Tall weeds. A path in the woods. The gear grinds as she shifts into low. The truck straddles the path and Dorothea weaves right and left, carefully creeping along.

"It's a little ways." Reuben wonders what his cousin is going to think when he sees a pickup coming down the path. Ezekiel acts so crazy most of the time, there's no telling how he's going to react to this invasion, of all things, by a young white woman. Reuben is out of his element. He doesn't like trouble. He doesn't want to be part of this, but sees he has no choice. His hand grips the doorframe hard. His other hand clutches his knee. He stares straight ahead.

"I don't mean to cause you no problem, Reuben, but I got to see this quicksand pit. I remember goatman talking about it and never knowed if it was true or not, but I ain't never forgot it."

"It's true, Miss Dorothea, and it's dange'us. I don't wants nothin to happen Miss Dorothea. You needs to be mighty careful out here." Beads of sweat are popping out on his forehead. "You know Zekiel, he ain't zactly well-minded."

"I reckon everybody knows that. His making like goat noise and kicking his leg like he's uh farting. He's kinda strange. But he ain't never hurt no one, has he?"

"No'm, he's gentle-like I reckon, but you don't never knows wit someone what is tetched." Looking ahead, Reuben can see a portion of Zekiel's hut through the trees. "He hear this truck, he may run off somewheres anyway."

Sorrows Road

Dorothea pushes the clutch. Stops and turns off the key. "That's it?"

"Yes'm." They both open doors and slowly climb out. Reuben walks ahead.

As they get closer, Reuben calls, "Oh, Zekiel."

Nothing. No movement. They continue slowly toward a structure the size of a hen house. It is a cluster of boxes, tree limbs, pieces of wood and corrugated tin for siding and roof. A stout, badly worn, wooden chair sits to the side.

"He might be clear to deh udder side, Miss Dorothea. He go all round dis here lake, cept he know how to stay outta deh quicksand." Reuben looks at her, hoping to change her mind. She continues cautiously stepping forward. Reuben knows now that the weather has turned cooler Ezekiel has a tendency to hide away more than usual. Now that hunting season is approaching, Ezekiel is sure to be doubly cautious.

"Zekiel." Ruben has his hand to the side of his mouth. They both have their eyes on the opening.

"Eieeaaah," Dorothea puts her hand to her mouth. Something has jumped from a tree off to the left. It's goatman. Crouching. Looking at them.

"Wuben." He utters in a mellow but guttural sound.

"Zekiel, it's me. This here be Miss Dorothea, Mista Jack's girl." Reuben stands stiffly, holding his hat in his hands, curling the edge of the brim. Ezekiel does not move. "You member her?"

"Hi, Zekiel." Dorothea drops her hands to her sides. She smiles, showing no fear. "I ain't seen you in a long time, you know it?"

He continues to look at her, still partly crouched, stiff and looking, as though nothing quite like this has ever occurred before. A person, other than Reuben, standing here on his home ground; a woman, a young white woman, out in this desolate place, standing here in front of him. He stares. Eyes like white holes. His mouth agape, the puzzlement showing on his dark, craggy face.

"I come to say 'howdy' and to see that quicksand pit you used to say was out here." Dorothea continues smiling. "You was telling the truth about that quicksand, wasn't you?"

TEN – September 1963

The streets leading to the university are lined with numerous small stores and an endless collection of bars and restaurants, many painted in brazen colors with even more brightly colored names scrawled across the upper façades. It's a bustling town. The streets are continually crowded with students dressed in unconventional and undeniably casual clothes, talking loudly and moving in every direction: bumping, turning, laughing. At night the town pulses with glowing neon lights.

Roy breathes in the atmosphere as he passes through the streets on his way to the library. "Sophisticated" may be the best way to describe how he feels living in a city so much more cosmopolitan than Cuttsville. Students from all over the country and several foreign countries are here, as well. A long stretch from Cuttsville, even though its only forty miles away. He started in September 1961 and now he's a junior into his third year.

As he enters the foyer of the library, the outside humming noises are shut off. It will take several hours to look up information for a report. He wants to get off to a good start this year and the cooler days energize him. He's eager to get busy and make a good impression early. Roy admires the high ceilings, heavy wood furniture and old-book mustiness of the library; he enjoys the quietness and the seriousness that permeates the air. It's not crowded. A few people sitting in isolated areas, a couple of people moving about.

In this environment, Roy is able to concentrate and time passes quickly. Later in the evening he looks at the clock high on the wall, it's almost eleven o'clock. Picking up his notebook, he walks toward the door. Outside he breathes in the cool evening air.

He walks among the dark trees, under the black night sky. Arching his shoulders to relieve the stiffness, he feels hungry. He follows the unlit sidewalk in front of the silent administration building toward the edge of campus, in the direction of the bright lights.

Across the street on one corner is a donut shop that stays open late. There's a damp chill in the night air, so the prospect of coffee and donuts is appealing. Not many cars on the streets tonight, at this hour. A couple of cars go by with their tires zizzing on the black pavement. The light changes and Roy crosses the wide street.

Windows wrap around the entire front of the donut shop. The inside lights spill out on the grass. Roy walks around to the parking side of the shop. A pickup and an older model car are parked near the entrance. Inside a long counter stretches the width of the building. One man sits at the far end of the counter; his left hand resting on the counter holding a cigarette, his right hand encircling a cup of coffee. A man wearing a white T-shirt, apron and paper hat holds a newspaper stretched across the cash register. He looks up; a toothpick hanging between his lips.

Sorrows Road

A woman backs out the kitchen door carrying a tray of glasses. The cashier puts away the newspaper and walks to where Roy is positioning himself on a vinyl-covered stool.

"Whata yeh have?" he asks. Thick black hair covers his arms. The toothpick dangles precariously from the corner of his mouth.

"Let me have black coffee and two chocolate cake donuts." Roy looks at the display case of donuts. The woman places a glass of ice water on the counter.

The man brings a cup of steaming coffee on a saucer. He goes to the display case and returns with two brown donuts on an onionskin tissue.

"Need any cream?"

"No. No thanks."

Roy sips the coffee, and then takes a bite out of one of the donuts. He looks around. Not much to look at. The cashier has his paper open again.

The waitress who brought the water comes back. Roy looks up.

"Do you know who I am?" She flashes a weak smile.

Roy looks at her face and swallows the piece of donut he has bitten off.

"Dorothea," she says. In the bright lights, her complexion is pale, her eyes framed by dark circles. Roy recognizes the familiarity of her face, delicate features. It has been several years and there's an obvious change.

"Well I'll be. How you doing?" Roy feels a tinge of excitement at meeting someone he knows, unexpectedly.

She lowers her eyes, slightly embarrassed. She has the same look of innocence in her eyes, but her disposition is more somber and apprehensive.

"Are you at the university?" She keeps her voice low. Her hair is pulled back and mostly covered by the white paper cap.

"Yeah, I've been here for a couple of years," he says, "but this is the first time I've been in here."

"I've only worked here a few months," she explains. She shifts her weight, places her right hand and a damp cloth she is holding on the counter and makes a nervous gesture as though she might wipe the counter.

"Are you married?" she asks.

"No." Roy smiles broadly. She smiles back.

"How about you?"

"Well, I was. And I got me two little girls." She quickly glances in the direction of the cashier. "The guy I was married to up and left. That's how come I got a job here."

"Oh." He takes a sip of coffee.

"But it's okay." She averts his eyes. "I'm doing just fine."

"You have two girls, huh?" Roy hunts for something to say. She appears to be thinner, her shoulders more rounded than he remembers.

"Yeah," she says softly. "How's your family?"

"Oh, they're fine. Everybody's fine."

"What was your sister's name?"

"Melissa."

"Yeah, Melissa. How's she doing?" She shifts her weight from one foot to the other; pulls her hands back from the counter. She glances to the side and then back.

"Good. She's doing good. She's a senior this year."

"Really? My goodness, I can't believe she's grown up already. Well," she says, backing away from the counter, "I better let you eat your donuts." The movement of her eyes to the side and down seems to signal an undercurrent of nervousness in talking with him. "But it was nice seeing you again."

"Yeah, nice seeing you." Roy watches her walk away. He notices the guy with the newspaper peeking over the edge of the paper and then quickly shifting his eyes back, giving the paper a shake to straighten it.

Roy picks up his donut and continues eating. He keeps looking up to see if she will come back out again. He drinks more coffee, savoring the taste. The donuts are good as well. He takes his time, his eyes on the kitchen door.

The man sitting at the end of the counter stands. With one hand on either side of his belt, he gives an upward tug on his pants. Satisfied with the adjustment, he walks along the row of stools. He hands the man at the cash register a handful of change. Without either of them saying anything, he walks out the door.

Dorothea has not emerged from the back since they spoke.

Roy takes a last sip of his coffee and then a few swallows of the cold water. He stands up and pulls a couple of coins from his pocket.

Dorothea walks back out carrying a wide metal tray filled with rows of donuts.

"Bye." She looks at Roy and smiles. She turns around and rests one side of the tray on a ledge at the base of the display cases.

Roy lifts his head. "Bye," he says. Moving to the left, he puts the change back and takes his wallet out of his back pocket. He hands the burly cashier a dollar bill. Putting out his hand for the change, Roy drops the coins into his pocket as he turns and walks toward the door. His hand pushes against the scarred silver plate at the door's edge and he walks out into the quiet night air. Moths are darting round the overhead lights, hitting against the glass. As he passes by the windows, he glances inside. The cashier stands in the same spot looking down at his paper. Dorothea lifts donuts off the metal tray and adds them to the ones on the shelves of the display case.

Roy crosses the street and walks under the canopy of tall dark trees toward the library parking lot. He sees a tiny glint of light twinkling on and off like a blinking star, only lower. A few more steps and he sees a leaf tangled in the silken threads of a spider web. He stops. The leaf twists back and forth with each breath of wind, and as it twists, flickers of moonlight reflect off the glossy filament.

ELEVEN

"Just before Billy left for good, he was acting real strange. He'd sit on the front steps with his rifle, drinking beer and shooting them chickens. They'd be squawking and running all over the place. No telling how many he killed. After a couple of days buzzards was perching in the trees till I dug a hole and picked up each dead chicken in the shovel and pitched it in that hole. Couple of days later he'd shoot a few more. It was a shame how he killed them chickens for no reason."

Sue Ellen shakes her head. "He sure sounds like a strange one."

"Well, he was. But he was nice at the same time. I mean I never really was scared of him. But it was like you never knew what was coming next."

"Shit," Sue Ellen says, looking at Dorothea with a puzzled expression, "most men are that way. My damn boyfriend lived with me for nearly two years. I thought we would get married. Soon as he got his degree, he was gone; no goodbye, kiss my ass, nothing. Got his stuff out while I was at work and left a note: Said, 'I'll be in touch.'"

"Lordy, he ain't called or nothin?" Legs straight out in front, crossed at the ankles, Dorothea sits upright in the stuffed chair.

Sue Ellen clenches her teeth, her brow lowers. "Hell no. Son of a bitch ain't gonna be back. He just used me. Pussy and groceries was all it was to him."

Dorothea's mouth purses with sympathy and in a somber tone she says, "Well, least you never got pregnant." Dorothea intertwines her fingers; she rubs one hand over the other. "Once I got big, Billy wouldn't have much to do with me. In the two years we was together on the farm, we wasn't in bed together more'n a dozen times. Sometimes I'd ask him to sleep with me because I wanted us to be close, kinda like I thought a husband and wife should be.

"But he'd say, 'No,'" Dorothea says softly, her head bent downward, staring as though she can see through the bare pine floor and beyond. "He'd say, 'I don't feel like it. Leave me alone.' And I would, because if we wasn't gonna be husband and wife-like, I hoped we could at least be friends."

"Man, I don't see how you put up with him as long as you did." Sue Ellen sits up on the couch, reaches for her bottle of beer. She feels sorry for Dorothea, hopes to learn more about her and be a friend. This is the first real conversation they've had, even though she lives right above.

"Course it made me sad, the way he acted, but wasn't nothing I could do about it. Seemed like nothing was turning out how I hoped it would." Dorothea looks at Sue Ellen, glad to have someone she can talk to about things. "But Patsy would come over sometimes and that really helped me."

"And Patsy is your aunt?"

"Yeah, and she's my best friend, too." Dorothea smiles faintly. "But, I was nearly always by myself. Course after Donna come, I stayed busy tending to her. I'd never let her outta my sight, I was so scared something would happen. And Billy just wasn't around that much. I never knew when he would leave or when he would come back."

"Did he go to see his parents?" Sue Ellen asks, sitting her beer on the table, leaning back.

"I don't think so. They would come out to the farm maybe every four months, maybe six months. And then after he left the last time, they came out and I told em Billy went off a little while ago and I weren't sure when he'd be back."

"And they never thought it was strange?"

"I reckon not. Least ways they never did say so, even though it was two years he was gone before they found out he'd been killed. I reckon they figured since I was there everything was the same. I don't know as they really cared. Maybe his ma, but she was always kinda sickly. His pa just didn't care."

Sue Ellen's eyes were fixed on Dorothea. "So he got killed and never did come back?" She took another swallow of beer, sat the bottle down and reached for her cigarettes; the pack was empty. The plywood board that served as a table rested on a stack of six red bricks on either end. It was low, only a foot or so off of the floor.

"No, I wasn't sure when he left the last time, because he was gone so much of the time that I just didn't pay it no mind anymore."

"Well I declare. You had sex with him just enough to get pregnant."

"Seems thata way. I feel sorry for him though. I wish I coulda figured out what was wrong. But I think he was mad at hisself and mad at the world. He never would talk. And then his pa . . . It may of been just that what made him act the way he did, because he couldn't do nothing to suit his pa. He was an awful spiteful person, times I was around him."

"You mean Billy's father?"

"Yeah, they come out and told me Billy had been killed." The words come rushing out as though Dorothea wants to unload the puzzlement and hurt she feels. "Said that a lawman in Chicago had called them. Asked them where they wanted the body sent. He asked me how long Billy had been gone and I told him Billy went off time to time and I wasn't sure when he left, which was truthful, because I didn't. And his ma looked at me pitiful-like, but his pa was ah glaring at me like he believed I was lying. And I don't know if they buried Billy or what they done. They never told me nothing."

Sue Ellen's mouth gapes open, her eyes unmovable and kind. "Did they tell you what had happened to Billy?"

"His pa went outside after awhile. And his ma was tearful and she said that this here Chicago lawman had told them Billy musta been fightin, because he was just beaten bad. And he was taken to the hospital there, but it was too late." Dorothea's voice falters and tears run down one cheek. "He was beaten so bad that it killed him."

"That is sad," Sue Ellen's voice is low and soft. "No matter what he did, it's not right for someone to do that. I'm so sorry, I know it hurts you to think about it."

"And then about a week later Mr. Yarborough come out there by hisself and told me I was gonna have to leave. Well, it like to scared me to death anyway because Dwayne had been there the night before and there was beer bottles sittin round and cigarettes in the ashtray and I reckon Mr.

Yarborough knowed I didn't smoke. At least he'd never seen me smokin."

Dorothea pulls her legs up, puts her elbows on the chair arms. "He said, 'What you plan on doing now, with Billy gone?' I told him, 'I hadn't really thought on it.' And he come closer to me, and I didn't like the way he was lookin at me, like he was wantin to see right inside my dress."

"That son of a bitch," Sue Ellen bristles, cocks her head as if preparing to learn the worst. "He was going to try screwing his son's wife."

"Well, I said, 'Just a minute,' and I hurried into the bedroom where Billy's pistol was by the bed. I was worried he might follow me, but he didn't. I knew it was loaded, so I come back out." Dorothea's eyes narrow in an uncharacteristically hard, serious look. "I said, 'If you're thinkin what I think, you ain't about to have your way with me.' Well, he backs up and has this scared look on his face, like he knew I was ready to pull the trigger."

"Would you have pulled the trigger?"

Dorothea is tense, her jaw tightens. "I reckon I would have. I'd done been raped before, I wasn't gonna allow it again."

"You had someone rape you?" Sue Ellen thrusts her shoulder back, her eyes jump. "I declare! When did that happen?" She scoots forward, sitting at the edge of the couch.

Dorothea lowers her head. "It ain't nothin I wanna talk about. It was just a bad thing that happened. That's how come I moved in with Billy. It's what started all my troubles."

She looks up at Sue Ellen. "I reckon Billy's pa thought, since Billy wasn't around, he could do what he wanted. But when he saw that gun pointing at em, he took out his wallet and threw some money on the floor. And he said, 'Looky here, bitch,' that's what he called me, 'bitch.' He said, 'Looky here, bitch, you be outta this house and offen my property before I come back out here. Cause if you ain't, I'm coming back with the sheriff to throw you off.' But I held the gun on him and never said nothin. He turned and got out the door in a hurry."

Sue Ellen blurts out quickly, "You know, you probably didn't have to leave, you being Billy's wife?"

Dorothea is momentarily silent. Then in a low voice, "It don't matter. I can't believe I stayed there as long as I did. Of course at that time I had me two girls. Maybe somehow Mr. Yarborough knew that Darlene was not Billy's girl. Maybe he found out about Dwayne coming out there."

Sue Ellen stands quickly. "Damn, I gotta have me a cigarette." She holds her hand upright toward Dorothea as though putting a halt on the conversation. "Let me run upstairs and get some cigarettes and I'll be right back." She starts to leave and then turns. "You have to get up early?"

"The girls always get me up early." A wide grin spreads across Dorothea's face. "But don't worry, I ain't going to bed yet. Go on." She jerks her head with a motion toward the door. "I'll look in on the girls."

Sue Ellen climbs the steps two at a time; she is intrigued by Dorothea's affair with Dwayne. When Dorothea was in the grocery store, Sue Ellen was going to give her and her girls a ride home; that's when she saw Dorothea talking to Dwayne. It really struck her as strange because this guy had flirted with her before. She was curious about what he was saying to

Dorothea. So Dorothea told her a little about the situation. Now she's anxious to learn more.

Remembering that she hasn't eaten anything since coming home, Sue Ellen opens the refrigerator door and quickly decides on a wedge of cheese. She removes the wax paper and begins nibbling at the cheese; picks up a pack of Winston's and heads back out the door.

"How are the girls?" Sue Ellen asks as she walks in the front room. She taps the pack of cigarettes on the table and opens the top. Tapping the pack again on the edge of her hand, she picks out a cigarette and then lights it.

"They're fine. Sleeping like angels."

"Well, I want to hear more about Dwayne. You don't mind telling me about you and him, do you?"

"No." Dorothea gives her a glance of casual indifference before sitting down. "It ain't nothing to hide from. Leastwise not from you."

"Well, when did Dwayne come to the farm? What was he doing out there?"

Dorothea leans into the side of the chair, pulls her legs up and under her. "Lordy, it wasn't long after Billy had left, that he come out there. I mean the last time Billy left. He was looking for Billy cause he said he owed him money. And I told him Billy left that morning and should be back anytime. I was kinda lonely, it being just me and Donna, so I was friendly toward him. We talked for a little bit and then I asked him if he wanted something to drink and he said, 'What yeh got?' And I told him beer and water. And he said he'd take a beer.

"He come in the house and we drank a beer and I guess I looked good to him and he put his arm around me on the couch. My breasts had gotten bigger since feeding Donna and I wasn't wearing no brassiere or nothing. And he put his hand inside my dress. Well, he sure had me a going and his kisses were real good. I stopped him because of Donna and asked him could he come back at night. I allow I shouldn't, but I was lonely."

Dorothea's eyes drop down and she looks at her hands as one touches on the other. "Wasn't no one to ever talk to. I turned on the radio from time to time to listen to music, but it worried me about what would happen to me and Donna if Billy wasn't coming back."

Dorothea puts her hand to her mouth to stifle a yawn. "I was just getting up every day, wondering what would happen. I tried to keep myself busy, cleaning in the barn, feeding the chickens. Then at night I would hear things and lay awake, and the moonlight coming in the window would make things move along the walls, and that ole house a creakin. Lordy, I was scared that someone knew I was there all alone." She giggles, but it instantly fades. Her eyes close, then open part way, laggardly.

"I better get outta here and let you get to bed." Sue Ellen stands and says, "But I'll tell you what, you have to tell me more about this Dwayne Sizemore."

"Sizemore?" Dorothea rises up from the chair.

"Yeah, that's his name, Dwayne Sizemore. You didn't know his name?"

"No. Reckon all I ever knew was Dwayne."

"Well, what is Darlene's last name?"

"It's Yarborough. Just like me and Donna. We're all Yarborough."

"Yeah. I guess that makes sense." Sue Ellen walks toward the door.

"Oh, wait," Dorothea says and rushes to her. "I brought home some donuts. Let me give you a couple." She tugs at Sue Ellen's arm and they walk together toward the kitchen.

"Don't mind if I do." Sue Ellen laughs.

"Well, I get em free. So if you like donuts, I'll sure have some for you."

Dorothea turns the light on in the kitchen, walks to the box on the table and pulls up the lid. "Take the kind you like."

"Ahh, these look good." Sue Ellen picks up two of the donuts.

"You want to put them in something?"

"No, this is just fine. Hey, when's your day off?"

"It'll be on Tuesday."

"We'll get together on Tuesday. I know where we can get them girls some real cute clothes. And they don't cost much at all." Dorothea flips the light switch and they walk through the hallway to the front room.

"Thanks for coming down and talking." Dorothea puts her hand to her mouth to cover another yawn. She realizes she probably should have gone to bed earlier.

"Hey, I enjoyed it. We'll have to do it more often." Sue Ellen smiles a pleasant, warm smile. "I like having you for a neighbor," she says, opening the door. "I'll see you Tuesday morning." She holds the donuts up. "Thanks."

TWELVE

Dorothea wraps both hands around the warm cup of coffee. She stares at the cuts and blemishes etched into the surface of the plastic tabletop. It is her day off and she is anxious to see Sue Ellen again, maybe take the girls out somewhere instead of just sitting at home.

A rapping on the front door makes her smile. The heavy wooden door has a distinctive high-pitch moan as it opens. "Hey, you up yet?"

Dorothea is cheered by the sound of Sue Ellen's voice. She stays seated and calls out, "Back here."

The coffee aroma hits Sue Ellen walking through the front room. "Got any more of that java?"

"Good morning. Sure, I got more coffee." Dorothea is relaxed, still smiling. She scoots her chair back and goes to the cabinet for another cup. "It really tastes good this morning. It's kinda chilly in here."

Sue Ellen pulls the other chair away from the table, sits down and lays her pack of cigarettes and matches on the table. "Yeah, it is. Girls still asleep?"

"Un-huh, reckon they won't wake for a little while. They were still up when I got home last night."

"Well good, you can tell me more about you and Dwayne. When I saw you talking to him in the store, I was kind of curious. From working in the store, I know a little bit about him."

Dorothea sets the steaming cup of coffee in front of Sue Ellen. "You use milk?"

"Sugar and some milk. You got regular milk?" Sue Ellen picks up a spoon lying beside the restaurant-style sugar container and shakes out a heaping spoonful.

"Well I told you Dwayne would come to the farm after Billy left." Dorothea hands her the milk carton. "At first it was really something," she says, reminiscing, "but, after I got big with Darlene, he'd come less often. Then I got kicked off Billy's place and everything sort of ended."

Sue Ellen pours in the milk. It overflows. "Oh, shit." She quickly slides back in the chair. Dorothea hands her a small towel. "Damn, I can't even fix my own coffee." She laughs.

Dorothea puts the milk in the refrigerator. "It's kinda strange the way Dwayne has treated me, but I've gotten used to men acting in strange ways."

"Well, it's because he's married. You knew he was married, didn't you?"

"No," Dorothea turns to Sue Ellen with a blank face, "No, I don't reckon I did. But I knew there must be something. He never talked about anything outside of his coming to the farm. And I was so glad for him being there, I never asked."

"Well, at least he's still talking to you."

"Yeah, he helped me find this place. And he helped me buy some old pieces of furniture. I reckon he's tried to help some. But when you saw me talking to him in the store, it had been several months since I'd seen him."

"I've seen him several times in the store, sometimes with his wife. I asked George, who works there, and he said 'Yeah, that's his wife.'" Sue Ellen lifts the cup, swallows coffee and makes a smacking sound with her lips.

"Well, it don't matter. It was good while it lasted."

Sue Ellen reaches for her cigarettes. Takes one out and taps the end on the tabletop. "You said he came out to the farm looking for Billy?"

"Yeah, said he owed him some money. It was strange too, because when I said I was Billy's wife, he said, 'I didn't know Billy liked women.' I didn't know whether he was making a joke or what."

"Well, Billy liked you enough to get you pregnant." She strikes a match on the black strip, lights her cigarette.

Dorothea lifts her eyes and looks at Sue Ellen. "Yeah, he did that. So did Dwayne, I reckon. But I didn't mind none because he sure did make me feel good."

Sue Ellen snickers, smoke coming from her lips in a series of rapids puffs. "Tell me about it."

"Well, he come back that first night," Dorothea's voice is low and quiet as she leans toward Sue Ellen, "and I had put Donna to bed, and we sat on the couch listening to some music and drinking beer, and he started kissing on me and running his hand in under my dress and rubbing on me. I tell you, I got hotter'n a firecracker." Dorothea makes her head and shoulders shudder. "I got off that couch and took his hand and led him to the bedroom. And I undressed and he did too, and we got under the covers because it was kinda chilly. But, lordy, it sure warmed up fast. He took his time. He wasn't like Billy, he done everything real slow. I mean I didn't know lovemaking would be that good. When we were done, we were both plumb tuckered out." Dorothea was glad Sue Ellen was interested. It felt good to recall those times.

"Whew," Sue Ellen sits up straight, grinning, "girl, you got me horny just listening to you. How often did he come out there?"

"Oh, I don't rightly know. It was a surprise every time. And when he would leave, I never knew if it was the last time I'd see him or if he'd come back again. Of course I hoped he would, because I was plumb head-over-heels crazy about him."

"You liked that lovin, didn't yeh?" Sue Ellen reaches out and lays her hand on top of Dorothea's hand, looks directly into her eyes and smiles.

"And he kept coming back," Dorothea says meekly.

"Course he did, he liked it too." Sue Ellen laughs.

"I reckon. Then too, Billy's pa was still sending a check to Billy every month and . . . Now don't you never tell nobody this, but Dwayne asked me if I had a copy of Billy's signature around anywhere. I found a paper Billy had signed and Dwayne got so he could copy it so as you couldn't tell it wasn't Billy's. And he would sign them checks and take em and then bring back groceries and baby food and beer and magazines. I didn't like taking that check because it wasn't meant for me, but I didn't have no way else to get any money, even for food. I guess I could of just eaten chicken and eggs till I run out."

"Honey, you deserved that check, putting up with what you did. Anyway, Donna is their grandbaby and Billy shoulda been supporting his wife and child."

"Yeah, I reckon that's true. I don't know. It's just that Billy had been gone for weeks and weeks and I didn't know would he ever come back or not. I was worried for Donna mostly. If it had been just me I coulda walked to Patsy's. I know she would get me some money for myself. I could always count on Patsy. I wish you could meet her. You'd like her. She's the only friend I truly had. I mean like a sister. I had other friends from time to time, but never anyone like Patsy." Dorothea turns to look at Sue Ellen and smiles. "And now I got you."

"You sure have. Me and you are gonna do okay, come hell or high water."

"I sure am sorry what happen to Billy." Dorothea put her fingers to her lips and then her chin, "I don't know why he went away like that. Why he didn't stay home. I don't even know where Chicago is, some big city way up north. I don't know why he went there or what he coulda done to get killed.

"His ma said he got beat so bad it killed him. That's so terrible. Who could do such a thing? And Billy wasn't all that big. I don't reckon he could defend hisself against someone who was much bigger. He shoulda taken his guns with him. I mean, I'm glad he didn't because I sure felt safer having them there with me. I just don't know. I don't understand what happened." Dorothea moves her hand from her chin and her shoulders slump forward. She looks at the linoleum in front of the refrigerator; the small, pebble-like pattern is nearly worn away from years of wear.

"Hard to know," Sue Ellen says, "lots of strange people in a big city like Chicago. I've never been there. Been to Chattanooga. Been to Birmingham. Even went to Atlanta once.

You get lost on one of those streets and don't know where you are, there's no telling what kind of freak you might run into."

"I sometimes think about it at night when I'm by myself and I cry." Dorothea has a look of perpetual misery, as though her inner core knows no other expression. "I cry for Billy. He was a blessing to me when I had nowhere to go."

"Well, honey, things will get better for you. I just know they will." Sue Ellen stands up, hoping to dispel this depressive mood. "Anymore coffee?"

"Yeah, I think there's more," Dorothea says, looking toward the coffee pot.

Sue Ellen pours. "You want some?"

"No. I've had enough." Dorothea stares ahead, hands in her lap. In a lighter tone she says, "You know I would of never learned to drive, if Dwayne hadn't taught me. Billy had an old truck out there on the farm and Dwayne did some tinkering on it and got it to running. And I cleaned it all out. Durn chickens had been nesting in there, even found a couple eggs on the floor."

"Didn't Billy ever drive the truck?" Sue Ellen pours milk into her cup, puts the milk in the refrigerator and comes back to the table.

"I never saw him drive it. It was in the barn." Dorothea puts her arms on the table, lifts one arm up and rests the side of her face against her hand. "Billy had his own truck to drive, I reckon he didn't need it."

"So Dwayne showed you how to drive it?"

"Yeah, that was so much fun." She smiles as she remembers. "Reckon it wasn't all fun for Dwayne. I was grinding them gears so much he started to holding his ears. It was one of them that shifts on the floor. Had a clunkity sound every time you shift. Course I couldn't get used to using that clutch. I swear, I'm surprised I ever learned. I know Dwayne was surprised."

"Were you pregnant then?"

"Yeah, I wasn't showing too much." She tries to visually recall how she looked, how Dwayne looked. "The bigger I got, the less he was coming out there.

"Love em and leave em," Sue Ellen says.

"When I went to the hospital to have Darlene, he never did come there. I wished he had. Of course, when I had Donna, Billy didn't come to the hospital neither. I just figured it was that way with men. Patsy was there for me. She helped me through, both times. I swear, if I could, I'd give her a pair of angel wings. Ain't anyone ever deserved it more."

Sue Ellen shifts in her chair. She looks at Dorothea, being attentive, enjoying the conversation. "When you left that farm, how come you moved to Parksdale? Why didn't you go back to Cuttsville?"

"Well, there wasn't nobody in Cuttsville that coulda helped me. Besides, Dwayne is the one asked if I wanted to live in Parksdale. Said he figured it would be easier to get a job here. And I had that money Mr. Yarborough gave to me. Wasn't no way I could go to Patsy. I reckon I felt I didn't have no choice. Seems like that's the way things always turn out for me."

"Things'll get better, believe me. And you have those two sweet little girls who love you." Sue Ellen smiles softly.

"Sometimes—I hate to say it—but sometimes I wished I didn't have em. I'm so afraid they're gonna grow up to be white trash just like me."

"Girl, you shouldn't talk like that. You're not white trash; you're just as good as anybody else."

Dorothea looks at her with doubtful eyes.

"You'll get through this okay. You just have to stay strong." Sue Ellen pulls another cigarette out of the pack and lights it. Lifts her chin to blow smoke toward the high ceiling and looks through the window above the sink. "Dang if it ain't raining. Look at that."

"Lordy, I hope it don't rain hard." Dorothea turns her head toward the window. "It's turning colder, won't be long before winter's here." Dorothea hears the bedroom door and, as she looks, Donna squeezes through. First she looks right, then left and sees Dorothea. She slowly walks toward her, still wearing the dress she had on yesterday and fell asleep in. As Donna climbs into her mother's lap and snuggles close, Darlene appears and walks toward Dorothea dragging a small blanket with frayed satin edging. With some difficulty, Darlene also climbs into Dorothea's lap. She holds the two girls one on either side.

"There's them little angels," Sue Ellen leans toward the girls, extending her arm until she touches Donna's leg, squeezes lightly, and then does the same with Darlene. Both girls look at her, but do not change their expressions. Donna rubs her eye and then yawns—mouth wide open.

"I kind of like Parksdale," Dorothea says, "there's a lot going on here. Lots of college people, that's for sure." She pulls with both arms, trying to keep the two girls balanced on her lap. "Most ain't much younger'n me, but they sure are lucky to go to the university. They must have lots of money."

"Well, not always, I went for awhile."

"You did? Oh, I didn't tell you, the other night a friend of mine from Cuttsville, his name is Roy, he came into the donut shop." Dorothea perks up in recalling the event. "I hadn't seen him since, lordy, I guess since we was still kids. And he goes to the university."

"Is he cute?" Sue Ellen raises her eyebrows.

"Yeah, I always thought so. And he's real nice, too." She holds a girl with each arm and lets them slide off her lap. "Donna, you and Darlene get down now, it's hard for mommy to hold both of you." She holds them until their feet reach the floor. "Want some cereal for breakfast?" Dorothea rises from her chair.

"I got some donuts too. Sue Ellen, I'm sorry, I forgot about the donuts. Do you want one with your coffee?"

"Heck yeah, I never turn down a free donut." Sue Ellen plunges her cigarette into the ashtray and pushes down.

Dorothea brings the box of donuts to the table. "Help yourself, there's plenty more where they come from." Dorothea goes to the refrigerator, takes out the milk, and then reaches for two glasses.

"Speaking of the university," Sue Ellen says, "I've managed to save a little money. I need to call my parents and see if they'll send some." She pulls a donut from the box. "I need to get back in school, myself." She bites into the donut.

Dorothea brings the glasses of milk to the table. "Gosh, you went to the university too?" She goes to the corner and drags a high chair to the table and lifts up Darlene.

"I've made it to sophomore, just barely." Sue Ellen reaches for her coffee cup. "I got three more years to go."

"You sit here, Donna." Dorothea helps her into the chair she was using and pushes strands of hair away from her face. She looks across the table at Sue Ellen. "Wow, just think, you're gonna be a college graduate." Her eyes open wide, she moves her head side to side in awe. "Just think, Sue Ellen."

Sue Ellen looks past Dorothea and out the window. "Looks like the rain has stopped already."

Dorothea turns her head to look. "Good," she says, "I don't want it raining on my day off!"

THIRTEEN

The ringing phone startles Roy. He is not expecting anyone to call in the middle of the day. He just came in from classes and is trying to get a jump on one of the reading assignments. He picks up the receiver.

"Hello."

"Roy?" The voice is demure. There's a funny scraping sound in the background.

"Yes." He responds hurriedly. He doesn't recognize the voice.

"It's Dorothea."

"Oh!" Caught off guard, he pauses. "Hi, Dorothea," he answers cautiously as though bad news can be the only reason for this unexpected call. "What's up?"

"I have a favor to ask." The voice continues its modest, soft tone.

"Uh." He wonders what he's getting into. "Yeah. Okay." He can't think of an honest reason to say no. He pictures her in his mind, not sure he wants this friendliness to develop any further.

"Do you have time to meet me somewhere?"

"Now?"

"Well, I go to work at six."

"Where at?" He draws the question out slowly. He feels an obligation, although only the same as he would if any person asked for his help.

"Would you mind coming to my house? I can't leave the girls."

"Sure. Where do you live?"

Roy jots down the directions. It's not that far. Near downtown. He tries to decide whether he should go right away or wait. He does not want to appear too willing since he isn't sure what she wants. However, if he does not go now he knows he won't be able to get it off his mind. He might as well go, then when he returns he'll be able to concentrate on the reading. He places a bookmarker in the book and closes it.

As he drives, he tries to imagine what she can possibly want. Is she having problems of some kind? Could it be something with her ex-husband? She did say he left her. Isn't that what she said? What if he has come back and she has refused to take him back? Maybe he's belligerent, a wife-beater. Maybe it has to do with her work. She probably doesn't make much money there. Does she think he can help her financially? What if she has romance in mind? Truthfully he doesn't find her that attractive. She has let life take a hard toll on her looks. She is thin and round-shouldered. She looks haggard and tired for her age.

He follows the main street through the old downtown area. This section of town probably hasn't changed in twenty years; most of the new buildings and new businesses are near the university. He passes massive buildings, brick and limestone, tan and gray, heavy, solid.

Even if she has romance on her mind, what would come of it? What if she told people in Cuttsville? Roy shakes his head. You haven't seen her in years. You don't know anything about her life and yet you're thinking her circumstances make her weak and vulnerable. Maybe she just wants to talk and be friends.

Could it have to do with her family in Cuttsville? With Uncle Jack gone, she has no one to rely on. Roy worries that he might be pulled into something unsettling. Something that he doesn't have time for.

He jams his foot on the brake, then the other on the clutch. Damn. Car in front stops suddenly for a red light. Not paying attention to the traffic, Roy almost doesn't stop in time. The near-accident rattles him.

Still shaky, he puts his arm out the window to signal a left turn. Waits for two cars to pass and then turns the corner onto First Street. The street is quiet. He looks for numbers. The huge trees are very old, the large houses ancient. It's the type of street that would have been a prestigious neighborhood seventy-five years ago. Only the town's wealthiest could have afforded to live here. Now it's quite different.

He pulls up in front of a large frame house—706 First Street. Many of the large homes in this area are still well cared for and some are not. Some are divided into apartments and rented to college students and others. This one is a faded white; the paint is obviously old and has no luster. Large trees are on either side, making the house appear secluded and dark. The handrail running the length of the porch has a baluster missing near the steps. As he looks farther down the porch he sees two more missing near the end.

Dorothea walks out on the front porch as he opens the car door. He looks carefully at the buckled sidewalk so he won't trip over a bulging chunk of concrete. As he approaches, the screen door opens slightly and a little girl runs to Dorothea. She wraps her arms around her mother's leg, holding tight and looking at Roy. Dorothea reaches down, putting her hand on the girl's head.

"Hi, Roy."

"Hi." He walks up the steps. She is smiling, seems relaxed, and looks better than she did at the donut shop. The work uniform and silly hat were not very becoming. Her dress is plain. She is barefooted, as is the little girl. "This is Donna," she says glancing down.

"Hi, Donna." Roy bends over to give importance to his greeting. But the little girl's face is buried in her mother's dress, which she clinches with tight fists.

"Will you come in?" Dorothea reaches for the screen door handle. She walks inside, stumbling slightly as the little girl clings to her. "Donna," she scolds.

Roy follows her into the dim interior. One faded couch and one stuffed chair in a large room. Two wooden chairs sit in disorderly fashion in one corner. Toys are scattered on an avocado-green rug. There are three or four boxes lying helter-shelter around the toys. There is nothing on the wallpapered walls. The room is sparse.

Dorothea goes to the stuffed chair. Roy moves sideways to the couch. She sits down, legs together, and the little girl lays her head on Dorothea's knee, still clutching her dress.

"I sure was surprised to see you in the donut shop." She smiles softly. Looking at him she shakes her head side to side as though it is hard to believe that she is seeing him again.

"Yeah," Roy lifts his head in agreement. "After all these years, I never would have guessed." His words trail off.

"I'm sorry I couldn't talk longer, you know how work is. They watch us all the time, don't like no one not working every minute."

"That's usually the way it is." Having said it, he feels awkward, knowing that the jobs he has had were never anything like hers.

"Well," she says, lowering her eyes, "I thought maybe you could help me." She is obviously uneasy about asking, after not seeing each other for several years.

The house is drab. It is also stuffy, no air moving. Roy feels apprehensive as well, overcome with the sense that he doesn't belong here, that he is out of his element. At the same time, she seems so vulnerable—the tall ceiling, the large empty room—her alone with the little girl clinging to her.

"In what way?"

"Well, you remember Rosemary and John?"

"Who?" Roy asks.

"My sister and brother, Rosemary and John."

"Oh. Oh, yeah."

"Well, our daddy left them some money. Rosemary, she's married and lives in Tennessee, she wrote to me and said she got five thousand dollars. She said she is sure that John got the same. In fact, he is going to college in North Carolina and she said that is how he is doing it. He got that money."

"Oh, wow." Roy jerks his head slightly, showing interest.

"What I don't understand," Dorothea continues, "is why I never got nothing. Not one cent. Nobody has called me or wrote me about no money." Her voice gradually becomes louder and more forceful. "I know Poppa woulda left me money too. He treated me like I was his own, he always did. It just doesn't make sense that I wouldn't get nothing." Tears well up in her eyes. Donna looks up at her mother.

"I called Rosemary long distance to ask her about it. She said there was a will and it said something about the children, I think she called it a trust. She said she didn't know no more than that. She said her husband, Danny, said they need to come down here and check up on it, because there coulda been more than that. He said how was they to know how much Poppa left to Rosemary. There weren't no papers, no nothing. Just the check and a note from a person that works for the county. It said that's what Poppa left her and she was supposed to get when she turned eighteen. She don't know why it didn't come sooner because she's nineteen and almost twenty. And John he's eighteen. I guess that's why he got his money." Tears from both eyes make wet tracks over her cheeks.

"Mommy." The little girl sees the tears.

"Hush now Donna." She places a hushing finger on the child's lips.

"Well, uh, how do you think I can help?" Roy can see she is upset. And why shouldn't she be. It sounds a little strange.

"Well, I just thought maybe you could ask your ma and pa if they know anything about it. I know your ma and pa are honest folks and I could trust what they say. I don't reckon I know who else to go to. I could ask my friend Patsy," she pauses and bites her lip, "but she's married to D.W., my uncle, and I'd hate that he ever found out. I wouldn't trust that sonufabitch, excuse my French, as far as I could throw em." She looks into the distance. "And if it was up to my ma and Ned, they'd keep any money they could to themselves." Her voice is sterner. With a quick move, she wipes the tears with the back of her hand. She is sitting up straight, her arms tight against her sides.

Another little girl comes walking into the room rubbing her eyes and her lower lip pushed out. A baby blanket is tucked under one arm and hangs to the floor. She walks quickly to her mother, lays her head on Dorothea's lap, causing her sister to move to the side. "Hi, angel. Did you have a nice nap?" Dorothea lightly strokes her left hand across the top of the little girl's head.

Roy remembers now that she said she had two children. "Sure, I can ask Mom and Dad. I'll be going over this weekend and then I can let you know what I find out."

"I sure would appreciate you doing it for me. I don't want to be a burden, but it hurts me not to know what happened." Dorothea swipes the back of her hand over her cheek again.

"No. It's no trouble at all."

Dorothea struggles to rise. The little girls hang on to her legs. She bends down and picks up the smaller girl, who clutches to the blanket and pulls it up to her chin.

"Thank you for coming."

Roy rises from the couch. "Oh, I don't mind. Glad I can help."

"This is Darlene." She gently bounces the little girl up and down against her chest. "Mommy's gonna need to get ready for work," she says to the two girls as she steps in the direction of the door.

Roy walks to the screen door and pushes it outward.

"I hope you don't think it's bad of me wanting you to do this. I just don't know how else I can find out," she says as he steps out onto the porch.

Roy glances back. "Noooo," he draws the word out, emphasizing his willingness to be helpful. "I just hope I can find out something."

Dorothea leans over and lets the little girl's feet touch the floor. As soon as she releases her, the little girl throws her arms around Dorothea's leg.

Roy descends the worn steps and follows the sidewalk to his car. Opening the car door, he waves with his free hand and slides onto the seat.

Dorothea bends down and nudges the girls away. "Stay here." Then she turns and calls, "Roy." She skips down the steps and hurries to the car.

"Don't go to no trouble on my account," she says.

Roy looks at her. Her face is pale, frozen hard with worry, yet her eyes and mouth are tentative and apologetic. He smiles. "I'll let you know what I find out."

"Thanks for coming over. I really appreciate it." She backs away, arms hanging down, her hands joined in the front.

"Glad to meet your little girls," Roy says.

She flashes a quick smile. The paleness of her skin, the dark circles around her eyes unveil an underlying sadness. She appears frail and despondent. Plain and barefooted, she stands on the uneven sidewalk with towering trees and the large, shaded house looming behind.

He pulls away from the curb and doesn't look back. Though the little girls' hair has not been brushed and their dresses are dingy and faded, they are cute. Who stays with them when Dorothea has to go to work? He wonders if someone else lives there with her.

Roy hopes he has not come across as too softhearted and pliable. At the same time he doesn't want Dorothea to think he is not willing to help. He drives through the streets feeling important, his own spirits lifted. She is placing trust in him to get the information. Still, he wonders how much help he can be. She could certainly use the money. He knows his father can probably find out something; he knows a lot of people, city officials, the sheriff. Roy just hopes it doesn't lead to a dead end or that Uncle Jack actually did not leave her any money. Dorothea doesn't need more bad news.

FOURTEEN

It is Saturday and, his class assignments all caught up, Roy has to make the trip to Cuttsville. He needs money (never an easy subject to bring up) and he is also taking his dirty clothes for his mother to wash. And now he has to go because he told Dorothea he would try to find out something about the inheritance money.

He carries a large cardboard box to the car and puts it on the front seat. He puts his clothes in the box as they get dirty and after his mother washes and folds the clothes she will stack them in the box for him to take back. Not very posh he realizes. A little more awkward than having a dresser, but since he lives alone, he keeps things in their place and organized.

Roy looks at his Mercury; it is clean and still looks good for a 1951 model. It has had a few problems. He just bought a new battery about two months ago. He goes back to the apartment and locks the door with his key. The car starts right up. Only ten o'clock and he is headed home.

He hopes Dorothea is right about Uncle Jack leaving money to her too. It seems the right thing to do. He was the only father she ever knew; leaving her totally out of his will would be a cruel thing to do. Roy never knew Uncle Jack to be cruel. Didn't know him all that well, however. Roy thinks back, tries to remember what his uncle was like, the few occasions he was around him.

The car is running fine, which is always a relief. Cool temperatures on October mornings are to be expected, but it always heats up by afternoon. He has the windows part way down and chilly wind is blowing in. Roy turns on the radio to pick up some music as he makes his way out of Parksdale to the highway that runs to Cuttsville. Eyes scanning one side of the road and then the other, there are a lot of familiar sites along the way, since he has made this trip so many times.

After arriving and unloading everything Roy offers to help his mother hang the clothes. Standing by the humming washing machine, she glances at him and says, "We'll see." He takes this to mean he should not concern himself with it.

When he pulled into the yard, he noticed that the grass is high and he knows his father appreciates it if he cuts the grass on his visits. This may be the last time it needs cutting this year and, if he does it, he will feel better about asking for money.

His father is in the den listening to the radio and reading the newspaper. More than likely, he is waiting for a baseball game to start on television. It's a little early yet.

"Hey," Roy greets his father, "looks like you're taking it easy this morning."

"Yeah," he says, looking up at Roy, "while I can."

"How's the juke joint doing?" Roy knows his father works long hours on weekends. His mother comes into the den.

"Oh, it's okay, I guess." His father is not enthusiastic, but Roy knows he would probably say more if it was not going well.

He sits down on a hassock. "You'll never guess who I ran into in Parksdale."

His mother looks at him. "Who?"

"Dorothea, Uncle Jack's daughter. She works in a donut shop near campus."

"Well, I'll be," his mother says clearly surprised. "How is she?"

"Truthfully, she seems to be a little down on her luck. She said her husband left her and she has two little girls."

"Two!" his mother exclaims. "My goodness she got off to an early start. She's not much older than you, is she?"

"A year or two, I guess."

"Oh, that's too bad." His mother moves her head side to side. "She was always such a sweet girl."

"She wanted me to ask if you might know anything about an inheritance she could be entitled to. She said Uncle Jack left his kids some money. She told me Rosemary and John both got five thousand dollars, but she hasn't gotten anything."

"Well, I'm sure Jack had money." His father pulls his pipe off of the tobacco stand. "If they sold off some of those properties, it should add up to more than any ten thousand dollars." He bangs the pipe face down into the palm of his hand.

"Wonder how much of it Eula Mae traded off," Roy's mother asks, "or gave to her family? You know her dad and D.W. aren't paying any rent on that store."

"If that family got their hands on it, there may not be anything left, that's for damn sure." His dad brushes tobacco ashes from his hand into a waste can.

"I thought," Roy's mother raises her voice to a higher pitch, "I thought Melissa said she heard from John that Cletus Henslowe had something to do with Jack's will." Neither Roy nor his father respond. Roy looks at his mother for clarification.

"You remember John?" she asks.

"Some," Roy answers, "but he was a couple of years younger than me. Now Dorothea says he's starting college."

"Melissa knew him at school. Said he is really smart; did real well in school." His mother rises. "Melissa should be home sometime this afternoon. You're going to be here for a while anyway, aren't you?"

"Why sure." Roy stands and walks up behind his mother and puts his arms around her. "I came home to see you," he says in a teasing fashion. "Also," he says, letting go of her, "I'll cut that grass out there. Looks like it is getting high."

"Yeah," his father says, "it's all that rain we've had." His father pushes tobacco into the bowl of his pipe.

Roy strips off his outer shirt on the way toward the back door. He has a T-shirt on underneath. He doesn't mind cutting the grass and he almost always does it, except when he doesn't get home often enough, then his father cuts it.

Once the yard is mowed, Roy pushes the silent mower toward the open garage. Just then, Melissa pulls in the drive in her little Ford Falcon. She honks the horn, maybe a greeting, probably hoping Roy isn't paying attention and she'll make him jump.

"Hey, brother." She has a broad smile that automatically causes him to smile. She goes to hug him and stops.

"Better not." He puts his hands up. "Got a little sweaty cutting the grass."

"You staying tonight?"

"Probably not. Head back to Parksdale; maybe go out tonight. That is if I can con Dad into giving me some money." He raises his eyebrows and grins.

"Ah, shoot. Me and Janice are going to a movie. We'll let you come along."

He opens the screen door and they walk inside. "We'll see. Say, I need to ask you about a lawyer named Cletus Henslowe. Mom said you mentioned he had something to do with Uncle Jack's will." Roy reaches into the refrigerator for a pitcher of tea. Gets a glass out of the cupboard and sits down at the kitchen table.

"Just a minute. I need to powder my nose." Melissa leaves the room.

Roy gets up, picks up his glass of tea and goes to the den. "Got the grass cut. Anything else you need done?"

His father turns away from a baseball game on television. "Hey, great, thanks for doing that. I really didn't feel like getting out there."

"Well, I did it for money, you know."

"Huh," his father halfway chuckles, halfway grunts. "Yeah, okay, we'll see what I can do, later." He turns back to the game. Roy knows he won't get any money as long as the game is on. He doesn't worry about it; his mother always makes sure he has enough money before he leaves. He ambles back to the kitchen, adds more tea to his glass and puts the pitcher in the refrigerator. After sitting down, Melissa walks in.

"John told me he took his father's will to Mr. Henslowe. Said he found it with some other papers in an envelope in a box of old stuff he was looking through. The envelope had Cletus Henslowe's name and address on it. Said he read it and put it back in the envelope. Didn't tell his mother and took it to Mr. Henslowe to find out what it all meant. Henslowe told him the children would be getting some money."

"Including Dorothea?" Roy asks.

"I guess; he didn't say."

"Well, Dorothea lives over in Parksdale now. She works in a donut shop near campus. She called me and told me that John and Rosemary had gotten $5,000 apiece, but she hasn't gotten anything. From the look of things, she could really use the money."

"Wow, $5,000 apiece. I haven't seen Dorothea in years. Hardly remember what she looks like."

Roy's mother is standing in the doorway. "Couldn't you go to Mr. Henslowe and ask him about it?"

While Roy thinks about the question, Melissa says, "Well I know John must have gotten his share of the money, because he's going to college in South Carolina. You know Eula Mae and that guy she married aren't paying for it."

Roy looks up at his mother. "This being Saturday, I wouldn't expect Mr. Henslowe to be in his office."

"You know," Melissa says, "your buddy Timmy Evans knows Mr. Henslowe pretty well. Why not call him and see if he knows where you might find him?"

"Probably wouldn't be too hard to track him down," Roy's mother adds.

Roy isn't anxious to face Mr. Henslowe; doesn't know if he would agree to talk about Uncle Jack's will, let alone give him details, since he isn't even part of the family.

"Go call Timmy," Melissa urges.

"Oh, okay." Roy gets up slowly. The phone is in the den; he watches the ball game for a minute. "Dad, can I turn this down a minute? I need to use the phone."

His father gets up. "Yeah, sure, I need to get something to drink."

After talking on the phone, Roy returns to the kitchen. Melissa and her mother are talking about Eula Mae and Ned and their venture at running the store. Rehashing that old story once again.

"Timmy says Henslowe goes to his office on Sunday afternoons. He said in the morning he goes to see his mother; she stays in a nursing home near Crowder. She's in her eighties and her health isn't too good. Timmy says Henslowe is very loyal and dedicated to his mother; says he never misses going to see her on Sunday. He thinks Henslowe drives back, eats lunch and then goes to his office."

"See I told you," Melissa chides him, "now you can go to the movie with me tonight." She tilts her head and feigns an exaggerated grin.

Later, after Roy has taken a shower, his mother has dinner ready. They eat and Roy and Melissa get ready to go. She is driving and they will pick up her friend Janice. Roy admires how nice his "little" sister looks. Already a senior and very popular in school. She and Janice have been friends for a long time, but when he sees Janice he is surprised by how much she has changed; her hair nicely curled, bright lipstick, very attractive, he thinks to himself.

"Hi-i, Ro-o-oy," Janice intones in a superficial manner, somewhat overly excited by his presence. Roy lifts out of the front seat, so she can sit in the front. "I didn't know you where coming." She shows even, white teeth.

"Hi, Janice, nice to see you." He gets in the back.

"I made him come," Melissa interjects. "He was going to go back to Parksdale and would have missed going out with us. He just doesn't know what he would have been missing!"

"Yeah, really." Janice laughs. Puts her arm on the seat and looks at Roy. "How you been?"

"Great. Great, staying busy." Roy smiles.

"I'll bet."

Melissa starts the car. "He has to study sometimes, he doesn't like that part."

"Can't blame you." Janice laughs again.

"How are things with you? Still going with that football player?"

"Clarence? Yeah, same ole guy. He's off fishing tonight. He'd rather go fishing than take me to a movie."

"Fishing in the dark?" Roy asks.

"Uh-huh." She nods her head. "He gets a couple of his buddies to go with him. He's crazy."

"Hey," Melissa pats her on the arm. "He's a man's man."

"Yeah, I reckon." Janice pushes her lips out as though pouting. "What about you Roy. Are you dating someone?"

"I'm looking. I was dating a girl named Kellie last year, but she graduated and went back to Illinois."

"Graduated! How old is she?" Melissa asks.

"Well," Roy pauses, "she's 21. That's the problem. There's no way I'm ready to get married just yet."

Melissa turns her head and frowns. "What are you doing dating older women?"

Roy smiles, but doesn't offer a response.

"Shoot," Janice says, "I wouldn't worry, you'll find someone else."

Coming out of the movie, the streets are dark as they walk away from the theater. It was twilight when they went in. The car has tiny beads of moisture on top. Melissa unlocks her door and reaches across to unlock the others.

Roy slides toward the middle of the back seat. "That movie wasn't too bad."

"I liked it." Melissa puts the key in the ignition.

"Me too," Janice adds, as she pulls her door shut.

"I guess that guy got what he deserved for running around on his wife."

Janice looks at Roy. "You're right, and you know what?" she asks in an excited voice, "Clarence, the guy I date, his sister Clarice is divorced and she's running around with this guy who is married."

"Really?" Melissa asks quickly. "Is he an older man?"

"Well, she's about twenty-three or twenty-four, but I think he's older. Clarice told Clarence he's got money. I guess that's what she's after. I think he has some kind of business, maybe."

"Hmmm." Roy raises his eyebrows. "Did she tell Clarence the guy's name? Not many things like that go unnoticed for long in Cuttsville."

"No. I don't think Clarence has any idea who the guy is. The sad thing though," Janice says, "Clarice told him this guy's wife has some kind of illness."

"Oh, so that makes it okay for him to run around with other women?" Melissa grimaces. "What a dog."

"Well, Clarice is pretty wild, from what Clarence tells me. I think he worries about her, even though she's a lot older than he is."

Melissa looks at Janice and in a joking manner says, "Maybe Roy can find out who this guy is. He's doing some detective work for a girl we know—well, I guess she's really not a girl anymore—a woman we know who's from Cuttsville."

"Really?" Janice looks to Roy for elaboration, but Melissa continues instead.

"She thinks she was supposed to get an inheritance and she didn't. Oh . . . Say, do you remember John Durso?"

"N-No. Don't think I do."

"He graduated, but he was on the football team. I'm sure Clarence knows him."

"I'd probably know him if I saw him," Janice says.

"Anyway, it's his older sister. Or I guess Dorothea is his older half-sister. Roy is going to talk to the lawyer tomorrow—the one who is supposed to have handled the father's will. He's going to see if he can crack the case! Right?"

"What I'm probably doing," Roy says, "is getting myself mixed up in a mess that I don't have any business being mixed up in."

"Hey," Melissa calls over her shoulder, "there could be some real simple explanation. And besides, you're being a nice guy, trying to help out this poor, defenseless girl—woman!"

Janice smiles.

Admittedly, Roy thinks his sister's teasing him about being helpful is justified. "We'll see," he responds and then raises his eyebrows as though considering what might happen tomorrow.

FIFTEEN

Sunday morning Roy eats a good breakfast and goes to church with Melissa and his mother. He has his car loaded, ready to head back to Parksdale.

He isn't sure what time to expect Mr. Henslowe to be in his office; he forgot to ask Timmy what time 'after lunch' would be. He guesses everyone eats around twelve or one o'clock. Anyway, his mother is fixing food and she won't let him leave before eating. His father is sitting in the living room reading the Sunday paper.

Roy picks up the comics. "What do you know about this lawyer Henslowe?"

"Not much, really." His father looks up. "I've only seen him a few times. As far as I know he's well thought of around town. Don't really know much about him."

After dinner, it is almost two o'clock. Roy hugs his mother. "Thanks, Mom. "Thanks for everything."

"You are welcome." She kisses his cheek and holds onto his arm momentarily. "Let us know what you find out from Mr. Henslowe."

"Yeah, I will." He is skeptical about having any success. Maybe Henslowe won't even be in his office; this Sunday could be an exception.

Downtown Cuttsville exists primarily of the two sides of Main Street. Henslowe's office is 205. He has never looked for it before, but knows it won't be hard to find. Not sure whether it is 205 East Main or West Main. There is little traffic, so he goes slow, looking left at the odd numbers. After crossing Walnut, he sees the sign on a door: "Attorney-at-Law, Cletus Henslowe". Roy parks his car. There are only five or six cars parked on both sides of the street. No stores open. A small-town Sunday afternoon.

Roy feels nervous because of Henslowe's importance. A lawyer or anyone with a college education carries an elite status in a small town; people such as attorneys, bankers, politicians—people who wear suits and ties to work. These are the people everyone thinks of as the leaders in the community, usually wealthier than most people, a little more fastidious than regular folks.

He re-reads the name on the door. No windows. He knocks. Waits patiently. Knocks again and hears some shuffling inside.

The door opens slightly, enough for Roy to see Henslowe's face. "Yes?"

"Mr. Henslowe, my name is Roy Orchelle. Timmy Evans said I would find you here. I'd like to talk to you about my uncle's will."

The door opens wider. "You Hank's boy? Come on in."

"Yes, I am." Roy walks into the room as the door is pushed shut. He follows Henslowe down the musty-smelling hallway and turns left into the first office.

"What uncle are you talking about?" He walks behind a large walnut desk with several stacks of papers. The walls are without windows and lined with books.

Henslowe sits in a large leather chair, his arms draped over the padded chair arms. The chair tilts back. He motions with an upturned hand for Roy to sit.

"It's my uncle, Jack Dorso. He passed away several years ago, but I understand his son recently found his will."

"Oh yes, Jack Dorso; a will and a trust for his children. Yes, we took care of that several months ago. What did you need to know about it?" Henslowe puts he fingertips together and raises his hands to his chin. A contemplative look.

"Well, I understand that two of his children, John and Rosemary, received five thousand dollars."

"Yes," he spoke sharply. "We arranged to sell off some property."

"Well, there is another daughter, Dorothea. She has never received any money from the will and . . . "

Henslowe's brow wrinkles. "I don't know where you are getting your information, Roy, but Dorothea received the same amount, five thousand dollars." His voice was stern. His stare direct and unwavering.

"Well," Roy is unnerved. "Uh, I just talked with Dorothea a few days ago. That's why I'm here, she asked me to find out why she has never gotten any money." Roy knows his face is red.

Henslowe slowly stands up as a matter of indicating that the meeting is drawing to a close. His white shirt is starched, his striped tie impeccably knotted. His thin-lipped smile is almost a sneer. "We-l-l-l, someone has given you some wrong information. This person, Dorothea, was right here no more than six months ago to claim her inheritance. I personally handed her the check for five thousand dollars."

Something is wrong. Roy knows Dorothea was not lying about the money. "I'm sorry, Mr. Henslowe, but that couldn't be." He grips the chair arms and raises himself up.

"Look, young man, uhmmm, uhmmm." He clears his throat. "I guess I know what can be and can't be." He straightens up to full height, his blue eyes glaring. He walks in measured cadence to the side of the desk.

"Mr. Henslowe, I don't mean to disagree, but Dorothea, if you saw her, you would know she never got any five thousand dollars."

"Young man." His face is contorted in disbelief. "Roy." He controls his voice so it is firm, yet calm. "This lady Dorothea was here with her uncle, a Mr. Crawley, P.W., I think he was called, and she had proper identification. There's no question about it, she did get the money."

Roy looks down, sees Henslowe's shiny brown cap-toed shoes; they look new. The carpeting, a light tan, is plush and soft. He feels out of his league.

Henslowe takes another step toward him, hoping to urge him out the door.

"There's a problem here," Roy persists, "her uncle, D.W., is not her friend, she dislikes this guy."

"Well, I wouldn't doubt that. I can see how just about anyone would dislike Mr. D.W. He's quite overbearing. A hot-tempered rogue, but, but that's doesn't change the situation. Dorothea was here and she did get her money."

Roy's mouth is open. He is perplexed, unable to think of how to get his point across.

"Mr. Henslowe, if you know what D.W. is like, isn't it possible he cheated her out of the money?"

"I don't see how, the check was made out to her, not him. You think he made her sign the check and then took it from her? Is that what she told you?"

"No. She never got the money. It wasn't her, she was never here in your office."

Henslowe looks disbelievingly at Roy, thinking maybe he just doesn't have the story exactly straight. "What are you saying? She was here, son, I told you she had identification, her birth certificate. She had her birth certificate and her uncle was here to verify that she was who she said she was."

"Her birth certificate? Did she have a driver's license or a social security card, anything like that?"

"No, she said she didn't have a job; she had never worked. She didn't have any other identification." Henslowe seems to be softening a little now. Doubts are taking hold and he begins looking at the situation more analytically. He brushes his hand over his hair, trying to remember the events that took place in his office. "You know, it's fairly common for people to have no identification at all." His lips pull back to show contempt. "They can't even write. At least she had her birth certificate. Yes, I remember, it was authentic, it had the state seal, I'm sure it was an authentic birth certificate."

"Could be." Roy is thinking out loud.

"Well, that D.W. was being so forceful, ranting and shouting, I made damn sure the birth certificate was authentic. He was attempting to bully me. I've never seen such a disrespectful person. He said, 'That's all the identification you need. Unless you are trying to cheat her out of her rightful inheritance.' That's what he said to me. I said, 'I can assure you, Mr. Crawley, that I'm not trying to cheat anyone.' And he kept up his tirade, he said, 'How do we know that's all she has coming?' And then he looked me right in the eye and said, 'What's your take in this? How much you getting paid for doing this?' And I told him my fee was set by the judge, which it was. Then he came right back and said, 'Yeah, I'll bet you and that judge is old fishing buddies, too.'"

Henslowe backs up a step, puts his left hand on the desk. "He was getting to me, so I said, 'Look here Mr. Crawley if you are going to make accusations and question my integrity, you can get out of my office.' And he sneered at me and said, 'Well you give her the money and we'll do just that.' So this Dorothea, she took the check and the birth certificate and they walked out."

"I guess you were glad to see him go."

"Was I ever. What a bizarre, well, anyway, I was glad to see him go."

"What did Dorothea look like? Do you remember her?"

"Yes, well, she was attractive, sort of. Shapely, I guess, but she was not well dressed or poised or anything, a little rough around the edges, I'd say. Blondish hair. Her gum-chewing and eh, her tight clothes were a little revealing." Henslowe opens his eyes wide, raises his eyebrows.

"Hmmm, that's not Dorothea."

Henslowe backs away, puts his left hand on the desk and then leans against it.

Roy feels they have found the problem. He is comfortable with Henslowe now that they are thinking more or less along the same line. He relaxes; leans toward the front of the solid desk. "Could he have brought someone other than the real Dorothea here? Maybe he got the birth certificate from Dorothea's mother or from her house."

"I can't believe he would try such a thing." Henslowe raises his voice, "He would be committing a crime. He could go to prison for doing something like that."

Roy can tell that Henslowe is considering the details carefully. "Well, you said he was trying to bully you. Maybe that's why."

"Well, I just took him to be a big mouth. I had no idea. Of course, I have seen worse over the years." Henslowe goes back to his chair. He and Roy sit simultaneously.

"If that's the case, what do you think Dorothea can do?" Roy leans forward in his chair to garner what information he can.

Henslowe takes a deep breath, breathing through his nose, expanding his chest. "She needs to get an attorney. If she's telling the truth. If it wasn't the real Dorothea that came in here to get that check." He is thinking about the possible ordeal that will follow. "Of course, she is going to have to prove her case. Prove that it wasn't her."

"You would know once you saw her, don't you think?

"Well, it has been a while. I would hope to remember, to be able to tell . . . However . . . "

"But," Roy tries to bolster him, "if the woman you saw had light hair, Dorothea's hair is dark."

"Some of these girls color their hair now, so you never know." He is being careful, not wanting to commit. Leans forward, elbows on the desk. "She'll have to get counsel. If she wants to pursue it. That's the way to go."

"Could the sheriff do something?"

"Can't see what. He can't make an arrest if he doesn't have some proof."

Roy is tired of asking questions. He stands up, holds out his hand. "Well, Mr. Henslowe, I really appreciate you talking with me."

"It was good meeting you, Roy," he draws the name out slowly, in a smooth, amiable tone. He stands, shakes Roy's hand and walks to the side of the desk.

"I'll tell Dorothea what you told me." Roy shakes his head side-to-side slowly. "She is really going to be disappointed."

"Well, yes, uh, I certainly hope she can get this sorted out. I would not want to be a party to any kind of scheme." He puts his hand on Roy's shoulder. "Even if it was unknowingly. I did everything I could to carry out the judge's orders," he says in a low, calm voice, "so if there is any type of fraud, I would want to see this resolved."

Roy opens the door and is surprised by the brightness of the afternoon.

"You let me know if I can be helpful."

"Yes, I sure will. Thanks again." Roy walks across the street to his car. Unbelievable, he thinks to himself. What is Dorothea going to think now? He dreads having to tell her that it seems her uncle has taken her money.

He starts the car and pulls away from the curb. He was looking forward to getting back to Parksdale, relaxing, maybe doing something with friends. But now, on the way back, the only thing he can think about is the problem his meeting with Henslowe is going to cause. Not much that can be done at this point except let Dorothea know what he found out. He keeps turning Henslowe's words over in his mind, trying to retain as much as possible. If he could think of some way to avoid putting the burden on her shoulders he would do it. He wonders how she is going to react.

SIXTEEN

Monday is a busy day and Roy doesn't have time to think about what he will tell Dorothea. That evening he does think about it and decides to call her tomorrow before she has to go to work. It is certainly not good news, almost unbelievable to think that D.W. would pull something like this. Maybe he thinks no one will find out. But why take the chance? Is it worth going to jail or possibly prison for five thousand dollars? Does he think that even if Dorothea does find out she won't challenge him?

Dorothea had reason to hope this might finally be a lucky break; a large sum of money that is rightfully hers would be coming her way. It is probably more than she can earn in the donut shop in two years' time.

Roy knows she will be upset. He feels partly to blame. He knows it isn't his fault, but he can't get over the feeling that he has let her down. She trusted him to help her and he was so upbeat on the way to Cuttsville. Now his ego is completely deflated.

Not only does he have bad news, he is unsure what it will take to finally get the money back. He has his doubts that she is capable of pursuing this. And, if she asks for his help, what can he do; how much time can he afford to take away from his classes?

Roy calls on Tuesday, hoping she has time to talk.

"Hello," she answers.

For an instant he thinks about making an excuse to avoid seeing her face-to-face. "Hi, Dorothea, it's Roy. I thought I'd come over and tell you what I found out about your inheritance."

"Okay, that'll be good, it's my day off. Did you want to come now?"

"Yes. If that's okay." There is a shade of hesitancy in his voice.

"Sure, come on over."

On the way there, he tries to imagine her reaction to the news. He hopes she won't break down, start crying and get really emotional. Maybe she'll just calmly decide to take action. However, if she talks to Henslowe or tries to get the law involved, it will take time and effort. How can she do it with two small children and having to work?

She is smiling as she opens the door. She doesn't speak, just walks away from the door expecting him to enter.

He attempts to return the smile. "Hi."

"Hi." Her arms are folded across her chest. She has a pleasant, but apprehensive look. "Have a seat." She motions to the couch. She sits in the stuffed chair, arms still folded.

"Well, it's kind of an unusual . . . " He can't think of the right words. "My parents didn't know anything about the will or the inheritance. But my sister knew John in school and he told her that a lawyer, Cletus Henslowe, in Cuttsville, had handled the will and gave out the inheritance."

She sits quietly, anticipating, leaning forward, elbows on her knees.

"Anyway," Roy pauses, searching. "Mr. Henslowe said that your uncle, D.W., came into his office." He notices her eyes narrowing and a steady glare at the mention of her uncle. "And D.W. brought this young lady in and . . . And he said she was Dorothea, that she was you!"

Dorothea doesn't speak; she stares hard, her jaws tighten.

"Mommy, Mommy." The youngest girl comes out from a side room and waddles on chubby legs straight to her mother. She is wearing a smock and has on white socks. Her hair is tousled. Dorothea's expression softens as she looks down. Darlene clutches at her lap, and then lays her head down so she can look at Roy. He smiles at her. "Sweety, what did Mommy say, you and Donna stay in the room and play. Mommy needs to talk with Roy. Will you do that?" She pats her back end lightly.

The little girl lifts her head. "O-kay." She slowly turns, takes a couple of small steps and then runs across the floor and back into the room. Roy watches Dorothea as her eyes follow the little girl's steps. She still has a look of innocence. Her skin is smooth and her features delicate; however, her eyes are darker, deeper and less assured.

Dorothea looks at him. "So what happened?" Her lips seem to tremble.

"Well, Henslowe said she had a birth certificate to prove that she was you."

"I never knew I had a birth certificate. I went to Ma to ask her about it when I was getting married," she says scornfully, "and she told me there wasn't none." Her eyes drift to the side as she thinks back in time. "She told me I'd have to get Dr. Lewis to get one. He's the doctor over in Butler. Billy drove me over there and we paid the secretary there to send for one. A few days later a birth certificate come in the mail. I still got it."

"I wonder if she, whoever it was, or D.W. could have gotten one the same way."

"Or maybe my ma was lying to me." She held the cold, hard stare. "Damn. Sonufabitch!" She spits the words out in frustration, her voice quaking. "So I reckon this lawyer gave them my money?"

"Yeah," Roy says despondently.

"I knew damn well something happened." She rises from the chair, hangs her head in thought, her hands clasped together tightly. She reaches, grabs a beer bottle that is setting on a small table and forcefully slings it against the wall. An explosion of shattered glass ricochets off the wall. She bends, resting her weight on the chair with one arm, holding her stomach with the other arm and struggling to hold back painful sobs.

"Dorothea." Roy is on his feet. "Dorothea. You can do something about this. It's not over," he says.

She looks at him. Her face red with anger, eyes glistening with tears. "No. No, it ain't over, that's for damn sure!" She shakes with bitterness, tears trace down her cheeks. She looks away.

"I, I mean," Roy stutters, he is shaken by the outburst. "There are ways to . . . " He doesn't know what to say.

Both little girls appear in the doorway after hearing the glass splatter. Together they begin slowly walking toward their mother. The oldest, Donna, is on the verge of tears, her lower lip puckered out.

"DON'T," Dorothea shouts, holding out her arm and hand, palm up. "Don't come over here. Donna, y'all stop and go back. There's glass on the floor."

They stop side-by-side, looking into their mother's tearful face. "It's okay. Y'all go back to the bedroom; Mommy just broke a glass. Yeh hear now?" her voice quivers. "Go on back."

Darlene holds onto Donna, whose eyes are brimming with tears, "Mommy . . ."

"Go on back." She moves toward the girls. "I don't want you to get glass in your feet." The girls turn around and Dorothea lays a hand on the shoulder of each girl and guides them back to the room. She closes the door.

When she comes back out alone she walks across the floor carefully. "I'm sorry. If you just knew. It ain't only the money." She stares at the dark window to the side of Roy, talking as much to herself as to him, "I hate him in my bones." She stands stiffly, her face and neck taut, fists clenched.

"Well, I believe you can correct the situation," Roy's tone is calm, "if you got Henslowe or another lawyer to take care of it."

She relaxes some, but the hurt is still obvious. "I ain't getting no lawyer," she says matter-of-factly. "I don't expect you to understand. Besides, you don't know what there is between me and D.W." She is talking softly. She looks at the floor between her and Roy. "You don't know what kind of poison he gave me." In a very defiant, but quiet voice she says, "I gotta get it out or it'll kill me for sure."

Roy doesn't understand. What kind of poison could he have given her? He can't imagine what her life has been like in the past several years, but to look at her now, to hear the intonations in her voice, he can only wonder what she has been through.

"Oh, shit," Dorothea blurts out at the sound of heavy footsteps on the porch. There's a knock on the door. Roy moves aside as Dorothea crosses in front and reaches for the door handle.

"Hi Mac, what you doing here?" Her tone is sharp, without enthusiasm.

Mac stands there, a large hulking figure. He looks past Dorothea at Roy. Then back at Dorothea. "Just thought I'd stop by. Everything okay?"

"Yeah, everything's fine." She wonders if her eyes are wet. "Roy stopped over because he had some things to tell me. Things he found out over in Cuttsville."

Roy is expecting her to introduce him to Mac, but she doesn't. Mac looks at Roy again and then his eyes shift quickly from one side of the room to the other.

"We got things to talk about, Mac." She is abrupt, obviously wanting him to leave. "I'll see you at work tomorrow."

He listens with no change in expression. He looks at Roy, intensely, a cold stare—a basic, primordial message that one male sends to another who threatens to invade his territory or come too near his possessions. Without saying another word, Mac turns and walks away. Dorothea closes the door.

She walks back to the stuffed chair and sits again. Putting her elbows on her knees, she brings both hands up, one on either side of her head, to hold and push. Her head droops, eyes shut.

"Maybe I don't even understand myself. I don't understand why things happen the way they do. It ain't what I wanted," she says the words slowly, dimly, as though thinking out loud. "I don't know what's gonna happen in the future, but I know everything I've ever done has stayed with me. I can't forget. I can't go back and change anything. I have to go on and do what I feel is right."

Roy stands silently, still trying to grasp what this is about. Certainly the money, but there seems to be more to it than the money. "Well, there's no doubt he cheated you out of what was rightfully yours. But you need to go to a lawyer or the sheriff where they can look into it."

"That lawyer'll just say it was me that went and got the money. How can I prove it wasn't me?"

"Well, the attorney, Mr. Henslowe, he knows what the woman looked like. He'll be able to testify that it wasn't you."

"If it wasn't me, who was it? If I can't show them who did it, how can I make them believe it wasn't me?"

"Well, I'm sure there's a way to do it. He can't do something like this and get away with it. Mr. Henslowe will know it wasn't you." Roy is standing erect, arms to his sides. "I'd talk to him or another lawyer or the sheriff."

"Lawyers and sheriffs don't help people like me. They walk over people like me to get where they are." Her face shows disbelief, as though she's trying to enlighten him. "They're concerned with their own hide, not nobody else's, specially people that don't have a pile of money. There's other ways to deal with things such as this."

"Not all lawyers are like that." Roy hopes to reason with her. "I mean that's what they do; they have to enforce the law, otherwise people would just go around breaking the law all the time."

"Well," she says, with a defiant smirk, "they may treat college people that way, but it ain't how they treat everybody." She turns her head to the side. She becomes flustered; she didn't intend to be offensive. She lets her head fall again.

"Well, I wish I had better news," Roy says, apologetically. "But given what D.W. has done, I think he can be sent to jail."

She stands up. "Look, Roy, I'm sorry. I really appreciate what you've done. I ain't gonna let it go. But I reckon I don't like depending on cops and lawyers to take care of my problems." Her demeanor is back to normal, her face stern, thinking. "Anyway, tell me, what's that lawyer's name again?"

"Cletus Henslowe. He has an office right on Main Street, 205, I believe. You can't miss it; he has a sign on the door. If you have a piece of paper, I'll write it down."

"Yeah, right over here." She walks toward the fireplace mantel, "Shit!" She sidesteps the bits of glass. "Reckon I better clean this mess up."

Roy notices shards of glass and glossy liquid on the wall. The stuffed chair hides most of the glass from his view. She hands him a scrap of lined paper and a stubby pencil.

He writes "Cletus Henslowe, 205 Main Street" on the page and hands the paper and pencil back. "Well, guess I'll go. Let me know what happens," he says, not really sure he wants to know any more than he does now. He pulls the door open.

"I really appreciate you talking to that lawyer for me."

"I just wish I could have brought you better news." He walks across the porch.

"Naw. Don't think nothing of it, you did what you could." She steps outside, holds the door. "Thanks."

At the bottom of the steps, he turns slightly, raises his arm in the air in a goodbye gesture and walks to his car.

As he pulls away he feels relief that this part is over. At the same time, he is disturbed by how volatile and bitter Dorothea was. He is still unsure about what kind of life she leads. Mac and D.W. are obviously different than the people he is accustomed to. It makes him feel vulnerable and unguarded, unable to predict their actions. This is a part of society that he has never really mixed with, a reckless, grittier element that he generally tries to steer clear of.

SEVENTEEN

The following evening, just as Roy arrives at his apartment, the telephone rings.

"Hello." He reaches for the refrigerator door.

"Hi, it's your mother."

"Oh! Hi, Mom, what's up?

"I wanted to find out what you learned about Uncle Jack's will from Mr. Henslowe."

"Oh, it's not too good. I was at Dorothea's house yesterday to tell her about it."

"Yeah, what happened?" Anything involving lawyers and inheritance is bound to create curiosity.

"You're not going to believe this. He said that . . . "

"Shhhh," his mother admonishes someone who is with her. "I'm sorry Melissa and Janice are here and I couldn't hear you. What were you saying?"

"I said you're not going to believe what I found out. Henslowe said there was also five thousand dollars for Dorothea, and that D.W., you know D.W. Crawley, at the store, he came in with a woman who said she was Dorothea, and she had a birth certificate for identification. So, Henslowe gave them a check for five thousand dollars."

"You mean she had already collected her share of the money?"

"No. No, it wasn't really Dorothea. D.W. had brought someone else in to say she was Dorothea."

"Oh my goodness," she says in disbelief. Then she informs Melissa and Janice, "Eula Mae's brother, D.W., brought some woman into the lawyer's office and claimed it was Dorothea, when it actually wasn't. But the attorney gave them the five thousand dollars."

Roy can hear muffled responses. He pulls a loaf of bread out of the refrigerator and then takes a package of lunchmeat from the drawer. He shuts the refrigerator door.

"I'm back," his mother says. "I had to tell Melissa and Janice what happened. What did Dorothea say? I mean the real Dorothea?"

"Well, she was pretty upset, naturally." He doesn't want to tell her about Dorothea throwing the beer bottle; she would worry about him if he told her. "I could tell she was hoping that something good would come of this. You know, that she would get her inheritance just as Rosemary and John did."

"I know," she says sadly, "that's really terrible."

"I can't imagine that he thought he could get away with something like that. You know there's something really strange about Dorothea and D.W., she really seems to hate his guts."

"Well, I never knew much about him. And Dorothea was always a real sweet girl, I thought. Of course, I haven't seen either of them in several years. Didn't you say Dorothea was married and has children?"

"Yes, she has two little girls. Real cute girls, one's about five and I guess the youngest one is about two. Don't know what happened to her husband." He hears voices in the background.

"Melissa wants to know what Dorothea plans to do."

"Oh, well, I did give her Henslowe's name and address." Roy tries to balance the phone between his head and shoulder so he can make a sandwich. "I guess she'll go talk with him."

"Didn't she believe you?"

"Oh, yeah. It's not that. Henslowe says she needs to talk with an attorney to figure out how she can get her money back. I would guess the sheriff or police can arrest D.W. and that woman who impersonated Dorothea, if they have good evidence that a crime was committed. I mean, according to what Henslowe told me, well, I guess he would have to be the prime witness. He knows what the woman looked like, and when he sees Dorothea, I would guess he'll be able to tell that she isn't the one who came to his office."

"What a mess. What a mess. Lord, the kind of people in this world. It makes you wonder."

In his mind's eye, Roy can see his mother's expression as she makes the comment. He smiles. "Yeah, it takes all kinds," he says, repeating another cliche he has heard his mother use many times. "Anyway, I guess I've done my part."

"Yes, I'd stay away from this if I were you. No need in you getting mixed up in something that doesn't really concern you. Wha . . . Just a minute."

Roy takes a big bite out of his ham and bread sandwich. It's cold, but he's hungry. His eating habits are erratic.

"Melissa says that D.W.'s wife Patsy has been sick and they did some tests here, and now she's in the hospital over there in Parksdale."

Roy can hear some other chattering in the background, but it's muffled. He bites into his sandwich again.

"Well, Melissa has a friend who works after school in Dr. McConnell's office and she knows Patsy. But then Janice was saying that her boyfriend . . . What's his name? Clarence. Clarence is his name and he has a sister who, rumor has it, has been running around with a married man . . . And what . . . ? And this married man owns some kind of store and his wife is sick, too. Oh, so you think maybe that married man could be D.W.? Oh, okay, she says she doesn't really know, but she mentioned it to her boyfriend and he's going to find out who his sister is running around with."

"Hmmm," is all Roy can say, his mouth half full of lunchmeat and bread. He remembers Melissa and Janice talking about this after he went to the movies with them.

"Well, Janice says if Clarence finds out that she's mixed up with this jerk who has a sick wife, he'll really blow his stack."

Roy hears his sister in the background say, "And you don't want to get Clarence mad." She says it with an exaggerated gruffness to lend humor to the statement, but it has a serious undertone; like you might joke about a growling dog behind a fence knowing that if the fence was not there, you wouldn't want to be there either.

"Well, I'm gonna let you go," his mother says. "Hank'll get mad at me talking on the phone so long. He'll say it costs a fortune. But I just wanted to see what you found out. When are you coming back over?"

"Well, gosh, I was just there. I don't know, I guess in about two weeks. When is Thanksgiving? I'll have a long weekend, so I might wait until then. Not until the twenty-fifth. Well, I may come before that—I'll let you know."

"Well, we miss you. You be careful now. And study real hard."

"I will."

"Alright, well, good night."

"Good night, Mom."

Roy continues eating his sandwich. He goes back to the refrigerator to look for a drink. He remembers Dorothea saying that Patsy, D.W.'s wife, was her friend. It seems strange that she has such a hatred for D.W. and yet it sounded like his wife is a good friend. Maybe that's why she hates D.W., maybe she knows he runs around with other women.

Roy wonders if Dorothea has heard about Patsy being in the hospital. He doesn't like the idea of opening himself up to Dorothea again, but if Patsy is her friend and she doesn't know she's in the hospital, he would feel bad about not telling her. Seems she would have mentioned it last week when she brought up Patsy's name.

The next morning, Roy picks up the receiver and dials Dorothea's number. It rings four times.

"Hello."

"Hi, Dorothea, this is Roy."

"Oh." It surprises her to hear from him so soon. Roy wonders if Mac might be there.

"Look, I was talking with my mother last night and my sister said that your friend Patsy was in Parksdale in the hospital."

"The hospital?" she questions the message.

"Yes. She said Patsy has been sick, and there were some tests, and they sent her over here to the hospital."

"Lordy, Patsy in the hospital. Lordy, I can't believe it. I mean I knew she was sick." Dorothea is genuinely befuddled by the news. "But I never guessed it was something bad. Lordy, you reckon I can find out where she is?"

"Well, sure, as far as I know there's only one hospital. I can't tell you the name of it, but if you look in the phone book I would guess it might be up front with the police. You have a phone book?"

"Yeah, yeah, there's one here. Okay. Well, I'll do that; I'll call the hospital and see can I find her. I can't believe she's in the hospital. Lordy. Well, Roy, thanks for letting me know. I wouldn't have known if you hadn't called. Thanks."

"Okay. Well, I hope it's nothing too serious."

"Lordy, I hope not, she's the best friend I ever had. I wouldn't know what to do if something happen to her. I just, well, I really appreciate you telling me, thanks." Dorothea hangs up the phone.

"Her best friend," Roy thinks. And D.W.'s her worst enemy, and they're married. It's hard to understand exactly what is going on. As he thinks about it, he realizes he knows other families like that—it doesn't always make the newspapers, but the stories spread. So maybe it's not all that uncommon.

EIGHTEEN

After talking with Roy, Dorothea is determined to find out why Patsy is in the hospital. She feels disheartened and selfish that she had not made an effort to call or go see Patsy since finding out that she was not doing well. She just expected her to get well. What could be wrong that she has to be in the hospital?

She picks up the telephone book and begins looking for a hospital number. She finds the hospital listed inside the cover, but it says "Emergency." She doesn't want to use that number, but now she sees the name: Waggoner Community Hospital—how could she forget? She flips through the pages and doesn't find it. Then she remembers that businesses are in the back. She mutters nervously, "Damn." Begins thumbing through the back pages, finds a couple of listings for Waggoner, and finally the hospital. She dials the number.

"Waggoner Community Hospital, may I help you?"

"Yes, mam, I want to know if my friend, Patsy Crawley is there, in the hospital."

"Does she work here or is she a patient?"

"She's a patient and I was told she was there."

"Just one moment." There's a pause. Dorothea waits, anxious to know for sure. "Yes. Patsy Crawley, Room 212."

"Can I come see her?" Dorothea asks hurriedly.

"Visiting hours are from 6:30 p.m. until 8:30."

"But I have to go to work at night. Can't I come over in the morning? I need to see her."

"Just a moment, please."

"Damn it," Dorothea stands, paces back and forth. Nervous and worried.

"Miss."

"Yes'm."

"Are you a family member?"

"Yes, I am. She's my aunt. And she's my best friend, too!"

"Okay. Then I'm told you can come in after ten o'clock, but you'll only be allowed a fifteen-minute visit. And Miss?"

"Yes'm."

"Only adults are allowed. No children."

"Yes'm. Thank you, mam." Dorothea hangs up. What'll I do? What'll I do with the girls? I'll have to call a cab. Maybe Sue Ellen. Lordy, I hate to ask her. Who else? I've got to. I've got to get over there to see Patsy. Lordy, she's helped me so much, I've got to see if I can do something for her. Dorothea calls Sue Ellen.

In the morning, after getting dressed, the girls wake up. Dorothea is putting cereal in bowls when Sue Ellen arrives. She insists that Dorothea take her car while she stays with the girls.

Dorothea accepts her offer. She pulls away from the curb in Sue Ellen's Mustang, nervous about driving her car. She doesn't feel that she can drive very well, although occasionally Mac allows her to drive his truck. She grips the steering wheel and leans forward as she maneuvers through the streets. Arriving at the hospital, she sees Visitor Parking and pulls in.

Since this is where her babies were born, Dorothea believes she remembers the way to the rooms. She looks from side to side at the people and two women behind a desk, afraid that someone will stop her. She takes the steps to the second floor and walks down the hall. The door is ajar at room 212. She raps lightly and carefully pushes on the door. Patsy looks up from the first bed and smiles. There are other beds and other people.

"How'd you find me?" Patsy holds out her arms.

Dorothea, nearly in tears, bends down and wraps her arms around Patsy. She is overwhelmed and begins crying softly.

"Honey, it's okay. There's nothin to worry about."

"I was so scared at what I'd find." Dorothea releases Patsy but holds onto both of her hands. Then she reaches up with her right hand to wipe tears away.

"Well, it's just tests. They don't exactly know what's wrong. That's why the doctor sent me over here."

"The doctor in Cuttsville?" Dorothea asks, sniffing to clear her nose.

"Yes. Dr. McConnell. Do you know who he is?"

"I'm not for sure."

"Well, I got here day before yesterday and they said I'd be done tomorrow." She smiles at Dorothea and holds onto her hands with a tight grip.

Dorothea notices that Patsy's eyes are tired; dark rings encircle them. Her skin is pale and she is much thinner. She does not look well. "Well, have they told you anything yet?"

"Naw. Don't reckon they'll tell me. They'll call Dr. McConnell with the results. Here, pull up that chair and sit down."

"I can't stay but fifteen minutes. That's what they told me."

"They won't run you off. I've missed seeing you." The tendons in Patsy's neck stand out as she leans back. It seems an almost painful effort.

"Well, Grandma said you were just feeling tired. That's when I was over to see you that time and Grandma said you were at the doctor's then."

"Well, I haven't got no better. The last time you came, after you had moved to Parksdale, it seemed I was doing good for a few days, then I just got worse again."

"D.W. bring you over here?"

"Yes, he did. Didn't even come in the hospital. Said he had to get back to the store. I think he just don't like hospitals —or me being sick. It's costing him money for me to have these tests." Her face has a soft, artificial smile; she raises her eyebrows for emphasis. "He's probably wishing I'd just drop dead," she says caustically, the smile still in place.

"Patsy, don't you say such a thing. There ain't nothing gonna happen to you."

Patsy lowers her head, closes her eyes. "I know he ain't never happy about anything I do."

"I guarantee that ain't your fault," Dorothea says. "Don't you think it is. Ain't no women could make any man like that happy."

She opens her eyes and looks at Dorothea, "You really hate him, don't you. Has he ever done anything to you, and you ain't told me."

"No. It ain't me. It's how he treats you. There ain't ever been a kinder, sweeter person in God's good world than you

Patsy Crawley. You deserve a better man than what you got. That's the damned truth, you deserve better."

"Oh, now don't go on. It ain't worked out for the best, it's true. But it wasn't always that way. I married him right out of high school. In fact, I was pregnant with James Earl before I ever graduated. And for a while I was as happy as a girl could be. And I wouldn't take it back for nothing because of James Earl. The Lord blessed me with James Earl and can't nothin take that away."

"Well, I have something to tell you. But maybe I shouldn't say nothing while you're here. It's about D.W., but I don't want to upset you."

Patsy looks at Dorothea, a quizzical look on her face. "Now don't you go holding back on me." She braces herself for the worst. "What did he do?"

"Well, I don't know if you know Roy Orchelle, he's the one that his daddy owned the grocery store."

"Mister Hank's boy?"

People across the room are saying "Goodbye." An elderly man and woman are leaving. They turn and walk past Patsy's bed. The man looks at Patsy and Dorothea and nods his head; the woman doesn't look.

"Yes. Well anyway, sometime ago I had a call from my sister Rosemary. You know how she's married and living up in Tennessee now." Dorothea looks around to see if anyone is near. "Well, she said that she and John both got a five thousand dollar inheritance, and did I get mine? I told her I didn't hear nothing about any inheritance. And I was wondering how come I didn't get any money. You know Poppa always treated me like I was his own daughter."

"Why Lordy, yes. He loved you just like you were his own."

"But I couldn't figure how come I didn't get nothing. It didn't seem right. So I asked Roy. I hadn't seen him in years and then one night he just walked into the donut shop, and I saw him and I said I know who that is. And I talked to him. And then I called him and told him about the inheritance. Because I figured if he was to ask his parents, that they might know something. I didn't know what to do. It seemed that was my only chance to find out. And he said he would."

Dorothea looks around again. "Well, yesterday he came over and he said he talked to the lawyer that did Poppa's will. Well this lawyer said he gave the money to Rosemary and to John," she leans closer to Patsy, talking in a whisper, "and he said this woman Dorothea came in with D.W. Yes, he said it was D.W. that came in with this person who claimed to be Dorothea and that he gave them a check for five thousand dollars. It was a check written to me. And, and he said, this lawyer told Roy that this Dorothea had a birth certificate for identification." Dorothea pauses, mouth open.

Patsy lets her head fall forward. "It wasn't you, it was D.W. and some women, and she said she was you?"

Dorothea raises her arms and shrugs her shoulders. "I reckon. Can you believe? I mean, Roy says this lawyer told him if D.W. did such a thing, well, maybe I shouldn't say."

"Dorothea, don't you . . . If D.W. did something like this, he'll get what he's got coming to him." She puts her hands flat on the bed and pushes so she is sitting straighter. Suddenly, she falls to her side.

Jumping from the chair, Dorothea grabs her arm and then reaches around and pulls her upright. "Patsy, you okay?"

"Hand me a drink of water." Patsy's face has no color, her lips are pale with a light purplish tone. Her eyes seem to be sinking, wanting to close. "I'm sorry, honey, I, just a minute, I'll be okay." She leans back on the pillows.

"Lordy, Patsy, I didn't mean to upset you. I wished them doctors would find out what's wrong," Dorothea spurts the words out in frustration. She puts her hand on Patsy's.

"It's okay," Patsy says weakly. "Tell me what you was saying about D.W."

"Well," Dorothea talks softly and slowly, "Roy says this lawyer told him if D.W. did this, I forget what he called it now." She rubs her hand over Patsy's. "But he said that D.W. could go to prison, if that wasn't me. But anyway, Roy says they stole my money. Don't know if they were able to cash the check. It had my name on it, but I reckon if she had a birth certificate, maybe she could."

"Lord." Patsy tightens her jaws. "If D.W. and that, well, guess there ain't no if. That lawyer says they done it." She stares ahead. "I know he's been seeing another woman. It ain't the first time."

Dorothea looks at Patsy's haggard face with sympathy. "I asked Roy what I could do." She continues patting her hand. "He wants me to get a lawyer for myself. I told him there wasn't no way I could pay no lawyer. He said maybe I could go to the sheriff or something."

From behind, a voice says, "Miss. Miss."

Dorothea turns.

"Miss, you'll have to leave now."

"Yes'm, I'm just saying goodbye." She stands. "Anyway, don't you go fretting about none of this. Maybe I shouldn't uh told you, I don't want to worry you." She leans over and hugs Patsy, squeezes tenderly, kisses her on the cheek. "You just worry about getting better. That's all you gotta do."

"I'm so glad you come." Patsy holds onto both of Dorothea's hands. "Soon as they find out what's wrong, I reckon they'll figure out what to do." She is forlorn, resigned to letting fate take its course. Dorothea begins backing away.

Patsy looks up at Dorothea. "You be careful." And then says more forcefully, "I mean it now. You be careful. No telling what D.W. would do if you try to corner him. You do as that Roy says; maybe he can find a way to help you get your money."

Dorothea begins sidestepping toward the door, making quick glances to see if the nurse is returning.

Patsy points her finger at Dorothea. "You just need to be careful. You hear?"

"I hear." Dorothea tries to force a smile. "You don't worry about me. You just get well. I'll come to see you. The next day I get off, I'll come over." She blows kisses and then holds her hand up and waves.

Dorothea turns, goes through the doorway and steps quickly down the hall. She thinks about Patsy's warning, thinking there's not much anyone can do to her that hasn't already been done, unless the devil himself pops up.

Her mind jumps to D.W.—thinking about what he has done, to her, to Patsy. Their frailty. Her face warms and blushes with heat, her throat catches. Tearfully, she pushes against the force of the stout door at the end of the hall. Slowly feeling her way down the steps, in a daze, her hand slides along the handrail. Her mind seems to swell with frustration and defeat, knowing D.W. is about as close to the devil as she can imagine. She wipes her eyes with the back of her hand.

NINETEEN

When Dorothea leaves the hospital she feels a damp chill in the air and knows this time of year she should remember to wear a sweater. Some mornings are cool. If the sun doesn't come out, the cold can be piercing. Of course it's not only the weather. Finding her dearest friend looking so sick and weak leaves her mind and heart cold, as though a wintry frost has invaded her body.

If something happened to Patsy, D.W. would be rid of her. He seems to have the upper hand. It sends a shiver up her back as she walks toward Sue Ellen's car.

She decides to go to Cuttsville next Tuesday and talk with that damn lawyer. She has a fear of highfalutin people, people who seemed to always have unexpected answers. She knows right from wrong, she knows what her thoughts are, and she isn't stupid. It's just that some of these fancy-ass people have a way of manipulating words and ideas that can throw a person off balance. Even though you think your head is clear and you know the truth of a situation, they can twist it and turn it, so as you can't think to respond. It confuses you, so you look stupid if you answer and you look stupid if you don't answer.

The hell with it, she thinks. I'm gonna fight D.W. with every ounce of energy I have. He's done just about as much as he can to ruin my life, and taking my rightful inheritance, and treating my dearest friend as though she's no better than a piece of trash. It ain't right for a person to have that kind of power over someone. I might as well be a mangy dog that hangs around waiting for D.W. to kick me just any time it pleases him to do it.

God knows it's unnatural for me to hate. I can't go through life being hateful, and I can't go through life allowing someone to just walk all over me as though I ain't nothing worth spitting on. I'll get my revenge or I'll damn sure die trying.

The following Tuesday Dorothea is up early. She gets the girls ready and lets them lie on the couch while she calls Mac.

"Mac?"

"Huummm, yeah," a groggy voice moans.

"I'm sorry to wake you. I'm taking the truck over to Cuttsville." She isn't asking. She doesn't want to listen to a lengthy sermon. "I need to see this lawyer over there about something important. I'll be back before it's time for you to go to work." She quickly puts the receiver down before his sleepy mind is able to grasp the message and react. She hears her name trail off as her arm swings the phone downward.

Mac lives only two streets away. She takes the girls by the hand and they walk to his house. He leaves the keys on the floorboard, and if he isn't outside to stop her she'll take the girls to daycare and head to Cuttsville.

The ride takes nearly an hour. She tries to find country music on the radio and ends up with Pat Boone instead. Since the station is clear she leaves it, knowing it will soon fade and she'll need to try rotating the dial again.

She can't help but feel peaceful seeing tall woods alternating with cotton fields and open pastures on either side of the road. Cattle are lazily grazing. It all looks so relaxed and restful. Then she thinks back on the farm and Billy. And then Dewayne. A feeling of loss washes over her, as though her life is slowly sinking down a dark hole. Her mind visualizes the quicksand at Ezekiel's and she sees her arms flailing; she gasps for breath as she is pulled down into the slimy muck.

She turns the music up; pounds her hands on the steering wheel. Makes herself think about those days of sunshine when she didn't have to work, didn't have to worry, only play all day with Donna. Then for a short time, Donna and Darlene, watching them grow from warm loving bundles into beautiful little girls. They were fascinating to watch: always amazed at everything their eyes fell on, that their tiny hands touched. They were part of her and her heart is in them—hurting when they hurt, happy when they laugh. Why couldn't life have stayed that way?

She feels a little frazzled by the time she reaches Cuttsville. Not getting enough sleep and driving in the early morning, Dorothea yearns for a cup of hot coffee. At the intersection of Main Street, she turns right, looking on the left for Henslowe's office.

Roy's note with the name and address is in her left hand when she enters the office. The stained wood interior is lit with soft lighting, but dark in the corners. She glances at the note and faces the lady behind the desk. The air is perfumed.

"Is Clet-tus Hens-lowe in?"

"No. Mr. Henslowe went to the courthouse this morning." No smile. Lips cocked up like it hurts to talk to someone like Dorothea.

"Is he gonna be back?" Dorothea doesn't know what to do with her hands and arms, moving them in several unsatisfactory directions before putting her hands together behind her back.

The woman is not looking at her. She arranges papers into a pile. "I really can't say." She stands and takes the papers to a nearby filing cabinet, her back to Dorothea.

Dorothea raises her voice, "Well is he coming back to this office sometime today or not?"

Realizing that her attitude of disinterest may be a little offensive, the woman decides not to push it further. Looking at Dorothea, she says, "Oh yes, I'm sure he'll be back. He never knows for sure how long his work at the courthouse will take."

"You think he'll be back by ten?" Dorothea asks sternly, looking at the grandfather clock by the filing cabinet.

"Well, I'd say it's likely that he will, but . . . "

The sound of the front door opening causes both of them to stop and wait. In steps a short man in a brown suit, walking quickly. Nose like an owl's beak, eyes darting quickly, side-to-side. He glances at Dorothea and then his secretary, but doesn't stop.

"Mr. Henslowe," his secretary's high-pitched call stops him. He doesn't answer, simply turns toward her. "This girl was asking for you." Dorothea glares at her.

He looks at Dorothea as though seeing right through her. His expression doesn't change, nor does his stance, obviously keeping his thoughts to himself.

"Mr. Henslowe." She moves her hands back to the front. "My name is Dorothea Yarborough. My friend Roy Orchelle was here to see you a week or so ago." She hates the way she feels, her stomach tight and vibrating. "He talked to you about my inheritance money. My, you see, Jack Durso, he was my father." She stops abruptly, hardens her jaw. "Can we sit down and talk about this for a minute." Her hands tighten into fists.

"Well, sure, come on in." He motions with his hand.

Dorothea walks past him and into his office. He is looking at his secretary, his eyes showing displeasure. Dorothea doesn't wait to be asked, she immediately sits in the chair facing his desk.

He slowly walks behind the desk, his hand gliding over the back of the leather chair, reaching for the arm. In a casual, fluid movement his sits and then crosses one leg over the other. Then he puts his hands together in front, looking self-assured and relaxed.

"As I was saying, my dad Jack Durso left me money, five thousand dollars, the same as what he left my sister Rosemary and my brother John. Roy said you told him you gave my money to D.W. Crawley and some woman who said she was me, but she wasn't."

The words gush out. But Henslowe doesn't respond. Hands together, fingers interlocked, he just stares at her.

"Well?" She almost shouts the question, "Did you or didn't you?"

He sits up, rests his elbows on the desk. "What did you say your name is?"

"Dorothea. Dorothea Yarborough." She braces, perturbed by his calmness.

"So your name is not Durso?"

"No, Durso is not my name."

"Then why would Mr. Durso leave an inheritance to you?" He smiles, seeming to have found a weakness.

"My married name is Yarborough, my born name is Dorothea Sheets. He left the money to Dorothea Sheets, the name that's on my birth certificate."

"Well, Dorothea," he speaks in a carefully measured manner, his voice even and unhurried, "I think I remember a conversation with Mr. Orchelle, but the details are not very clear. You see I deal with a number of complex legal cases day-in and day-out. What exactly are you asking of me?"

"Shit," Dorothea says, jaws clenched. This soft-peddling crap irritates her. "You gave my damn money to D.W. Crawley and some woman who said she was me. She wasn't me. Have you ever seen me before Mr. Henslowe?"

He leans back, his face reddening, "Well, I uh, I can't say for sure. You look somewhat familiar, but . . . " He shrugs his shoulders. The same calm, but his eyes are moist and they reflect a glint of fear.

"Well, let me tell you, you ain't never seen me before. I don't know who the woman was that came in here, but it wasn't me." Her teeth are clenched, her eyes like darts.

"If you're expecting me to remember the person who came in here," his face twitches faintly; his voice still even, but not quite so calm, "I can't say that I do. I don't know how long ago this event happened, but it has been a while."

She stares hard, trying to read what was going on in this tidy little man's brain. He has all the trappings of education and success, but—as she remembers Billy saying about people—he wipes his ass the same as anybody else.

"Bullshit," she snaps, "you told Roy that you knew what this other woman looked like. That was only a week ago. You telling me that you knew, but now you've done forgot?" Her hands are clutching the arms of the chair. Heat radiates over her skin; she is ready to lunge at this bastard and pound on him with her fists until he answers truthfully.

Henslowe senses the anger and pushes himself further back in his chair. "He misunderstood," his voice louder, more defiant, "I don't remember what the woman looked like. It, it could have been you for all I know."

She rises out of the chair. This dark, closed-in office with its odors of books, polish, and stale cigarette smoke makes her stomach unsettled. Her eyes are beaded on him like a hungry cat waiting to pounce. His body tenses and she feels him drawing back. Her back straight, she thrusts her hands on her hips. Her eyes never leave his face as she sidesteps away from the chair.

"Has D.W. gotten to you?" Slowly the words are drawn out. The anger continues burning, but she exerts control. She tilts her upper body in his direction, "Did that sonufabitch threaten you, Mr. Henslowe? Is that what it is?"

He quickly slides out of his chair and stands behind the large desk. "Look," he says, his fingers pushed against the polished desktop, "it has been a while since this all transpired. It's just that I can't be positive about the identification at this point." He looks to the door, questioning if he moves in that direction will she leave or will she turn vicious and attack him. He tries to balance his options, find some way of getting her out of his office.

"I shoulda known." Her steady gaze keeps him pinned in place. "I don't know if he's paid you or if he's threatened you, but you're damn sure lying about not remembering. You told Roy you knew what the woman looked like and you damn well know she wasn't me. You gave D.W. money that was mine." Her chest expands and contracts with heavy breathing.

"Miss Yarborough," Henslowe smiles weakly, attempting to keep his composure, "you're sadly mistaken, and your accusations are highly offensive. You can leave now. I'm afraid there's nothing I can do to help your situation." He moves back in front of his chair and sits on the edge, picking up a file folder on his desk. He opens a top drawer in the desk and pulls out several sheets of blank paper. He avoids looking up.

Dorothea takes slow steps toward the door; hands still on her hips, she turns. She feels no fear of him or D.W., only disgust at how small some folks are when it comes to lying and cheating. How some folks, no matter who or what they are, will try to elevate themselves by beating others down—and do it without shame or remorse.

"If you think this is the end of this, you're damn sure wrong," the words are spoken forcefully. "You ain't seen the last of me."

As she walks away, Henslowe takes a pen from the walnut holder, wanting to write something down. He wants to take some action that will distance him from this incident. He hears the front door close. His lips quiver. His hand drops the pen and he props his elbows on the desk. Arms raised, he lowers his forehead into the palms of his hands to ease the tension.

TWENTY

"Sonufabitch," Dorothea mutters as she opens the truck door. She knows he's lying. She turns the key, eases up on the clutch and pulls out of the parking space. Haannnkk! A horn blares behind her. She doesn't look, shifts into second and turns right at the next street.

She doesn't feel like talking to anyone, but knowing that Patsy should be home from the hospital, and being this close, she can't just drive away. Driving out to see Patsy might help ease the frustration. "Damn," she grunts. She can't believe this shit. She fumes. Looks around. Doesn't want to get stopped in Mac's truck, so she drives carefully on the way out of town.

She rolls the window part way down. It groans and stutters. The air blowing in helps. It's not as chilly as it was in the morning. She worries about running out of gas and looks at the gauge. There is still half a tank.

Dorothea stares blankly at the road while her peripheral vision picks up fields and trees, familiar landscapes, blurred at this speed. But in her head she plays back the scene in Henslowe's office. The air feels good. Her eyes are puffy. She could cry easily but won't; doesn't want to upset Patsy with this. She focuses on the road ahead. Thinks about seeing Patsy.

Dorothea turns left on Sorrows Road and takes solace in putting some distance between herself and that asshole

Henslowe. Jaw still clinched. How to deal with it? There's an answer somewhere. She decides she'll worry about that on the way home, not now, because she is eager to see Patsy and make sure she's okay.

It's quiet and peaceful out here. She slows down and turns on the road to Patsy's. She misses Patsy's company, they had such good times together—their girlish prattle and playfulness, doing little things that made them both happy. She misses those carefree days. She misses Patsy.

She drives into the yard. No sounds, only stillness. She notices a few chickens poking around behind Granny's house. She walks up the steps and knocks on the door. Waits. Knocks again. Listens for footsteps. Maybe Patsy's in bed. She opens the door cautiously, "P-a-t-s-y." No sounds. Waits. Calls again, "Oh-h P-a-t-s-y." No answer. She pulls the door shut and walks toward her grandmother's house.

She doesn't like not finding Patsy at home. She's beginning to think the day may turn out to be a total loss. Knocks on the door. She hears a scraping sound that indicates movement and tells her someone is home.

The door opens slowly. "Dorothea?" The voice is low and tremulous, as though from illness or just waking.

She looks at her grandmother, momentarily, pausing without speaking.

"That you?" Her grandmother squints, steps forward.

"It's me, Granny." She smiles a soft smile. "I stopped by to see Patsy. She told me she'd be home from the hospital."

"Naw . . . They never did let her come back," the voice is hoarse and raspy, filled with pathos. "Doctor told her she had cancer." She tries clearing her throat.

Dorothea's lips pull back in a grimace. "Cancer? What the heck is that?"

"Hit's bad. They ain't got no cure for it. Tumors inside. Doctor says she's got maybe two weeks, could be less." She pauses and steps back. "Why don't yeh come in a minute?"

Dorothea is dumbfounded. She steps slowly into the house. "Two weeks. You mean she could die in two weeks?" Her mouth hangs open; she is dazed. She turns a wooden chair away from the oilcloth-draped table and sits down.

Shuffling her feet in scruffy shoes with the backs worn flat, the older woman slowly makes her way to her rocking chair. "Hit's bad. Woman that young." She turns before sitting. "James Earl's uh takin it hard." With hands on each arm of the chair, she lowers herself, straining to keep her balance.

"Where is he?" Dorothea asks.

"Out back sommers."

The house is dark and musty. Cooking smells and dust permeate the atmosphere. Light coming in the open door turns cloudy with tiny floating particles; it fades quickly as it moves away from the doorway.

"He don't say much. I reckon he's tryin to understand the whole thing. He's scared too. You know he's always had his momma right there to take care uh him."

"You sure that's what the doctor said?" Dorothea's eyes are misty; her chest feels tight and anxious.

"We was there last night. Pa drove me and James Earl." Her head lifts, her pale eyes focus on Dorothea. "That's zackly what they told us." Her face is limp and frail, dotted with brown spots, mouth sagging at the edges into rounded jowls, creases down and under her chin.

"What about D.W.? He didn't go?"

"Naw, he says he can't stand teh see people what's sick. Says he ain't never going into no hospital lessen they drags him in there unconscious." She pauses to think about D.W.'s attitude, her face haggard and expressionless. "His pa's the same way. Don't like teh be in no hospital, nervous as a worm on a hot stick, fidgitin and all. Reckon D.W.'s waiting teh see what she don't come home."

Dorothea stares hard at the old woman: Reckon she don't know any better? A man that won't go see his own wife in the hospital, knowing she might be dying.

Dorothea rises and walks to the door without looking back. "I'll see if I can find James Earl," she says in a somber voice.

She walks behind the house. Chickens cackle and scatter as she walks near them. Stopping, she hears a faint thumping sound, something hitting against a tree. "James Earrrrl," she calls.

No sound. She walks toward a stand of large trees; watches her steps, because of the chickens. She steps into higher grass, steering clear of the bare wet ground. Looking up, she sees James Earl in the distance, leaning back against a stout oak tree. He holds the handle of a hunting knife in one hand, lightly tapping the blade in the palm of the other.

He straightens up, but his shoulders are hunched, head hanging forward. Dorothea approaches. "Granny told me about your ma." She tries to pick her words carefully.

His eyes meet hers and she reads the sadness. He moves his mouth and jaw, pondering, averts his eyes. Dorothea watches, he looks so much different than the last time she saw him. He must be several inches taller and lankier. He doesn't look like a little boy anymore.

"I seen her a few days ago," she says. "I thought she didn't look bad."

He moves his feet but his posture stays the same, shoulders drooping. "We went last night," he says weakly. His hair is a mess, patches sticking out in different directions.

"Yeah." She stands in front of him. "Granny told me. You know, sometimes them doctors don't get it right. They're mostly guessing, cause nobody knows for sure." She puts her hand on his arm. "Only the Lord Almighty knows for sure," she says in a voice barely above a whisper.

He lowers his head further, looking at the ground. Pushes his lips out and turns his head slightly.

"You know you're nearly as tall as me." She puts her hand on his shoulder. "You're nearly a man, James Earl. Won't be long."

All is still, a few unseen birds chirping, a hen in the yard is clucking. She squeezes delicately and keeps her hand on his shoulder.

"Well, I have to leave. I'll go to see your ma tonight. I'll tell her I saw you."

He glances at her quickly, not wanting to meet her eyes, not wanting her to look into his. "Bye," he says softly. He moves his body slightly as though on the verge of saying more or maybe feeling edgy about not knowing what to do.

As Dorothea stops at Sorrows Road, she decides to make another trip to Ezekiel's place. Wants to take another look at the area, the quicksand—what you can see of it. She looks at the gas gauge again, turns right and pulls onto the wider road to head out past West Fork Creek. Her remembrance of the trail into the woods is vague. Her head is cloudy, filled with disgust. She hopes she's not wasting her time.

Small snatches of white cotton are scattered along the roadsides. Flying off the trucks going into Cuttsville or blowing out from the fields, she wonders. The stalks in the fields haven't been picked clean either; seems there's still plenty of cotton left. Maybe it's better to move fast and get as much picked as you can. Then if you have time and the weather holds you can come back later and clean up the leftovers.

She doesn't know for sure. Never picked cotton, although plenty of folks in Cuttsville do. Knows it's hard work and little pay, even worse than selling donuts. Of course, people living in Parksdale don't pick cotton.

Since it was her day off, a Tuesday, when she met Reuben along the road, she keeps looking, hoping she'll see him again. She doesn't want to go into Ezekiel's hideaway by herself, although she will if she has to.

She stretches her arm out and leans to the side to open the glove compartment. Remembers that Mac keeps a ball cap in there. She pulls it out, shakes it, slaps it against the seat to dislodge any bugs or spiders. She puts it on her head, thinking people won't recognize her or know she's a woman with the hat on.

She tries to remember the spot where she was walking when Billy stopped to pick her up; it seems like such a long time ago.

Her head aches with the news about Patsy. She refuses to think about it. Can't. What's done is done. She let's her eyes roam over the landscape; just needs to think what to do next. Think ahead and do what needs to be done. Don't let it get inside; hold it off.

West Fork Creek is up ahead. She can see the brown water already, since recent rains have swollen most of the creeks and rivers. The news tells of flooding farther north.

She looks at the thick growth of trees near the water. Sweet gum leaves have a reddish tinge, but the other trees seem unchanged, maybe a little more yellow.

Passing the creek, a large truck loaded with stacked bales of hay is coming toward her, blocking her view. She knows the turnoff is not long after the creek, before you get to Sandy Bottom.

Not much traffic, so she lets the truck slow down. She keeps her eyes on the left shoulder, hoping she'll be able to identify the spot when it appears. Putting her foot on the clutch, she shifts into second, thinking it's near. Going very slow. No other cars. She sees an opening into the woods, so she pulls to the other side of the road and eases toward the ditch. She pushes the gas pedal to pick up speed so the tires won't slip and spin in the mucky bed of the ditch.

Got stuck plenty of times at the farm, once or twice when Dwayne was teaching her to drive and when she practiced on her own. One time, she had to leave the truck stuck in the mud until Dwayne came back out. He showed her how to get it unstuck using planks of wood under the back tires and shifting gears rapidly to rock the truck back and forth. It wasn't easy.

Moving cautiously in second gear, she doesn't want to make any new scratches on Mac's truck. Pretty beat-up already with dents and scratches, but that's not her fault. She can't see the hut and can't remember how far back it is. Maybe Reuben will be there.

The pines are tall, but some of the other younger trees—tulip trees, sweet gum and scrub oak—scrape against the truck, making eerie sounds like fingernails on a blackboard. Gives her the heebie-jeebies.

The opening comes suddenly. The makeshift shanty is off to the right and looks deserted. She pulls past the structure, looking for Ezekiel; doesn't see him anywhere and carefully inches forward. She cuts the engine, gets out and looks around. Even though she is out in the open, except for the inlet, tall trees surround the area. The inlet is swampy with high grasses and reeds and it winds between isolated trees and merges into the lake. The small gap between the trees gives a view of Paradise Lake—the far side of the lake is shrouded in a haze, with no clear definition.

Dorothea looks along the ground for a large rock. She wants to test the thick muck of the swamp again, see if the rock will sink. She moves over by Ezekiel's hut where pieces of junk metal, all sizes of twigs and sticks, and assorted debris clutter the ground. She is leery of snakes, particularly cottonmouths. She hears a faint sound. Is it coming from inside? Carefully, she steps forward, a few feet away from the haunt to peek inside. Ezekiel's dark head appears over the far side of the shack. "Eehhh!" Dorothea catches her scream, but her heart jumps to her throat. Her entire body is chilled and ridged.

She exhales, "Zekiel, Lordy, you near scared me to death."

Quizzically he examines her, not moving, not speaking.

"You remember me, don't you?" She puts her hand on her pulsating chest. Remembers the cap and quickly pulls it off, runs her fingers through her hair. "See, Dorothea. I come out with Reuben, your cousin Reuben. Weren't that long ago. Mr. Jack's girl, you remember me don't you?" He holds his position, doesn't blink.

She lowers her arm and the ball cap not knowing if she should run to the truck or wait to see what he does. Ezekiel's head turns and she can't see his body until he walks a few feet away. He sits on a wood-slat box and picks up what appears to be a small pan of boiled peanuts. Picks a peanut out and puts it between his teeth, presses down and, holding onto the shell with thumb and finger, he sucks the soft peanut and juice into his mouth.

"Zekiel, I just come to take another look at the quicksand."

He ignores her, doesn't look. "Lo-ree, lo-ree, ummmh, stop, stop dat, ummmh." His head moves side-to-side, his mouth smacking on the mashed peanut, his voice a low, humming incantation. "Lo-ree, lo-ree, ummmh, stop, no, ummmh, stop," he mumbles, reaches into the pan again.

Dorothea feels a shiver up her spine. Her hair becomes electric, as though it is standing up stiff on her tingling, cold scalp. Something in Ezekiel's gibberish sounds seems eerily familiar. She feels vulnerable and threatened. She begins slowly backing away. Better to get to the truck and leave. Ezekiel always seemed harmless, but this is his territory. No need to take risks.

She turns and walks unhurriedly to the truck. Closes the door, puts the cap back on her head and starts the engine.

She glances toward the hut, turns the steering wheel sharply to make a u-turn and presses on the gas pedal. As she passes, she looks over and sees Ezekiel calmly sitting on the box, eating peanuts, paying no attention to her or the moving vehicle.

TWENTY ONE

Head down, Reuben walks along Sorrows Road thinking about Dorothea and the dream his mother told him about. Normally, he would be coming out to see Ezekiel earlier in the day, but he and Esther had a long discussion this morning. Reuben recalls he didn't contribute much, he mainly listened to his mother. She would often tell him things and then he would think about what she had said for days. He was in awe of her; she seemed to know so many things and always had answers.

He wished he could study the Bible more like she does, but there are so many words he doesn't understand that it doesn't hold his interest for long. He could ask his mother about the words, but if she didn't know them it would be an embarrassment for her and, besides, he would have to ask her so many times she would think him stupid. And he didn't want his mother thinking that. He wanted her to think he was smart just like her. That is why he would try to remember everything she told him and then go over it again and again in his head so he would learn from her.

What she told him about evil was coming back to him. She said God told her He puts evil men on earth to test people, to see who lets themselves be drawn into hatred and destruction by evil men.

Then Reuben asked her, "What if an evil man forces hisself on people, don't a man got to defend hisself against that evil?"

"No," she said, "if you do you are as bad as the evil one. God wants us to avoid the poison that evil people spew at us. We got to have determination and control so we can overcome that evil. Don't do things cause someone else makes you do it," she told him, "do things cause you wants to do them and you know it's the right thing to do."

Then Reuben asked, "Well, what if someone gonna kill you or burn yo house down? Don't you gotta stop em from doin it?"

At this Esther paused. She put her lips together tightly. "Sometimes," she said, "when you sees evil comin at you and you knows it's gonna kill you or yo chil'ren, den the Lord allows that you protects yo'self. Dat's how come they is wars."

Then she spoke about Hitler: "What they done to him was the right thing," she said. "He was a crazy man and he would have gone on killin peoples til dey stopped him. Dey done the right thing killin him and the Lord in heaven give them the strength for it."

It was Americans, she explained, that done most of it. "And Americans is mostly Christian folks," she said. "Some of dem don't always treats us coloreds like dey should. I reckon dey gots they own way uh thinkin about what Christians should do, but you got to do the right thing and don't study on what other peoples do that ain't right."

Back on Sorrows Road, Dorothea heads toward Route 40, thinking about Ezekiel's mumbling. Deep wounds slowly resurface. Her mind flashes to the fishing trip and D.W., the start of her being trampled under his feet; now he has cheated her out of her inheritance and probably forced Henslowe to lie about not knowing who was with D.W. when he took her money. Her body involuntarily shudders, which surprises her because it comes so suddenly, as though her body is reacting independently, out of her control.

She clutches the steering wheel, realizing she's going too fast and not paying attention. She lifts her foot off the gas. A feeling of frustration muddles her brain, makes her head throb to think about her situation. Her life has not been her own since that day at the lake. It has belonged to D.W. He has used her like a worthless doormat.

Around a bend in the road Dorothea sees a figure walking along the edge. She slows down to see if it's Reuben. She is past before she realizes it is him, his head low, his limp not obvious. Quickly stopping, she puts the truck in reverse and backs up. She stops. A green pickup is coming toward her. She waits until it passes. Two men looking in her direction; she watches as they pass by. After they are around the bend, she backs until she is past Reuben. Pulls the hat off, leans to the passenger door and opens it.

"Hey, Reuben," she shouts.

Slowly, cautiously, careful of his step, Reuben walks to the open door and peers inside. "Miss Dorothea, that you?"

"Yeah, it's me. Get in."

He looks down the road, reaches for the door and steps on the running board. "Why, Miss Dorothea, you done surprised me again."

"Well, I was looking for you. You heading to Zekiel's?"

"Yes'm, dat's where I's goin." He smiles. "It sho nuff is uh thing teh see you, Miss Dorothea, what with my momma and me was jus talkin about you." He shifts his weight to sit straight in the seat, one hand on his knee, the other on the door.

She's glad to see Reuben, glad her thoughts about D.W. and Henslowe have been derailed. She puts the cap back on her head. Twists her head around so she can see the road behind. Nothing coming. She pulls left, backs up and then heads back toward Ezekiel's.

"Me?" she asks, glancing at Reuben, "Y'all was talking about me?" It lifts her spirits.

"Yes'm, I told Momma about seein you out here and she ask me how you doin." Dorothea looks at him and smiles. Reuben looks ahead, talking to the windshield. "I told her you is doin good, ceptin you likes teh study on quicksand."

"Studying quicksand? I just think it's interesting, that's all."

"It's dange'us, too," he issues a friendly reminder. "That's what my momma say too. She say it dange'us and she don't know why you want to see no place like dat." He turns his head to look more in her direction. "Deh other day she say she have a dream about you and dat quicksand."

"Really? She had a dream about me?"

"Yes'm. She say when I see you I should tell you about her dream. And I say, Momma, how you know I gonna see Miss Dorothea again. And she say, I jus knows it and you be sho teh tell her." Dorothea drives slowly, listening intently.

"Well, tell me, what's the dream about?"

"You drivin me to Zekiel's, Miss Dorothea?"

"Yeah, that's where you was going, ain't it?"

"Yes'm, we's almos dere, dat's all."

She doesn't tell him she was just there. She recognizes the path between the trees and takes her foot off the gas pedal. No one else is on the road, so she turns left into the ditch and presses on the gas.

Dorothea is excited to hear about the dream. Remembers how Reuben used to tell about his mother's dreams years ago and how he said that other coloreds set great store by how she could tell what was going to happen before it ever happened.

She drives farther into the woods, until the truck can't be seen from the road. "I'm gonna stop here a minute so you can tell me about that dream." She stops and turns the ignition key off. Dense trees bush out and cluster above, blocking the sun—only narrow beams of light poke through. A breeze tickles the leaves making them shudder and wink. She turns, looks at Reuben, watches a drop of sweat create a shiny line down the side of his face. Thinking it's warm and he is probably nervous as well.

"Yes'm, she tell me in dis dream she see you standin in deh quicksand. And den she say maybe it ain't quicksand cause they's a gator in there. And you has somethin in yo hand like a piece a paper, only shiny silver and dis keep deh gator from gettin at you."

"Lordy," Dorothea says, reciprocating to Rueben's enthusiasm.

"Yes'm, dat gator is ready to get you, but dat paper shine in deh gator's eyes and he can't get at you." Reuben pauses, picturing the tense images of the dream in his head.

He turns his head half way in Dorothea's direction, but keeps his eyes on the floor. "And I say, Momma, is dat a snappin-mouth real gator? And she say she don't rightly know what it is. She say deh devil can change hisself mighty easy. He can fool you into thinkin he be yo friend. Might be the person standin right aside of you and you would'n know it. She say deh devil is mighty tricky about foolin folks."

Dorothea thinks she hears something and turns to look out her window. Reuben, likewise, looks around. The trees are thick, with undergrowth waist high or more. The windows are down on both sides. In the shade of the trees, the air is cool, but there is only an occasional ripple of wind. They hear the sound of a car passing by on the road.

Dorothea leans back against the door, her left arm drapes over the steering wheel. "So, she didn't know what this gator was?" Her lips form a soft near-smile.

"No, mam, she say it some kinda danger. She say dat's why folks has to be careful and think on what they's doin." He leans forward and tilts his head slightly toward her to emphasize this warning. "Yes'm, dat's right, cause you don't and it can be deh devil trickin you. And she tell me be sure to tell you bout this cause it's some kinda dange'us evil and you don't guard yoself and it gonna eat you up fo sho." He seems to be exaggerating, over-emphasizing the danger, but his seriousness doesn't waver.

As puzzling as the message is, Dorothea takes it to heart. She doesn't comment, just continues looking at Reuben. His square jaw is set, there is no doubt that he is serious and believes in his mother's dream.

Dorothea remembers her. Ethel or Esther or maybe Lucille, she can't remember her name for sure. She remembers seeing her and hearing about her. She was not a wild and crazy looking person like you might expect, but quiet and nice. She was tidy looking, someone who had a way of holding herself that sets her off from others. Dorothea figures that is why people took her seriously; she had an air of confidence, looked as though she might know something that no one else knows.

"Miss Dorothea, I reckon I can walk from here to see Zekiel." He reaches for the door handle.

"Wait a minute Reuben." She puts her hand on his arm, but removes it quickly. "Is that all there was? Is that the whole dream?"

"Yes'm, dat's mostly what she say." He looks through the windshield. "But, now dat I thinks about it, dere was some more. I don't like tellin dis part, Miss Dorothea, but Momma say all she members is you drop dat shiny thing. She say she don't know what dat gator done, cause dere was thunder like an e-splosion and it woke her up. She say it was rainin, but she don't rightly know if dat e-splosion was deh thunder or it was in deh dream."

She listens open-mouthed, believing this has some meaning for her, that it isn't just an old woman's fairy tale. Reuben doesn't move. They are both still and quiet. The cawing of crows can be heard overhead, but it doesn't disturb, it fits in with the unsettling, shifting mood she and Reuben are both feeling—not from this moment alone, but from the weight of restless memories that each carries.

"And that was all?" Dorothea says, breaking the spell. "She didn't dream no more?"

"No'm, dat's all she toll me."

They continue to sit quietly, Reuben with his hand on the door handle, Dorothea with both hands holding the steering wheel, a blank stare, eyes pointed at the trees ahead.

"Miss Dorothea, I got somethin else to tell you. It's about Zekiel."

Dorothea swallows. "What about Zekiel?"

"Well, he say he know why you wanna see deh quicksand. He say somethin bad happen to you and he say he seen it."

She squares her shoulders and looks at Reuben with a wrinkled brow. "When'd he tell you this?"

"Next time I come out after you was here. He jus come right out and say he know why you wanna see dat quicksand."

Her face reddens; she feels a stinging sensation as though slapped by the comment. "What was it he seen?" She jolts the question at him.

"He didn't say, Miss Dorothea. He jus say it was somethin bad and he seen it."

"Well, I don't know what he's talking about. How could he have seen me?"

"I don't know Miss Dorothea." Reuben is sorry now for bringing it up, he can tell this irritates her. Maybe Ezekiel made a mistake; maybe he was confused about it. "I wasn't gonna tell you about it, but den I thought it might be bes iffen I did."

"He wasn't dreaming it was he?"

"No'm, he didn't say nuttin about no dreamin." Reuben has both hands in front of him, lying on his lap, thumbs overlapping.

"Well, I still don't know what he's talking about."

She wants to believe she doesn't know what it's about. He's half crazy, so maybe he's just making this up. She doesn't want this to continue. She clenches her teeth; she wants all this talk about dreams and bad things and lawyers to stop. She wants Patsy to be well so she can talk with her and sort things out. Without Patsy how will she figure this all out and make sense of what is happening to her? Who will help her understand it? Her head is in a fog; she feels as though her chest is collapsing inward.

"I reckon I best go now, Miss Dorothea." He opens the door, places his right foot, then his left, on the running board.

Dorothea wakes from her stupor. "Well, I'm glad I got to talk with you Reuben. I reckon I'll think on your momma's dream. I don't rightly know what it means." She hopes Reuben doesn't misunderstand. She appreciates that he and his mother are concerned about her. After the fiasco with Henslowe, it is nice to have someone show her some kindness.

He holds onto the door, one foot on the ground and the other on the running board. "Yes'm, I don't know." He pauses, looking down at the floor. "Sometime maybe it'll come to yeh, Miss Dorothea." He raises his left hand and scratches the wooly hair above his ear; his knuckles bump the brim of his hat. "I reckon she thinks dere is somethin dange'us and she tellin you to be careful. I reckon dat's mostly what deh dream is about."

"Well, I always did like your mom, Reuben. You know . . . " she starts to add more and then lets her words trail off.

Reuben's dark eyes look up at her. "Yes'm, I'm mighty glad to know dat, Miss Dorothea. I reckon I'll go on now." He doesn't move, waiting for a sign from her.

"Yeah, that's fine Reuben. I'll be seein you."

"Yes'm, I be seein you, Miss Dorothea." He backs up and pushes the door shut. He walks to the front of the truck, pauses and looks back.

She turns the key. Reuben continues to watch her. She waves her hand at him and starts backing up. She puts her head out the window to see her way out, but quickly pulls it back in, remembering the twigs slapping against the truck on the way in. Instead, she sits straight and focuses on the rearview mirror.

Once on Sorrows Road again, she steps on the gas even though there are plenty of ruts and bumps. She's not sure what time it is, but it seems as though it has been a long day. She'll have to hurry back to Parksdale to get the girls and get Mac's truck back to him. She's determined not to think about anything until she gets back home.

Maybe she will find a way to talk to Sue Ellen about all of this. They seem to get along well and she feels Sue Ellen is someone she can trust. She turns the radio on and fumbles with the knob as the truck bounces along on the hard-packed road.

TWENTY TWO

Esther's dream, Reuben, Ezekiel and the quicksand are all set aside on the way back to Parksdale. Even if Reuben's mother is able to see danger in Dorothea's future, it can't be any worse that what Patsy faces right now. The sadness in James Earl's eyes occupies her thoughts. She doesn't care what happens to her—Patsy being in the hospital is her only concern.

Since today is her day off, she thinks about going to see Patsy tonight. She worries about asking Sue Ellen to watch the girls again, but she has to see Patsy.

Being confined in the truck, with the hissing sound of the tires on the asphalt keeps thoughts about Patsy reverberating in her mind. Can Patsy really be dying? What is cancer, why can't they give her some medicine for it? She's such a good person, what will James Earl's life be like without her? The radio blares out music alternating with static and an occasional announcement or commercial, but Dorothea is oblivious to the sounds; her mind is a battleground of thoughts about Patsy.

The trip seems shorter going back. In her dreamy state, Dorothea doesn't even consider where she is until she reaches the outskirts of Parksdale. After picking up Donna and Darlene, she returns Mac's truck. Parks it in front of the house where he lives, but doesn't go in, doesn't want to talk to him. She takes the girls hands and walks the two blocks to their place.

Sue Ellen's car is not parked out front. She'll wait, maybe it's not as late as it seems, since it is getting dark so much earlier now. The girls didn't sleep at daycare and they are obviously tired. She fixes food and they eat. After a few bites of food, Darlene falls asleep sitting up. Dorothea picks her up and takes her into the bedroom. When she comes back into the kitchen, Donna is nodding off as well.

At seven o'clock she looks out the window for Sue Ellen's car, but it is already so dark she can tell if it's there or not. She opens the door and walks out on the porch. No car. Dorothea goes back inside and lies down on the couch to wait.

The next morning she awakens, her back aching and stiff from the awkward position in which she slept. During the night, she had wrapped herself in the cover that was lying on the back of the couch, but it didn't keep her warm, her feet feel like ice.

She missed her chance to see Patsy; she'll have to call in sick. She can't let another day pass without seeing her and she decides she damn well isn't going to go to the hospital for just a fifteen-minute visit.

That evening it is after six o'clock when Dorothea hears Sue Ellen upstairs. She looks outside and sees her car. She inhales deeply, it makes her nervous to think about asking Sue Ellen to watch the girls and use her car. She could take a cab, if necessary.

Dorothea climbs the steps and knocks on the door.

"Hey, there." Sue Ellen is drying her hands with a small towel.

"Hi, Sue Ellen."

"Come on in." Sue Ellen turns and walks away.

Dorothea clasps her hands in front, her arms hanging down. "I need to ask a favor."

"Well, what do you need, sweetie?" Her cheerfulness is apparent.

"Well, my friend Patsy is still in the hospital and it don't look too good. Granny told me she has cancer. I was wondering if you'd watch the girls for me, so I can go visit her again." She stands passively, shoulders sagging, eyes pleading.

"Oh, my goodness, cancer?" Sue Ellen lays the towel on a chair and turns and looks at her. "Well, ahh, sure. Yeah, I can do that."

Dorothea senses hesitation. "Now I don't want to put you out, if you got something planned."

"No, I don't have nothing planned." She reaches out and embraces Dorothea. "No. I'm just damned sorry to hear about Patsy. You take my car, too. I won't need it."

Dorothea looks into her eyes. "You are such a good person, I can't believe how lucky I am."

"Oh, hey, sometimes I'm just the opposite—at least that's what some people tell me." She smiles and takes several steps backward. "You let me fix myself a sandwich and I'll be right down."

Downstairs, Dorothea calls Mac at the donut shop. "I ain't coming in tonight. I gotta go to the hospital and see Patsy."

He doesn't answer immediately. "Couldn't you of said something earlier? You know if Mr. Simmons hears about it, he may fire your ass."

"Well, let him," she says in a belligerent voice, "I been kicked in the teeth by so many people, one or two more won't make a whole lot of difference."

"Okay, Okay, I don't want to start anything, I'll take care of it."

Dorothea taps softly on the door. Slowly opening it, she holds the edge and peeks in. The lighting is dim. Everything looks so organized and tidy. Dorothea is aware of a distinct odor she doesn't recognize. Sliding past the door, she quietly walks to the bed where Patsy is lying. She is on her side, her face turned away. Dorothea stands still, looking at the sleeping form. Heaviness crowds her chest, moves up her neck, tightening her throat.

Patsy turns as though knowing she is being watched. Saliva coats the side of her mouth. Her eyes open. Her face is pale and languid; her expression doesn't change. She looks at Dorothea and a telling message is there, in the watery blueness of her eyes.

Dorothea steps closer. Patsy pulls her arms from under the covers and Dorothea reaches down enclosing Patsy's hand between hers.

There is a soft rap on the door. A well-dressed woman walks in and stops at the end of the bed. Patsy's eyes follow her. The lady looks at Dorothea and smiles softly.

"Hi, I'm Patsy's sister, Evelyn." She holds her hand out.

Dorothea shakes her hand. "I'm Dorothea, a friend of Patsy's."

"Well, I'm so pleased to meet you." Her smile radiates. "Patsy talks about you all the time. Used to tell me about Dorothea every time I'd see her. I was even a little bit jealous." She continues smiling and then turns to look at Patsy who is smiling also, although weakly. Evelyn walks to the other side of the bed and leans over to kiss and hug Patsy. Her dress looks like silk, soft green.

"Doro-th . . . " Patsy can't get the words out. Evelyn reaches to the table and picks up a glass of water, holds the straw for Patsy to drink.

"Uhhm, thanks. Dorothea, this is my sister Evelyn. Ain't she pretty?" Evelyn grins, pats Patsy's hand.

"Beautiful," Dorothea replies, "just like you."

"Naw, I'm the plain Jane, she's the one who got the looks."

Dorothea looks at Patsy, then Evelyn. Not easy to tell they are sisters. Evelyn's hair is lighter, nearly blonde. She is a little heavy, but in a shapely way, and the dress is very flattering.

"I had plumb forgot you had a sister."

"I'm two years older," Evelyn says, "and I married a man from Florida, so that's why I'm not around very much."

"You ever heard of Chat-ta-hoo-chee?" Patsy asks in a raspy, unsteady voice.

"Yeah, I think I've heard that name. It ain't that far away is it?"

Evelyn smiles. "No, it's right on the border. They tease me about it because there's a state mental hospital in Chattahoochee. But that ain't why I'm there." Her grin widens. "My husband works for the gas company and we live out in the country, near the transmission station."

Dorothea turns to see if anyone else is nearby. "Did your husband come with you?"

"No, we have three children at home, so I came by myself, what with them being in school and all."

"Dorothea," Patsy reaches for her hand again, "I was talking to Evelyn about James Earl . . . I don't want him to stay with D.W. after I'm gone."

"Well," Dorothea doesn't know how to respond. She looks into Patsy's sad blue eyes and squeezes her hand tighter.

"Evelyn said she would take him." She pauses, out of breath. Dorothea and Evelyn both see that she is in pain. "Only thing is, D.W. won't let him go."

"Did you ask him?" Dorothea asks the question even though she knows Patsy probably did not ask him. They both know it would be useless; D.W. would never willingly let James Earl leave.

"You know as well as I do he ain't gonna let James Earl go. No, I ain't seen him since I been in here. And I don't wanna let him know what I'm thinking."

A nurse walks into the room, her white outfit bright and clean. She smiles at Patsy and says, "Hi there, dear, looks like you've got company tonight."

"This is my friend Dorothea." She wobbles her right hand, which Dorothea is holding. "And this is my sister, Evelyn." She wobbles her left hand.

"Well, I'm gonna give you some medicine, then I'll get out and let y'all visit." She walks to the side by Evelyn, and

Evelyn passes in front of her and moves to the end of the bed.

Dorothea looks at the hollows in Patsy's cheeks, gray-violet circles under her eyes, even her nose and mouth have changed, her whole face is bonier. She can also tell her body has shrunk, her arms thinner and pale—a noticeable change in just one week.

The nurse holds out a large pill. Patsy puts it in her mouth. Picking up the glass of water, the nurse bends over and holds the straw for Patsy to drink and swallow.

"There you go, honey. Not easy to get them big ole pills down, is it?" She puts her right hand on Patsy's forehead, lets it lie there, and then brushes her hair back even though it is not sticking up. She takes another pill from the table, gives it to Patsy.

"One more," she says in singsong tone. Her arms are freckled. Her orange hair, faintly tinted with streaks of white, is pulled back and held in a bright silver clasp.

"There, that wasn't too bad, was it?" She places the water glass back on the table.

"Thanks," Patsy says.

The nurse takes Patsy's hand in both of hers. "You visit with these nice ladies and then you get some rest, honey. You need anything, you just push that buzzer and I'll be right in." She exits quickly.

Patsy looks at Dorothea. "I don't know what to do about James Earl. You know what D.W. is like." Her watery eyes spill over, tears run down the sides of her face. "I want my baby to have a better life"

"We'll have to get his permission, Patsy, I don't see any other way." Evelyn tries not to show any emotion.

Dorothea breathes deeply; she has never felt so sad. "There might be a possibility," she says without thinking beyond the word 'possibility'. "Let me think on it some. But I guarantee, Patsy, I can find a way."

"You think he will agree?" Evelyn asks.

"He may not have any choice."

Patsy squeezes her hand. "Oh, Dorothea, if only you could do this, I would be . . . " Tears roll into the hollows beneath her eyes. She turns her head to hide her weakness and to conceal the grief.

Dorothea and Evelyn stand in silence, unable to think of any words that might provide some consolation. Their eyes are moist with emotion.

Patsy turns back and forces a smile.

"Dorothea, if there's anything I can do to help," Evelyn says firmly, "you let me know. James Earl would certainly be welcome at our house."

"Patsy, don't you worry none." Dorothea looks into her moist eyes. "I think I can get it done. In fact, I promise you I'll get it done." She bends down, kisses Patsy on the cheek." Patsy holds on to her, returns the kiss.

"I love you so much, don't get yourself into any trouble."

"Me? Get into trouble?" Dorothea's heart beats rapidly. Her head aches with sorrow as tears swell to the brims of her eyes. "I'm gonna get outta here and let you sisters have some time together." She sniffles and backs up.

"I'm so glad I got to meet you." The low light gives radiance to Evelyn's face.

"Same here," Dorothea replies, "and I'm glad you can be here with Patsy. I'll be in touch, let you know what happens." She throws kisses to Patsy as she backs away into the semi-darkness.

As she passes through the door, tears spill down her face. She momentarily closes her eyes. Lifting her hands to cover her mouth, she stumbles into the nurse.

"You okay, honey?" the nurse holds her by the shoulders. Dorothea doesn't answer, just silently cries. The nurse walks with her down the hall, her arm draped around Dorothea's shoulders.

In the days that follow, Dorothea thinks constantly about Patsy and how sick and weak she seems to be. She wonders how much longer she can hold on.

TWENTY THREE

At work the next day things are normal. Dorothea doesn't know what Mac did to smooth out her absence, but there are no problems. She tries to get to the hospital as often as she can, but working the night shift makes it difficult. Mac is helpful in letting her get away when they aren't busy or if he can get someone else to work in her place.

Dorothea realizes that Patsy's time is getting shorter; she is thinner and weaker with each new visit. Visiting on a cold December evening, Dorothea sits near the bed with her hand on the covers over Patsy's arm. She wonders why she can't transfer some of her health through the covers and into her friend's body to help her get well. It seems so unfair. Patsy doesn't wake, doesn't turn. Dorothea sits and stares at the unresponsive form. As Dorothea leaves the room she sees the red-haired nurse at the nurse station.

"She didn't wake up the whole time I was here. What's happening to her?"

"Well, honey, her condition isn't getting any better. Her pain is more intense, so the medicine the doctor is giving her is stronger than in the past." She places her hand on Dorothea's arm. "I wish I could give you some better news."

Christmas decorations hang in the hospital lobby and Dorothea looks at them as she passes through, but their festive colors bring no cheer. She walks slowly out of the hospital to Mac's truck. Feels a dull pain and stiffness in her bones. The night air is crisp and clear, the chill penetrating. On her way home, holiday decorations and lights are strung from light posts, giving a rare degree of luminosity to the city, but Dorothea drives through the busy streets ignoring them, her sadness poignant and deeply felt.

The following day, she calls Mac early to tell him she's not feeling well, doesn't think she will make it to work.

"Well, if you can't, you can't," he tells her, not offering any sympathy, not asking any questions. He is resigned to taking whatever happens day by day.

"It ain't that bad. I think it's just my nerves, I just need rest so I won't get really bad sick." She has been crying and her voice is hoarse and sullen. "I'll feel better tomorrow."

She mopes around the rest of the day, tears flowing every time she thinks of Patsy. She pats her eyes dry and blows her nose a hundred times, it seems. Exhausted, she sleeps while the girls are napping.

When she wakes up, her focus begins shifting away from her sorrow. The unyielding aggravation of her hatred for D.W., and Henslowe lying, continues to simmer in the back of her mind. Her body and mind feel the betrayal like a searing irritation, like a low-frequency agony that won't leave, staying just below the surface, under her skin, burning.

Knowing tears won't make things any better, she struggles with how to alter the situation. She doesn't want to wait for something to happen like she's done in the past, she is determined to take the first step. She begins thinking about how to get James Earl away from D.W. It would be a huge victory for her and for Patsy. She fixes dinner while the girls are playing. Stirs grits on the stove, mulling over the risky prospect of trying to outsmart D.W., committing herself to doing whatever it takes. After feeding the girls, she calls Roy.

He isn't in. She wants support to clarify her thoughts, make sure she isn't just blindly letting her hatred get in the way of doing things the right way. Half an hour later she calls again. This time he answers.

"Roy, its Dorothea."

"Hi, I was thinking about you, wondering if you ever went to see Henslowe."

"Yeah, I went. But I can't say it went too well."

"Really? You don't think he's going to be able to help you?"

"Well, his story has changed."

"Changed? How? What did he say?"

She pauses, thinking about how she can explain what happened without getting into too much detail. She lies back on the couch and puts her feet up on a box.

"Dorothea?"

"Yeah, I'm here."

"What did he say? I don't understand what happened."

"Well, it ain't that easy to understand," she says in a distressed tone. She knows her response is ambiguous and wants to keep it that way, to tease and purposely try to hold Roy's interest. "Reckon he's had a change of heart."

"Damn. I swear, Dorothea, what I told you is exactly what he said to me."

"Oh, I ain't questioning what you told me. But he's changed his story. I know that. And I think I know why."

"Well, is there something I can do? I feel like I should help you, but I'm not sure what I can do." Roy is feeling partly responsible for the predicament.

"You've done what you could and I appreciate it. I think now I just have to take care of it in my own way." She sounds self-confident, there's nothing timid in her voice.

"What do you mean?" he asks calmly. "What are you thinking of doing?" Roy is intrigued by the conviction in her voice. He feels himself being drawn in, but he's curious to find out exactly what she has in mind.

"Well, I haven't quite figured it out, but I know I'm gonna settle things the best way I know how." She lays her head back, stretches back her neck. The sound of Roy's voice is soothing. Having the day off seems to have helped, she feels relaxed, the tension and doubt gone. In talking with Roy she begins to feel energized. She rubs between her legs, her fingers pushing down on her dress, sliding smoothly over silk panties. Pushing down harder, she feels her face flush with warmness.

"Dorothea?"

Suddenly, her mood changes and doubts rush in. "Roy, I just wanted you to know what happened, but I gotta go now. Thanks for listening."

She replaces the receiver before he can reply. She tightens her legs and sticks out her chest. Her hand continues rubbing softly. With both hands she pulls her dress higher and stokes the inside of her legs, lightly, up and down.

"Rin-n-n-ng." The sound jars her.

"Hello."

"Dorothea, I'm coming over." She doesn't say anything. He hangs up.

She gets up off the couch and feels a shudder run from her ankles up her legs. "Donna. Darlene. Come on girls. Time to get ready for bed." She hears the clapping of their bare feet on the floor as they run in different directions, letting out shrill screams: "No-o-o-o-o, No-o-o-o-o." She smiles at their playfulness.

Her body tingles as she washes the girls. Her skin seems hypersensitive. Each step of her bare feet touching the floor brings a delicate sensation. She has not felt this flood of anticipation in a long time. Her mind is at ease, she relishes this sense of freedom: freedom from sorrow, freedom that allows her to dream of floating, drifting in air, yearning for relief, relief she can feel in every inch of her body.

She tucks the girls in bed. Begins picking up scattered toys when the doorbell rings.

"Hi, come on in." She looks briefly but can't keep her eyes on him. He takes off his jacket. "Sorry this place is such a mess."

"Oh, don't worry about it. I'm kind of barging in, but I couldn't help wondering what you plan to do about Henslowe." He stands upright, hands on his hips. "You said he changed his mind."

She walks to the couch, sits at the far end. He follows and sits at the other end. Turning in his direction, she curves her left arm across the cushion. Crosses one leg over the other. "Don't plan to do nothing about him."

"Well, didn't you say he lied to you about D.W. and the woman?"

"He said he can't remember what the woman looked like. Says it coulda been me. He can't be sure."

"Ohhh, man. He described the woman to me. Said she was blonde. How . . . "

"He ain't forgot." She maintains her poise, but her heart beats faster. "Hell no, he ain't forgot. Henslowe's not the problem. He's just lying because D.W. got to him. Henslowe's not the problem." She remains unemotional, but her eyes become stormy. "D.W.'s the problem."

Her eyes remain focused on Roy. "Somehow D.W. found out we were talking to Henslowe about Poppa's will. D.W. must have gotten wind of it."

"Well," Roy feels the problem is falling back on him, "I talked to my friend Timmy, asked him where I could find Henslowe, but nothing was said about you or the will. And then I told my mother about seeing him when she called me. I don't think she would tell anyone, especially D.W. Of course, my sister was there too, and her friend Janice. They know about it, but being high school girls it doesn't seem likely D.W. would find out from them." He thinks about it and then adds, "But I guess anything is possible."

"I don't know. I don't know how he found out, but I bet a dollar to a donut he found out and went to see Mr. Henslowe. It's just like something D.W. would do. He's the sneakiest bastard in the world," she says in a matter-of-fact tone.

"Well, you know, Janice was going to tell her boyfriend about it, I guess. The thing is, she and Melissa are thinking that Clarence—that's Janice's boyfriend—they're thinking maybe his sister could be running around with D.W."

"No kiddin?" Dorothea's eyebrows rise. "Could she maybe be the one what went with him to get my inheritance money?"

"I . . ." Roy jerks his shoulders forward and tilts his head to the side. "I don't know. I mean they're not sure she is actually the one. I guess they may find out something, but right now I don't think they know whether Clarence's sister even knows D.W."

"Well, he found out, somehow that sonufabitch found out. If you'd seen Henslowe's eyes you would know he was lying and scared." Dorothea's voice is steady, almost casual; not letting her suspicions about D.W. upset her. She continues to look at Roy and moves her left leg so it lies angled on the couch, the edge of her dress stretching tightly from thigh to thigh.

Roy notices the gesture. He swallows, moving his lips. "What are you planning to do?" he asks.

She exhibits the calmness of a tightrope walker. She doesn't answer. Pulls her leg back, raising the edge of her dress. She watches his eyes drop.

Roy tries not to look nervous, but can't help wondering where this is leading. When he came over his only thoughts were about her problem with the money and Henslowe. Now it seems to be turning into something else.

Dorothea continues her direct gaze. She says nothing, her expression is calm and serene, her lips parted, her posture invitingly open.

The girls are probably asleep and no one else is around, Roy surmises. He feels his temperature climbing.

"Dorothea, what are you thinking about doing?" He poses the question without enthusiasm, as though he is not expecting an answer. And she doesn't answer. Thinking about the question, he realizes it can be taken in more than one way.

"Do what I have to do," she utters softly. "Some people can afford to be careful and follow the rules. But I can't live my life one short step at a time, being careful every time I move. I don't have many choices in my life, maybe that's why I just choose what I think I need to do and then I do it." She pulls her other leg back, hiking her dress higher. "It's as simple as that."

Roy isn't sure that he's not shaking. His mind races: This could really get me into trouble. A woman with two kids, down on her luck. Damn.

He tries to slide over closer, feeling the blood rush to his face, but the cushion doesn't allow him to move. His eyes steady on hers; he thinks he detects a slight smile on her lips. Puts his hands down and with his legs rises up and moves toward her.

She moves her leg so he can get closer. Reaching and putting his hand on her leg, he bends forward, his mouth finding hers. Her lips part and the soft, pliable lips fill his head with a rushing pulse, a flood. He slides his hand farther up her dress.

"J-I-I-N-N-N-G-G-G!"

They both jump at the sound of the doorbell. Alarmed at their vulnerability. Frightened by the blaring intrusion.

"Ph-h-eeew," Roy lets air escape through his teeth, releasing the pressure, feels himself shaking—whether from fright or disappointment he isn't sure. He waits until she isn't looking then stands up, runs his thumbs around his belt line and then makes quick strokes downward to smooth out the front of his pants.

Dorothea is on her way to the front door. She looks down quickly to make sure her dress is down. She pulls her shoulders back and stands behind the door, opening it just enough so she can see who is there.

"Hey," says a man's heavy voice.

Dorothea opens the door wider. "Just thought I'd drop by to see how you are." Mac steps inside and then sees Roy and stops immediately. The smile he had for Dorothea fades.

"Oh, Mac, you remember Roy." She closes the door to shut off the cold air. "He's my friend from Cuttsville."

Roy steps forward and puts out his hand. "Good to see you again, Mac." Remembering Mac's coolness from the last time he was here, he wants to show that he is visiting as a friend and nothing more.

Mac shakes his hand, looking with a cold stare. "What's goin on?" he asks, turning his head to look at Dorothea.

Roy feels a little apprehensive. Mac is a big guy, over six foot and heavy set, and it looks like he is on familiar terms with Dorothea, especially since he seems to stop by often.

"Well, Roy just came over to talk about me seeing that lawyer in Cuttsville. Roy here is the one that told me about why I didn't get the money Poppa left me." She looks a little tentative standing in front of Mac. His hard look implying he may be thinking there's more to it than what she's telling him.

Roy is afraid that 'caught-in-the-act' sweat may pop out on his forehead if he continues standing here. "Well, I guess I'll be getting on home, Dorothea." He moves toward his jacket, which is closer to the front door.

Dorothea turns away from Mac. Roy puts his jacket on and she reaches for the doorknob. "Thanks for coming over," she says. "I reckon I'll let you know when something new happens." Her eyes could melt ice. Roy can see she is breathing heavily, her chest rising and falling. He's glad Mac is standing behind her and cannot see the soft, despondent look on her face.

"Okay, I guess I'll see you later then. Goodnight." Before passing through the opening, he looks back at Mac. "See yeh, Mac."

Mac gives an upward jerk with his head to acknowledge Roy.

Dorothea pushes the door shut behind him. As he zips up his jacket, he can hear Mac inside. "I thought you was sick."

"I was, earlier," Dorothea fires back. "I told you I just needed some rest."

As Roy walks down the sidewalk to his car, he dimly hears both voices. He can't make out the words and doesn't really care to try. It's comforting to be outside in the fresh, cool air. He is anxious to get away.

What if Mac hadn't interrupted them? Roy is certain that it is for the best that he did. Mac seems to be more of the type of man she needs, someone who may be interested in marrying her. Although she is a nice person. Maybe her actions are a little bizarre because of what has happened to her. But even at that, she is not someone he wants to get entangled with. He feels bad about D.W. ripping her off, but decides it's time to leave well enough alone. If she asks, he'll try to help her out, but he definitely will not be coming back over here to talk about it.

However, as he drives through the familiar streets of Parksdale, Roy has to acknowledge the change he saw in Dorothea; she was healthier looking and she sounded more assertive about handling her problem with D.W. She was certainly bolder. He envisions the scene on the couch, replaying it, trying to imagine what it would have been like if Mac had not shown up.

TWENTY FOUR

Roy is glad to be heading home for a breather. Leaving Parksdale, he crosses a street that leads to the section of town where Dorothea lives. He wonders what she'll be doing during the holidays; if it will include spending time with Mac. It is a little difficult to tell how she feels about the guy. He hopes the incident a week ago didn't stir up any trouble and add to her problems.

He packed books with the intention of studying during the break. When he returns after the first of the year, exams are only two weeks away. Maybe he can use his time wisely while at home—doesn't see any reason why he can't hit the books and be prepared when he returns. He also has a report to write, which shouldn't be difficult.

The only thing he dreads about this time of year is having to buy gifts; it's so hard to know what to buy Melissa and his parents. He usually thinks about it until the last minute and then hurriedly buys something. But he enjoys being back home with Melissa, his mother and father, and being able to see old friends occasionally. It is a nice change of pace and restful.

As he gets nearer to Cuttsville, his thoughts turn to the Hideaway. This being Friday, he knows his father will be there working. He's never been in there at night, so he decides to stop and say hello. It has been in the same location for years, but his father and Frank only reopened it about three years ago. They were hesitant, but decided they would open only on weekends and give it a try.

The many times he's passed it, he has taken cursory glances. The long, wooden building has no windows, so it's impossible to tell what is happening inside. Bars and juke joints are intriguing. With a mix of people drinking, dancing, talking, these places always have an interesting ambience. Frank's liquor store is a short distance away. He has never stopped there either, knowing that Frank is a friend of his father.

He slows down and sees headlights coming up from behind. The parking area is crowded; it looks like it could be a busy night. Nearly nine o'clock and it closes at one, so this is probably the busiest time. Dodging a couple of large dips in the dirt drive, he finds a spot off to the side near a tall tree. He locks the car.

As he opens the entrance door, warm air and honky-tonk music leak out. He walks in and looks around. A lady standing by a small table says, "Two dollars." He starts to tell her his father owns the place, but decides to fork over two dollars instead. She stamps his hand with the word "Hideaway" in blue ink, and then places the money in a cigar box and lays her hand on top.

Roy can see his father behind the bar to the right. He's talking to someone, but then moves to the counter edge where a barmaid is waiting. A band is at the left end of the building: woman singer, guitar, bass and drums. A din of music fills the enclosure, along with an underlying ruckus of voices, clattering bottles and shuffling feet. Roy notices some empty tables. Some people standing around the edges, mostly men, local rabble, surveying the dance floor and the tables.

He moves toward the bar and pulls out his wallet. His father is making change. When he turns around he sees Roy and gives a measured smile. "Hey, what in the world."

Roy smiles. "Just thought I'd stop in and say howdy." He holds a dollar bill up. "Can I get a beer? I might hang around for a few minutes."

"Put your money away." He moves to the center, dips his arm down and comes up with a beer in-hand. "Try this. It's kinda new."

"Who's the band?"

"They're from over Parksdale. A man and his wife, and they've got a couple of other guys in the band. They're not bad. Just hope enough people come in to cover the cost."

Roy turns to the side and looks at the room. "Looks like a good crowd." He takes a swallow of the beer. A barmaid brushes by.

"Just a minute," his father says as he attends to the barmaid. She rattles off a list of drinks. Roy can see that Frank is keeping busy at the other end of the bar. Every bar stool taken. A lot of back and forth movement, putting drinks on the counter, pulling empty bottles and clinking glasses off, and occasionally wiping up spills with a small towel.

"Well, it's picking up." His father wipes his hands on the white apron.

"Well, hey, I'm gonna hang around for a little while. I'll see you at home."

"There's Ned." His father raises his head with a subtle jerk, indicating the doorway.

"Eula Mae's husband?" Roy asks, looking.

"Yeah, he comes in every once in a while. Hey, I need to get busy." He moves away.

"Okay." Roy looks for a place where he can stand. Doesn't see anyone he knows, except Ned, but hasn't seen him in years. He moves to the side, backs up against the wall, and watches the couples on the dance floor. Two women dance together, one a little hefty, the other smaller, thinner. A better-looking woman is dancing in the center with a tall thin guy. Hips swaying, she has a nice figure—seems to know it too. Half the men who can see her are watching. She moves with confidence, loose and easy, like she has had a few drinks.

Ned walks past, up to the bar. Roy's father comes over to get him a drink. Gets a beer, comes back and they begin talking. Ned turns and looks in Roy's direction, then turns back. Roy looks around. Interesting just watching the people, a menagerie of shadowy faces revealed by touches of flickering light.

Out of the side of his eye he sees Ned coming back. He stops. "Roy?"

"Yeah. Hi, Ned, how you doing?" He reaches to shake his hand, thinking he hasn't changed much, looks about the same.

"Your pa tolt me you was here. Boy, I wouldn't a knowed you, if he hadn't tolt me." Ned smiles quizzically, like he's trying to figure something out.

"Well, you haven't changed much," Roy says, looking at Ned's tanned face. "It's been a while." Their voices are raised and then the music stops. The noise level goes down. Roy watches the shapely blonde walk from the dance floor to the bar, wonders if she is with the guy she was dancing with.

"Yeah, I say it's been a while. A few years for sure. You done growed up." He follows Roy's eyes. "Know who that is?" He jerks his head in the blonde's direction.

"No. Don't think so."

"Name's Clarice. She's ole D.W.'s girlfriend."

"Really?"

Ned has a knowing look on his face—inside information.

"Yep, ain't nobody supposed to know it, D.W. being married and all." Ned's eyes follow Clarice as she walks to the bar. "He knowed she was out here dancing it might not set too good. I heared he's knocked er around a time or two."

Roy reacts with raised eyebrows. "You know I think I have seen her before. I believe she was a couple of years ahead of me in school."

"Is that right?" Ned says turning back to Roy. "Yep, she's a pretty good-looker, considering D.W. ain't that much." He thinks about it, then adds, "But he has bought hisself a new pickup." Raises his eyebrows and puckers his lips to warrant this as a serious consideration. "Reckon him and his pa is making some money in that store. Don't know how, but reckon they must be." Ned takes a large swallow of his beer.

Roy doesn't want to talk about the store. Since Ned and Eula Mae failed to make a go of it, it is probably a sore subject. Ned's shirt is unironed, a little rumpled looking. He wears work khakis that hang loosely, cuffs bunched up on top of brown workshoes. Clean-shaved, he has on cologne and his oiled hair is parted and combed. Roy wonders about Eula Mae, but doesn't ask.

"Where you at now?" Ned asks.

"Over in Parksdale, going to college."

"Is that right?" He pulls his head back as a gesture of surprise. "I'll be doggone. You aim to get you some smarts, I reckon."

Roy smiles. "Yeah, I'm trying." He doesn't know how to gauge Ned. He holds his smile, hoping to avoid any awkwardness. The musicians are back on the stand, the bass player thumbing the strings, tuning. The mirrored globe hanging above the dance floor rotates with precision, throwing cascades of uneven light around the room, flickers of white spots moving across people's faces and clothes.

"Let me get yeh a beer," Ned says, reaching for his empty bottle.

"Thanks, I appreciate that." Roy knows they don't have a whole lot in common, but likes having someone to talk with in this den of strangers. Socializing with an older, more seasoned reveler makes him feel as though he almost fits in.

Ned walks to the bar and Roy looks around, trying to locate Clarice. Wondering why D.W. isn't here. If she is his girlfriend, why is she here without him? Considering the two players, maybe it's not such a tight romance.

"Here yeh go." Ned hands him a beer.

"Thanks."

"Yeah, I reckon Clarice is steppin out on D.W. Don't know much about it, cept I'm thinkin D.W. oughta be payin attention to his own wife, her doing so poorly."

"Really? Don't know much about her. I heard she was in the hospital."

"Oh, she's a right fine lit'l gal," Ned's voice has a somber tone, "but she ain't doin well. From what I hear, she's pretty bad off."

That said, he lifts his head, stretches his face into a grin, looking squint-eyed across the dance floor. "I'm gonna mosey over here and talk with a gal I know."

This catches Roy by surprise. "Yeah, well hey, thanks for the beer."

"Don't think nothin of it. It was good uh seein yeh." He pats Roy on the shoulder as he slides away.

Ned moves across the dance floor toward two women. They have drinks sitting on a table, but are standing. Both are unattractive, in their mid-thirties at least. One of them, leaning slightly, her hand on the table, has a slouching posture, her stomach sticking out, as though she might be pregnant. She notices Ned and smiles. Hard to tell for sure, at this distance, but it looks as though she is missing a front tooth.

Roy continues to gaze around, trying to catch the light on a pretty face. Unfortunately, it looks like most of the women are middle-aged or older; however, he notices that the woman singing with the band is attractive. He sips his beer as he listens to the music. It's a slow song and several couples hurry onto the dance floor.

He notices Ned dancing with the woman who smiled at him. His back curved so he can fit snuggly against the shorter woman. At the other end, Clarice is dancing with a different man, this one short and husky. He has on boots, blue jeans and a western-cut plaid shirt. Another pair dancing in a jerky manner with extravagant motions are probably in their sixties:

the man in faded overalls, the woman has on a plain dress and white open-toed shoes.

Clarice seems a little cool to the short guy, not letting him get too close. Roy wonders why she allowed D.W. to use her to take Dorothea's money. Obviously, it must have been her, her being D.W.'s girlfriend and blonde. Henslowe said she was blonde.

Doesn't know if he should get another beer or not. If his father is counting, he might have something to say. It's not that far to the house, one more won't hurt. He strolls to the bar, taking each step carefully, not wanting to sway or bump anything, and not wanting to have a one-drink-too-many grin on his face.

"I like that beer," he says when his father approaches, "gimme one more and then I'm heading out of here."

His father reaches for the beer, snaps off the cap, and hands it to Roy.

"When do all the pretty girls show up?" Roy cajoles.

"Huh-uh," his father laughs, "you'll be waiting a long time if that's what you're looking for." He looks out at the crowd. "We get the leftovers here." He sniggers rapidly.

Roy laughs as well. "I believe you got that right. Hey, I'll see you at home."

He turns and moves to reclaim his place at the wall. The music stops and Clarice comes barreling by, almost knocking the beer out of his hand. She pays no attention; swaggering, she heads to the bar. Roy looks after her, but then eases into his old position.

Seems there are more people now than when he came in. The gray walls more compacting. Cigarette smoke spirals into a haze, illuminated by tiny, intermittent flashes of mirrored light. Rumbling voices meld into a steady, rowdy monotone.

The music starts again. It seems to get better with each beer. Maybe he'll ask his father for the band's name and look for them when they're playing around Parksdale.

Suddenly there is a rattling of bottles and clanking brown empties hit the floor, bounce and roll. Across the room there is confusion, possibly a fight, Roy thinks. Then a man steps aside and the old man in overalls who was dancing is on the floor. His wife (it would seem to be) is bent, pulling on his arm to help him. Another man bends over and gets hold of the other arm. Together, they help lift him to his feet. The old man acts disoriented, shuffles one leg, hobbles a little using his wife and the man to brace himself. He sways and then steadies himself. Everyone is looking in that direction. The music has slowed in much the same way as someone's finger on a record would slow the sound. Then the musicians, realizing it is a minor incident, pick up the normal rhythm again.

The old man is laughing. Or maybe crying. It's hard to tell in the dim light, with all the ruckus back to full pitch. People continue passing back and forth, making it difficult for Roy to see what is happening. Some don't notice the bottles on the floor, kicking them spinning out to the center where no one is dancing.

"Drunk old bastard," Clarice says caustically to a man standing two feet from Roy. He laughs, casually leans back against the wall.

"Need teh take the old fucker home," her voice is rough and loud, "it's waaaay past his bedtime." The man she is talking to hoots, leans forward with spasms of laughter. Reaches up with his free hand to wipe fluids from his mouth.

Roy looks on. She's not as attractive up close as he originally thought—ruddy complexion and crooked teeth. He decides to speak up about Dorothea's money and see how she will react. She walks a few steps closer.

"Clarice."

She looks at him, smile gone, almost as though he pinched her. "Yeah?"

"Uh, just thought I'd say hello. I know your brother Clarence." He tries to think quickly, so as not to make a complete fool of himself.

"Good for you," she throws the words at him with arrogance. She probably has treated several men here tonight with the same snide indifference. It doesn't set well with Roy, makes him feel like rattling her.

Before she can turn away he says, "I know someone else who knows you."

She hesitates; left eye a thin slit and piercing, her lips in a tight smirk.

"You know an attorney in Cuttsville named Cletus Henslowe?"

Her expression softens. "Can't say as I do." Her lips open and close in a swallowing motion.

Roy steps closer. "You don't remember him? Somehow he was a little confused though, said he thought your name was Dorothea."

"What kinda bullshit you talkin?" She spits the words at Roy. Pulls her shoulders back in defiance. "I don't know your asshole attorney."

Roy can tell his probing has cut—even to the extent that she might throw a fist at him. He holds her gaze unflinchingly. "Well, just thought you'd remember, he says he knows you."

Her mouth contorts into an awkward grin. She moves away quickly, trouncing across the floor to the far side. Roy doesn't know what to expect. He swigs down some beer. His eyes focus across the room, but Clarice is lost somewhere in the crowd. He bends and sets the near-empty bottle on the floor against the wall. He straightens up and starts to walk in the direction of the door, but stops. Ahead of him, he sees Ned leaving with the oddly shaped woman. Roy waits a few more minutes and then he leaves.

TWENTY FIVE

A cold, January drizzle is keeping people inside the gravesite tent. Now that the coffin has been lowered, some are voicing a hard-faced note of sympathy and quickly exiting to cars and trucks. Evelyn is glad she said yes when the funeral director asked if she wanted them to bring the tent—just in case. They charge twenty dollars extra, but it has been worth it. The bill is going to D.W. anyway. Least he can do is pay for his wife to have a decent burial.

D.W.'s hand holds onto James Earl's shoulder as they walk a few feet to where Evelyn and her husband are standing. The preacher has just turned away to talk with another couple. Evelyn had called D.W. to ask if it would be okay for this preacher to officiate at the service, because he is her and Patsy's uncle. He has a church near Mobile and she and Patsy always enjoyed visiting him and their aunt. D.W. told her to do what she wanted, he had not made any plans.

Evelyn came to Cuttsville a week in advance just to make sure everything would be taken care of. She didn't trust D.W. to do right by her sister. She talked with him only when absolutely necessary for making the arrangements.

Evelyn and Tom's children stand behind them; the two boys in jackets and ties and the little girl, her coat open, showing a flouncy, blue dress. Shy of strangers and bewildered by the day's proceedings, the girl presses against her mother's leg for comfort and warmth.

"Bellman, how yeh been doin?" D.W.'s voice is high and whining like a circular saw cutting through hardwood. He reaches awkwardly to shake his brother-in-law's hand. He's not sure of his first name: Tom or Don, he can never remember.

"Not bad, I reckon. Sure hate this happened," his heavy tone cracks with unsteadiness, "Patsy being so young, it sure is hurtful." He holds Evelyn close, acutely aware of how difficult the last few months have been on her.

Evelyn looks at D.W. with woeful eyes, moist and red-rimmed. Sees a face that is blank and guarded, scurrilous eyes and thin lips. She tries to dispel the anguish she is feeling, for James Earl's sake. She reaches out to touch the side of the boy's face. His eyes momentarily lift to hers; his expression is one of nervous uncertainty.

"Yeah." D.W. looks at Evelyn and then James Earl. "Yeah, James Earl's sure gonna miss his mom."

Many of the women have understandably doted on James Earl, offering you-call-me-anytime-you-need-anything consolation. They can only guess how painful his mother's passing would be on someone his age.

His hands jammed in pockets, James Earl hunches his shoulders forward. His appearance makes it apparent that he has no mother to care for him. His shirt has not been ironed and a portion of the collar sticks up and out of the jacket. Evelyn wonders if he is eating okay. He seems to be shivering and sniffling; it is difficult to know what to attribute to cold weather and what to the funeral. His arms twitch and his eyes dart one direction then another. Maybe the movement keeps his mind from locking in place.

A gaunt man with tousled white hair walks up behind D.W., placing gnarled fingers on the sleeve of his jacket. The man's bony face and crinkled eyes seem to indicate years of hard living. D.W. turns and walks away. James Earl remains, looking at Evelyn's oldest boy.

"James Earl," D.W. throws a call over his shoulder. The boy turns slowly and follows.

The tent sags in large swoops and the air inside is thick with moisture and the smell of turned earth. Now that people are leaving it seems easier to breathe.

Stiffly, Mrs. Crawley moves in Evelyn's direction. As she approaches, her head wags slowly side to side. "Sure is shameful, us losing Patsy like that."

"Yes, mam. It's mighty sad," Evelyn says quietly, squeezing her hands together. "With our parents gone too, I thank God I got my own family to lean on."

"I thought right highly of your sister, you know that."

"Yes'm, Mrs. Crawley, I know you were close to her." Evelyn is not really sure how Patsy felt about her mother-in-law; it never came up.

"I reckon it'll be plenty hard on James Earl." The older woman pinches the edges of her black shawl closer to her neck, her face sagging with age and fatigue.

Evelyn looks across the tent at James Earl, an uneasy stance, his thoughts trapped inside. She notices D.W. as well; he keeps glancing over his shoulder in a guarded manner, as though someone might sneak up from behind.

"No one can replace his ma," Mrs. Crawley says, her eyes turning downward, her body rigid. "I aim to do as much for em as what I can. Old as I am, I reckon I can do for the boy."

"Yes'm, I know you'll do your best," Evelyn says. Of course she hopes Dorothea wasn't just talking; that she actually has some idea or some way planned to help her get James Earl, like Patsy wanted. Being around D.W., even for a short time, makes her feel all the more strongly about it. Though she never asked Patsy for any gritty details about their marriage, she surmised enough to know she will never feel anything but anger and disgust for D.W.

"Sure hate this weather," Mrs. Crawley says, looking through the tent opening and drawing her shawl tighter against her body. "Makes my old bones ache somethin awful."

"Yes'm, it's a miserable day in more ways than one," Evelyn says calmly, her voice vapor-soft. Her eyes gaze out at the bleak grayness, random rows of slanted, worn tombstones running to the distant fence, an occasional columnar shape with arches or triangular pediments at top, but mostly small, tilting markers stained with black splotches of moss and decay.

"You comin?" Mr. Crawly calls to her, as he waits at the opening.

Bent forward, slowly turning, with eyes sweeping the ground, Mrs. Crawley puts her hand on Evelyn's arm. Evelyn waits for a closing formality, but there is only silent resignation. The old woman pats her arm softly and walks away.

As the Crawleys slip through the narrow opening, Dorothea comes in from the opposite direction, avoiding them, looking corner to corner. She sees Evelyn, then notices

D.W. and James Earl toward the back. As she looks in their direction, D.W.'s eyes meet hers. She turns to Evelyn.

Dorothea reaches out to enclose Evelyn's hands in hers. "Don't know how I'm gonna get by without her." Dorothea breathes deeply, her face is winter-pale and her eyes, tinged with red, are sunken into dark hollows.

Evelyn steps closer and holds onto Dorothea's arm, offering her support. "We're going to miss her. I still can't believe it happened." They stare at the black walls of the rectangular shaft, its impenetrable secrecy. Precise. Unfathomable.

Softly, Evelyn pulls back. "Mrs. Moss invited us over for something to eat." She clutches Dorothea's hands tighter. "You coming?"

"No, reckon I gotta get back to Parksdale. But can you write out your telephone number for me and I'll call to let you . . . ," she hesitates, looks across the enclosure and then turning her back toward D.W., says quietly, "let you know about James Earl."

Evelyn lifts her purse in front and looks inside for pencil and paper. "I should have something in here to write on, seeing as how I got so much." Her hand pulls out a small wrinkled slip of paper.

She turns her back to the few remaining people and holds the short pencil and paper out to Tom and turns her purse flat side up. "Here Tom, write our telephone number on here."

"It may take me a little while," Dorothea says in a whisper, "but I will definitely call you."

"You sure you don't want some help in this?" Evelyn questions, "I . . ."

"No," Dorothea interrupts, "you don't need to do nothing. Don't you worry none. I got it all figured out."

Evelyn looks at her, swallowed in the faded brown coat, she seems frailer than the last time she saw her. "Okay, well you call collect if you need to talk to me." She glances at Tom. He nods his head.

"I hate to leave." Dorothea turns her head toward the grave and, in the pale light, the tears in her eyes glisten.

Evelyn struggles to keep tears back, clamps her teeth together and swallows with difficulty. She pats Dorothea softly on the back and then swipes her hand back and forth as though it will swish away the pain.

"Bye now." Dorothea's cheeks are puffed with sadness, her lips pouting.

Evelyn touches her head against Dorothea, then releases her.

Dorothea hurries through the opening, her head down, tears falling to the wet ground. As she steps quickly past several markers to the narrow gravel path, her eyes focus on black cows moving slowly, grazing just beyond the barbed wire fence at the edge of the cemetery. The cold, wet ground has numbed her feet. She wraps her arms across the front of her body, but the coldness crawls up her legs, over her arms and chest, causing her to involuntarily shake.

Her eyes scan the assemblage of weathered grave markers, quiet in their stoic resilience. She lifts her head to the wind and lets the coldness sting her face.

During the funeral she had been despondent, standing just inside the tent, trying to be inconspicuous, not wanting anyone to notice her—especially not wanting D.W. to see her suffer or know how much she is hurting. But now, the sadness is lifting. It's over. Patsy is beyond the grave. And now Dorothea envisions her floating above, serene, a warm smile on her face, looking down and watching over James Earl, and watching over her as well, offering her love and encouragement. The feeling is so strong that Dorothea's stride slows and she looks up, turning her head side to side, searching the gray sky.

TWENTY SIX

Roy has not seen Dorothea since before Christmas. Doesn't know what she is doing about Henslowe or D.W. Maybe nothing. He has resisted calling. It is easier letting the whole thing rest, avoid getting entangled and hope the messy ordeal will somehow resolve itself. Although he knows it won't.

Besides, there is the worry that by kissing her, she may have taken it as some type of commitment. It makes him nervous to think about how seriously she may have taken the incident. True, he took advantage of the situation. And maybe he shouldn't have, but it's just as obvious that she openly invited it. He's not sure if he precipitated the kiss or if he was purposely lured in by her.

Still he feels he shouldn't just abandon her. He considers her a friend. There is an unspoken bond because of their childhood connectedness and their family ties. He tries to put it out of his mind. Doesn't want to dwell on it all the way to Cuttsville.

In a telephone conversation with Melissa, he learned about Patsy's dying. She told him the funeral was at Paradise Lake Cemetery, sometime in January. He remembers Dorothea telling him how close she was with Patsy. No telling what affect it has had on her, and it's another reason not to be eager to talk with her.

Melissa had also said that Clarice was missing. Janice told Melissa that her boyfriend's family didn't know what to think about it—they were concerned, but didn't really think anything had happened to her.

It has been more than a month since Roy was home and spring break is still weeks away. So, tonight he's heading home for the weekend to get his laundry done and catch up on the latest news about D.W. and Clarice. From what he saw of Clarice at the Hideaway, it looked as though she could probably take care of herself.

He looks at the black darkness through the windshield. Two nights ago, the weather report said there might be snow. That has only happened a few times before, as far as he can remember. But it never amounts to much. Wednesday night he was walking back to his apartment and, in the moonlight, he could see small, sparkling flakes falling. Nothing accumulating on the ground, but you could definitely say it was snowing.

The temperature must be near freezing, so he has the heater cranked up. As he approaches the Hideaway, he briefly considers stopping to see his father, but doesn't feel up to it. If he goes inside, he'll end up hanging around for an hour or more, and it's already late. Cold weather this time of year makes winter seem endless; seems to sap his energy and enthusiasm. Roy is definitely eager for spring and warmer days.

Tonight he just wants to crawl into bed and sleep late Saturday morning. When he does get up, he knows his mother will have a nice, hot breakfast for him, something he is rarely able to enjoy when away from home.

When he arrives, his mother opens the door and gives him a hug. "Boy, I'm glad you made it safely. Are the roads slick?" Any indication that temperatures may drop below 32 degrees causes her to imagine horrific possibilities.

"The weather isn't really that bad; it won't go below freezing," he tells her.

"I hope not, Melissa is out on a date."

Roy watches television with his mother for a while, just to settle in. A fluttering glow from the television's changing scenes gives the room an eerie, oscillating light. The program initiates a mild stupor.

"Guess I'll hit the hay," Roy says, standing up and stretching.

"Okay," his mother looks up and smiles, "I think I'll stay up a little longer." Of course Roy knows she won't go to bed before Melissa gets home. His father probably won't be home until two o'clock or later.

The next morning Roy hears Melissa and Janice talking. He doesn't want to embarrass himself by appearing pasty-mouthed, hair in a mess and still not clear-eyed. He decides to lie in bed a while longer.

He wakes suddenly, realizing there are no voices in the living room. Climbing out of bed, he quickly slips on the jeans and flannel shirt he wore home yesterday. Timidly, he steps into the living room and, seeing no one around, he dashes into the bathroom. He washes, but decides to take a vacation from shaving—at least for today.

"Hey sleepyhead," Melissa calls as he walks into the kitchen. She and Janice are walking in from the back porch. Janice smiles.

"The-r-r-e you are." His mother, standing by the stove, draws out the words in a melodic tone to imply that there may have been some question about him ever getting up.

"Yep, and I'm mighty hungry." He wraps his arm around his mother. He looks at Melissa and Janice. "Hi, ladies," he says cheerfully.

"Hi, Roy. Good to see you again," Janice responds.

Melissa walks over and rubs her hand over his head ruffling his hair. "Glad to see you're up so early," she teases.

"How many eggs you want," his mother asks without turning from the stove, "three, four?"

"Nooo, no." Roy moves to sit at the table. "Two will be plenty." He knows there will also be grits and sausage or bacon.

Melissa and Janice sit on the opposite side of the table. Both look fresh and awake, like they have been up for hours.

"What time is it?" Roy asks while turning in his chair to see the wall clock behind him.

"Nearly noon," Melissa says emphatically.

"Hey, only eleven fifteen," Roy responds.

"What'cha been up to, college boy?" Melissa leans forward, her arms crossed on the table.

"Ummm, not much." Roy's mother comes to the table holding a woven basket with biscuits wrapped inside a cloth.

"You should see Clarence's car," Melissa says as Roy begins buttering a biscuit. "It's a really neat fifty-six Ford."

"Really?" Roy says and puts the biscuit to his mouth. He remembers Tommy Ritchie's brother had a fifty-six Ford.

"It's two-tone, blue and white. He has touched it up and waxed it. It's neat looking," Melissa assures him. She asks

Janice, "What's it called with that chrome going over the top?"

Roy listens, but watches his mother as she brings a plate and sets it in front of him: three eggs, instead of two, strips of bacon and a heap of steaming grits.

"I think he called it a Crown Victoria," Janice says, with a quizzical look. Then turning toward Roy, she adds, "He let me drive it today, because him and some other guys are going fishing."

"Fishing?" Roy cuts up his eggs. "A little cold to go fishing, isn't it?"

"Clarence said it isn't that cold, once the sun comes up. Supposed to be nice and sunny today."

Roy forks egg and grits into his mouth. Nods his head.

"Clarence said he'd go fishing every day, if he could," Janice continues. "He likes to get out there on the lake, especially with a couple of his buddies."

Roy looks at Janice and continues to eat. "Likes fishing, huh?"

"Y-e-a-h-h, says his daddy used to take him and Clarice fishing out to Paradise Lake all the time when they were kids. And now, him and his daddy go out there hunting, too. It's a big lake, but I imagine Clarence knows his way around out there as much as anyone," she says with a smile of admiration.

"That's a really nice sweater." Roy says, nodding his head toward Janice. Catches her by surprise. She quickly pulls her arms off the table and looks down at the pale pink sweater. She also has a fluffy, white angora sweater, open in the front, over the pink sweater.

"Well, thanks." She beams. Blushes some, so Roy looks back at his food.

"What's this about his sister being gone?" Roy looks at Janice again.

"You said you saw her at the Hideaway?" Melissa asks him. "When was that?"

"Oh, gosh, that was back before Christmas."

"Well, it's been more than three weeks now that she's been gone," Janice says. "They are really getting worried. Clarence said she went off once before and she was gone about a week before she called."

"Tell him where she was," Melissa urges.

"She called from Oklahoma." Janice stifles a giggle. Then she talks rapidly, in an excited voice, "Said she had met someone who wanted her to come with him on a trip out there. So she just up and went. Didn't say nothing to nobody. Of course, Clarence says she was over twenty-one, guess she can do what she wants. But his dad didn't think so. He told her as long as she's living in his house she better not do it again."

Roy and Melissa listen with interest. Roy's mother is busy washing dishes, but he's sure she is not missing any of the story. She likes gossip as much as anyone.

"You said they finally went to the sheriff and told him about Clarice being missing?" Melissa asks. Her elbow on the table, her head is leaning at an angle against her upturned palm.

"Yeah, Clarence said they didn't want people to know. Afraid, at first, of what people might say about her running off with men. But then when time passed they got so worried that something might've happened."

Roy has been eating while he listens to Janice, but now he leans back in his chair. His mother notices and is quick to ask, "You want more?"

"No, Mom, this is plenty. I'm just about filled up," he says as he rubs his hand across his stomach. "I need to catch my breath and then finish what I've got. Thanks, Mom, that was mighty good."

"Well, here, finish off this coffee. I'll wash the pot." She pours the remaining dark liquid into his cup.

"Where's Dad?" Roy asks.

"He went off about half-an-hour ago." Melissa swivels her head in his direction. "Something to do with one of the distributors not delivering enough beer. Said they were really busy last night."

"Oh." Roy senses he's out of touch, disconnected. At the same time, the ambiance of the kitchen, the aroma of his mother's cooking, the warm cup of coffee, talking with Melissa and Janice, these are the things he enjoys about being home. His stomach full, he feels satisfied, very comfortable.

He looks back at Janice. "Well, have they heard anything from Clarice yet?"

Janice has a somber look, eyes pinched closer together. "No, not a thing. Clarence said the sheriff has put a bulletin out to other law enforcement people, even in nearby states, but so far they haven't gotten anything back."

Her speech slows to a crawl. "Clarence is really upset. That's one of the reasons he wanted to go fishing, to get his mind off of it. But, knowing him, that's all he'll be thinking about. He really thinks D.W. has something to do with her being gone." Her tone becomes more emphatic. "Said he'd kill him if he did anything to his sister. He means it, too!"

"Wow," Roy says with amazement, "you hate to think something could happen to her." Thinking back to Clarice at the Hideaway, he wonders, "You suppose D.W. was jealous, maybe?"

"Clarence says they suspected D.W. has hit her before. But she wouldn't tell. Said she had a black eye and some bruises, but she made up some story about falling down steps. They knew it wasn't true, but couldn't prove otherwise."

"Boy, I found out someone did that to someone I knew I'd shoot them myself," Melissa says and bangs her fist on the table.

"You, young lady," her mother says while lifting her arms out at angles and putting curled fists on her hips, "would do no such thing." She stares at Melissa with squinted eyes. "You shouldn't even be talking about shooting someone, let alone thinking like that."

"Well, something needs to be done," Melissa emphasizes her point.

Her mother pushes her lips together in displeasure. Makes a low "uuummm" humming sound but has no retort. Sucking her breath in, she turns back to the stove.

"Hey, let's go look at that car." Roy takes a sip of coffee and then pushes his chair back. Melissa and Janice also push away from the table.

"Roy, you sure you got enough to eat?" his mother asks.

"Yeah, Mom, that was plenty for me. Got to watch my figure, you know." He reaches out with his finger to lightly poke her side.

She jumps. "Youuuuu . . . " She raises a shaking, wooden spoon in a false threat. Roy makes a dodging move to play along. The trio, laughing at his mother's playful gesture, continues through the kitchen onto the porch and then out the back door.

TWENTY SEVEN

More than a month has passed since Patsy's funeral and Dorothea has been planning, trying to carefully think through every step. Having to work and take care of the girls, there never seems to be enough time, but she's determined to take James Earl away from D.W. He is too sweet a boy to live out his life under the thumb of a hard bastard like D.W. Besides she owes it to Patsy. Nervous as she is, right now nothing matters more than making Patsy's dying wish come true.

At least she has Sue Ellen to buttress her. She wishes she could repay Sue Ellen in some way, for her kindness and her friendship. She always comes through when Dorothea needs her. Maybe, if she gets her five thousand dollars back, she can do something nice for Sue Ellen.

Sue Ellen has the radio on and neither she nor Dorothea has talked much during their ride toward Cuttsville. Remembering earlier conversations with Dorothea, Sue Ellen asks about Roy. "Have you seen him lately?"

"No." Dorothea tries to remember the last time she saw him. "I guess it was before Christmas, he came over," she says, scanning the passing landscape.

"Were you making out with him?" Sue Ellen asks jokingly.

Dorothea can't help but smile. "You are so crazy," she says, shaking her head to stress the silliness of the question.

"Nothing crazy about that, you being a nice-looking woman, him being an old friend."

"Sue Ellen, he's going to college," she says forthrightly, "he'll probably end up marrying a doctor's daughter or somebody like that."

Sue Ellen is sorry she brought up the subject. She quickly glances at Dorothea and then back at the road.

"That's why you better get back in college and finish up." Dorothea is somber, dispensing matter-of-fact advice.

"Going to college doesn't change who you are," Sue Ellen blurts out, challenging the idea that Dorothea has about the benefits of education.

"Well, it'll help you make your own way and get a good job." Dorothea looks at Sue Ellen. "You need to learn to take care of yourself, instead of letting others decide things for you. Look at me," she says in a calm-but-decisive manner, "my life's a holy mess and it's because of what other people have done to me. It's like it's my life, but other people have more control over what happens to me than I do."

Sue Ellen's sorry she let the statement rile her; maybe she was being defensive. "Yeah, you're probably right. It can't hurt."

Dorothea reaches over and rubs her hand across Sue Ellen's shoulder. "You're one of the sweetest people I know. I want you to have the best life you can."

Sue Ellen reaches up and touches Dorothea's hand. "And right back at you, young lady." She reflects on how strange it is that, just because events led them both to the same house, they've become such good friends. She's glad she has come along to help.

Dorothea feels the same way, especially now. She knew she couldn't pull this thing off by herself. "We're almost there," she says, to bring their focus back to the task at hand.

She told Sue Ellen part of her plan—enough to get her to help. Told her about D.W. taking her inheritance money and how she was meeting him at an out-of-the-way place at the lake. How she thought he would give her the money once she had James Earl. She didn't tell her about the pistol she wrapped in a cloth and secured up against her back with a wide elastic belt.

"You sure you're feeling okay about this?" Sue Ellen asks, worrying about what could go wrong. "You don't know what this son-of-a-bitch will do, you go there by yourself."

"I'll be okay." Dorothea flashes a calm smile to assure her. "As long as we have James Earl, he ain't gonna do nothing to me."

When they reach the corner of Sandy Bottom and Sorrows Road, Dorothea shows Sue Ellen where she should park and wait for her once they have picked up James Earl and Dorothea is dropped off at the meeting site. Driving to D.W.'s house, the sky is blank gray. There is no wind. The trees are still, nothing moves. It has rained nearly every day and it looks like more will come today. As they pull in the yard, James Earl is walking toward his house. He stops to look at the strange car.

Dorothea opens the door, glad that she didn't have to look for him. "Hey, James Earl, what you doin?"

"Dorothea? What you doin here?"

She puts her arm around James Earl's shoulder, surprised by how tall he is. He smells warm and earthy. "How'd you like to go visit your Aunt Evelyn in Florida?"

His squinting eyes and widened lips show confusion. "How I'm gonna do that? My pa won't let me go, will he?"

"I talked to him about it and he said it'd be okay." She cocks her head and playfully pushes against him. "So, lets get you some clothes and we'll get on our way." They walk to the house and go inside—so far so good. Dorothea rummages through his dresser drawers and closet quickly pulling out clothes and putting them in a box she found in the kitchen.

"Any special toys or games or anything you wanna take?" she asks.

"How long am I gonna be there?" He is dumbfounded by the suddenness of these plans; his face has a blank stare.

"Uh, don't know for sure." She grabs the pillow from his bed and puts it on top of the box. "For awhile, anyways."

"Can I take my knife?"

"Sure, take anything you want, just so it ain't too big."

They walk into the kitchen with Dorothea carrying the box.

"James Earl, can you take this box out?" She puts it in his arms and opens the door. "Ask Sue Ellen to put it in the trunk. Tell her I'll be out in a minute. And you and Sue Ellen wait for me in the car, okay?"

He turns back toward her. "Should I tell Grandma I'm leavin?"

"No. Not right now. Just wait for me to come out. I got to call someone and then I'll be right there."

"Okay." James Earl holds the box tightly, carefully descending the steps.

Dorothea walks to the phone. Looks around the room. It's the same as when Patsy was here. A feeling of solemnity overcomes her, she wants Patsy back, she wants the love and security that she knew when she was with her. Her eyes fill with cloudiness. She recalls those final days, Patsy dying slowly. Urgently, she turns back to the phone.

She calls the store and D.W. answers.

"I'm at your house, D.W.," she says in a now-stern voice.

"Who is this?"

"It's Dorothea. I'm packing James Earl's clothes. He's gonna be leaving."

"What the hell you talkin about?" His tone is tense, threatening.

"Patsy told me in the hospital, if she died, she didn't want James Earl living with a thieving bastard like you. So I promised her I'd see to it." Her voice is calm and firm, which irritates D.W. all the more.

He lowers his voice to a hiss, punching the words directly into the phone, "You stupid bitch, you ain't takin my son anywheres. If you're at my house you better get your ass outta there cause you're tresspassin on private property."

"Oh, I'm leaving and I'm taking James Earl with me. But I'll tell you what, I might make a deal with you."

"Damn you Dorothea, iffen this is a joke, it ain't funny."

"It ain't no joke D.W.," she says with unmistakable gravity. "No, I'm serious as hell, so you better listen. First of all, I'm taking James Earl fishing and if you wanna meet us, maybe we can work out a deal." She pauses. "You hear what I'm saying, D.W.? I'm leaving right now."

"Now wait, Dorothea," his voice changes its tenor, higher, less commanding. "Where you goin fishin? I'll meet y'all there."

Dorothea can hear the swagger in his voice even though he is trying to conceal it. She knows he plans to play along just long enough, just until he can get the upper hand. Her sudden realization of this fact sends a chill up the back of her neck.

"Well, I know where the fish are biting real good. Remember the spot, D.W.?" She quickly hangs up. She looks at a slightly curled picture of Patsy and James Earl lying on an end table. She picks it up, blows the dust off and tucks the picture into her pocket. As she reaches the door she takes one last look around. No turning back.

After Sue Ellen and James Earl drive away, Dorothea is left standing alone in the clammy weather, in the spot where she was raped. A distant memory, almost seven years now. She looks around trying to revisit the ordeal. It looks similar, but different; her remembrance is vague, clouded. No mistaking this is the place, though. She recalls the bite of the cold ground, the savagery ripping at her flesh, the brutish force that crushed her enthusiasm for life and the goodness of things. Stripped her of her innocent view of the world and the hopefulness that she naively believed was everlasting.

The dampness causes her to shiver. Maybe its fear, she tells herself. After not facing D.W. for so many years she's not sure what to expect. She runs her fingers through her hair, pushing it back.

She worries that he might not show, that somehow he will trick her again, that he'll sneak up behind her in a careless moment, that he'll send the sheriff out to get her or that he'll kill her on site. It chaffs her mind. Seems people always get the upper hand, finding ways to outsmart her. It's a constant uphill battle just trying to make it, always the aggravating doubts of "What is there I done wrong this time."

She almost hopes he won't show; it would be so much easier. Yet, her heart bristles with exhilaration. She forces her mind back to the plan—she knows everything is on the line because it has to be. There is no future until this is past her. There is no time beyond this time.

Her heart aches for her girls. But even if her life ends now, she knows she can never be a mother, never be any kind of person, if she can't see this through. She is where she has to be, doing what she has to do.

Dorothea walks slowly in a circle. She doesn't like being alone, with all the trees blocking the outside world from view. She has never felt so alone. The water in the lake is calm. The air so thick with moisture it is difficult to see far; the other side of the lake is a misty blur.

Even close by, the woods are hazy, hiding most details. Greenish-gray clumps of leaves dripping with dampness—thick brush and dark shadows all around. A soft, omnipresent hissing of rain or wind. No other sounds. No birds. No squirrels.

The sound of a car or truck on Sorrows Road makes her alert. The hum grows louder, and then fades. She realizes her heart is pounding in her chest. She opens her jacket and reaches behind to make certain the pistol is there. She grips the gun's smooth wood handle, pulls it at an angle—making it easier to reach, her thumb touches the cold, steel hammer. She thinks of Billy. His gun.

Another car? It seems to be getting dark, but that can't be. It was only four o'clock or so when they drove into the woods. The rain, no sun, that's all it is. She hears the humming of a motor. Now changing tones, slowing down. Silence. She waits. Again, she hears the hum, the screeching of branches on the side of a vehicle as it moves along the narrow path. Again, she reaches behind to touch the gun. She backs up slowly, taking position, readying herself.

She sees reflected flashes of light on the windshield. The truck comes into view. She plants her feet. In seconds the truck halts, the door swings wide. D.W. moves slowly, taking careful steps until he is standing ten yards from her.

"Where's James Earl?" he barks.

"He ain't here, I got him somewhere else."

"What the hell you mean, takin James Earl like that. Don't you know I ain't gonna take no shit offen a little bitch like you?" The bristly words come at her, hitting her skin like needles and pins. He takes a step forward. "I want him back now." His fists clench.

"Hold it right there," she hammers back, her left arm out, palm forward. Her right hand on the gun butt.

He stops.

"I didn't come here to be told what to do by you." Her voice iron cold. "I'm here to do you some tellin."

His teeth clench tighter, jaw muscles ripple. His lips force a cold smirk. "You dumb bitch. I don't know what kinda shit you think you're pullin." His eyes narrow, an amber glint, piercing with cat-like precision. "I'll make you wish you was never born." His body lifts, left foot steps forward.

Even though it is held tight against her back, she pulls the pistol from the belt with experienced ease. "I told you to hold it."

He freezes. Eyes jolt open, mouth gaping. "Wait, now wait here." His arms rise for protection. "Dorothea, what you got . . . Where'd you get that damn pistol?"

"I got a blank check here D.W. It's written out for five thousand dollars." She holds the gun steady, pointed at his chest. "I need you to sign it, so I can get back my five thousand dollars you stole." She pulls the folded check from her pocket and holds it out.

"What the hell you talking about? I don't know nothin about no five thousand dollars."

"You're a lying piece of shit, D.W." She moves the pistol slightly with an up and down motion. "You stole the money that my father gave to me in his will. You're a dirty, thieving sonufabitch, D.W.," she spits the words at him, "and I aim to make you pay." She rocks side to side in anticipation, anxious and tense.

He recovers from the initial shock, from looking foolish, like a limping bird dragging its wings. "What the hell you gonna do, Dorothea, shoot me?" he asks with nervous flamboyance.

"You don't want to find out." Her tone firm. "I'm settin this here check down and a pen. You best sign the check, D.W." She lets the piece of paper drop from her hand and reaches in her pocket for the pen. She bends at the knees, her eyes on D.W., and lays the pen by the check.

Dorothea backs up several steps. "I want my money that you took."

"Girl, you ain't shootin nothin." He stands straight, hard and bold, arms to the side in a show of cavalier confidence. "I can be on you quick as stink on shit; ram that gun up your ass un blow your stupid brains out." He grins, attempting to show his wittiness, emboldened by the feeling that he is invincible to her threats.

She puts her left hand up to steady her right. Just the way Billy showed her. "Any shootin to be done, D.W., I reckon I'll be doing it." Her thumb pulls the hammer back in one steady motion. "I'm givin you this . . ."

Quick step, he lunges through the air. She steps back and sideways, straining every muscle in her body, arms like taut wires. Lips slashing back as her finger squeezes.

Crack! She falls back, scrambling, she sees D.W. darting for his truck. **Crack!** She squeezes off another round. The sound resonates loudly in the opening, lifting up and out, echoing through the trees, dispersing, radiating farther and farther out over the water.

TWENTY EIGHT

Ezekiel wipes the dirt from his palms and fingers on the damp grass. **Crack!** The sound reverberates across the water. The hair on his neck bristles. That sound is rarely heard this time of year. **Crack!** He drops the tin can and fat, fleshy earthworms wiggle out of the black humus. He slinks toward his hut, stoops and squats just inside the doorway.

Hunting season, when white men come to the woods with guns, is at the time when cold weather moves into the woods to stay. Why are there shots now? This is the time of new leaves. The shots are coming from across the lake, the same place he once saw a white man doing bad things to the dark-haired girl, the one who came with Reuben, the one who wants to know about quicksand.

Ezekiel feels his arms shaking; the muscles across his chest and his back vibrate with electricity. He cannot feel safe in these woods during hunting season. He can climb trees and he has secret hiding places, but the fear is overwhelming. Several days he stays with Reuben and Aunt Esther. He doesn't want to, but he has to escape. He feels violated with each shot, sometimes several shots come rapidly and he lays prostrate in the corner, shivering, his sleeping blanket pulled over his head to muffle the bursting air.

He cannot forget about the dark-haired girl trying to get away from the bad man. How he threw her to the ground and did mean things to her; would not let her go. Ezekiel remembers and understands her helplessness. She cried hard and he wanted to do something, but was paralyzed. This was a very sad time for him. He could not understand the man hurting the young girl, water from her eyes wetting her face, her body shaking with fear like a snared rabbit.

He knew he could do nothing to a white man. He would be shot and his body dumped in the lake for the fish to eat, unless an alligator got there first.

If there are no more shots, he will sneak away to Aunt Esther's for the night. He waits. He trusts Rueben and Aunt Esther, they are good to him. But he is weary of anyone else. People, whether they are dark like him or white people, can be cruel. Even their children throw rocks at him and his bicycle. Why would they do this? He has never done them any harm.

His body, although tense, is no longer twitching. He stays alert. Always alert. Ears practiced at knowing the sounds of the woods. Even the snakes and alligators cannot be trusted. His hand clamped tightly to the post, his body feeling frail and weak. Water comes to his eyes, it runs down his dark leather-hard skin, snagging on scattered salt-and-pepper whiskers. He can never help anyone. He would like to get rid of the bad people, but he can only hide.

At times, alone and remembering, he sees himself in his head striking bad people with a hard stick, hurting them, making them sorry for being bad. He does this with water moccasins when they come too close, whacking them with a stick, watching them thrash about as he swings down again and again. Battered and bloody, they twitch in the grass, their mouths wide with white cotton inside. He uses the end of the stick to sling them toward the water.

The expansive gray sky grows darker. Yellow-green, spring leaves wave up and down with wafting winds and the hiss of drizzling rain can be heard touching down. The exploding sound no longer lingers in the open spaces. But Ezekiel knows the stillness can be shattered any second. His quick eyes move from tree to shadow, ground to sky, alert to any movement, waiting.

He trusts the trees. He trusts the weeds and brush. He trusts the ground and lays on it to hear its secret sounds. The woods protect him from bad people. Out here he has everything he needs, water, roots, fish, everything in its place. But in town things are always changing and the people are all strangers. He can never know what they will do, whether they will treat him badly or not.

Ezekiel reaches into the corner of his shanty where his denim jacket hangs limply from a wooden stob. The sky has been overcast most of the day. The lake is up higher; he knows to expect rain nearly every day. Although there are new leaves and wild flowers, the weather can easily turn colder, as well. It's the time of year when it can be blazing hot one day and just a few days later bitter cold.

Bent low, he moves toward his bicycle hidden in the brush and tied to a tree. He will ease out to the road, pushing his bicycle and staying to the side, cautious and alert for any sounds, any movements. If he sees anything or hears anything he will slip back into the woods to find a place to hide and lay still.

He hopes the shooting has stopped. However, if rain comes, it could bring thunder and lightening, which is nearly as frightening. He has to be vigilant, prepared to react. Once he gets past the lake, he can jump on his bicycle and ride fast until he reaches Reuben's house.

As he reaches the road, rain is falling lightly. The sky fades with darkness. No moon can be seen; there is not much light left. He knows he will have to move more slowly, allowing his eyes to adjust. He crouches, his back bowed, the bicycle seat rubbing against his ribcage. Lean and sinewy, his agility is a natural result of his living in the woods.

He guides the bicycle with both hands in the middle of the handlebars—very aware of the ringing bell near the right grip. He doesn't want his hand to slip up against it, accidentally making the shrill pinging sound. His eyes are focused just above the handlebars and the bicycle is as close to the edge of the ditch as he can get it. He feels his shoes slipping on the already-wet ground, but knows the ditch is the safest place for him to be.

He stops. Leans the bicycle against the side and takes his jacket out of the wire basket. The darkness and rain give him a chill.

As Ezekiel nears the other side of the lake, not far from where the evil man made the girl cry hard, he hears the low hum of a car. He eases into the high grass, bends his knees and lays the bicycle down, stretching out beside it. He holds his head up so he can see the car's lights. Maybe these are the people shooting guns.

His neck hurts; he can see no lights. The car does not sound as though it is coming nearer. It seems to stop. He pushes up with his arms, but still no lights. This is puzzling. Maybe there is a secret thing happening that no one is supposed to know about. Then he hears the motor go louder and it moves away from him, the humming becoming dimmer.

He reaches out to his side hoping he can find a stick, something to use if he is attacked. His body wants to freeze solid with fright, but he must make it to Reuben's. He finds no stick, but he will keep looking. Along the edge of the road there are always good-sized limbs or pine knots that can be used as weapons.

TWENTY NINE

Dorothea carefully steps in the direction of D.W.'s truck. Pistol held straight ahead, left hand acting as a brace under the right, tense as she nears the rear of the new truck. D.W. is not there. She notices a couple of small reddish splotches on the ground. Moving forward a few more steps, she sees drops of blood on green leaves.

Gun still pointed into the woods, she back-steps to the open door. Looks in, reaches with left hand and touches the dangling keys. She waits to see if there is any movement from the bushes. She will not attempt to follow, it's too risky.

Quickly, Dorothea gets into D.W.'s truck and starts it. She turns the steering wheel sharply, easing out on the clutch. Moving slowly, she follows the ruts heading toward Sorrows Road. Light rain and the dark sky make it difficult to see. Both doors locked, she watches to the side, halfway expecting D.W. to lunge at the truck. Gun tucked into her belt, the barrel still warm. Leaning forward, her chin is just above the steering wheel, her eyes darting back and forth.

She pauses at Sorrows Road. Decides to drive north to see if D.W. has made it this far. Mentally, she visualizes him lying on the road, she presses on the gas. When she comes to LaSalle, she makes a left to go by his house. She knows he couldn't make it this far yet, but she can't just leave. If he survives, what will he do to her now?

As she passes by his house, there is no light. A dim light is on at Granny's. She continues out LaSalle. It is now almost totally dark, but she decides not to turn the lights on. If she sees a car coming, she'll pull off to the side.

She stops at an open field. It seems to be safe enough to back in and turn around, although it's impossible to see much. As she backs in, she lets the truck idle in neutral to catch her breath. Blood pulses through her body, tingling every fiber, like a rush of tiny, tumbling pins. She breathes deeply, her heart still thumping loudly.

She goes back the other way to pass his house once again. No light. She turns south on Sorrows Road to continue looking. Mac told her a new truck can cost more than two thousand dollars. A lot of money. Her money that D.W. used to buy this damn truck. So it's her truck, but she sure as hell can't keep it.

No sign of D.W. anywhere. Driving slowly, she stays close to the edge.

She crosses the bridge at West Fork Creek, knowing that just beyond is the elusive path that leads into the woods to Ezekiel's hut. Luckily, she has not seen another car or truck on the road. Not a good night to be out; the rain falls steadily.

The wipers swing back and forth with a monotonous swish, thud, swish, thud. She rolls the window down so she can see better. The air is frigid. Wet drops pelt the side of her face and shoulder. Her hands grip the steering wheel tightly, her arms shaking.

Pressing her foot down on the clutch, the truck moves slower, rolling quietly. She doesn't want to pass the spot and have to back up. She's desperate to get off the road as soon as possible. She feels as though she is riding with a load of dynamite that could explode at any minute. Dorothea lets out on the clutch briefly to pick up speed. The fence posts stop. This is it. She presses the brakes, but realizing that the red glow of the taillights can probably be seen for miles, she quickly removes her foot. Turns the steering wheel hard left, the truck heads for the ditch and, if it's the right place, the path. She lets out on the clutch and gives it gas, plowing through high grass. She can't see. The trees block out any light. She pulls the knob and the lights shine ahead. All she can do is dodge the trees and hope somewhere in here she will eventually see the opening with Ezekiel's makeshift hut.

Having been out here only twice, neither time at night, she can only guess at the distance to the hut and then beyond to the quicksand. The truck jolts hard with each dip. No time to be timid. She has conditioned herself, deciding she would do it, deciding she would not back down, deciding even if it meant sacrificing her own life it was a risk she had to take. She vowed not to allow herself to think about her daughters, her only weakness, the only thing that could break her stone-hard determination.

The night is black with loneliness. Cold, wet and trembling, her daughters faces drift into her consciousness and her lips quiver.

She had plenty of time to reflect on her actions and firmly believes what she is doing is right with Jesus. Her wrong is justified by ridding the world of an evil, an evil that has deeply hurt people and would go on hurting others unless stopped. She also believes, right or wrong, she had to even the score for Patsy.

So far she has kept her focus. Her body shakes with tension and cold. She's worn and tired, but she tells herself soon she'll be able to rest like she hasn't rested in years. One way or another, when it's over, she will rest.

The truck jostles from side to side. She grips the steering wheel to keep from banging against the door or losing control. There's an opening; she quickly presses down the clutch and pushes the knob in to turn off the lights. She allows the truck to roll toward Ezekiel's shanty.

The truck stops just past the hut and rolls back slightly. She sits looking through the blurred windshield, trying to remember exactly which direction and how far. The drumming of hard rain on the truck is hypnotic. Her stomach is taut; she feels her heart beating harder. Ahead, nothing is clear; she can only guess. She wants to scream, "Help me." Her jaw quivers. Teeth clinched, she exhales with force through her nose.

She lets out on the clutch; the truck lurches forward and stops. "Damn," she says in anger. She turns the key and the truck starts. Giving it more gas, she eases forward. Desperately she tries to see what is ahead, but it is only a dim mass of darkness, a blur, nothing distinct. Keeping her foot on the gas, she sticks her arm and head out the side window; things seem clearer. She keeps moving, turning the steering wheel one way then the other, trying to feel her way to the edge of the quicksand.

The truck comes to a sudden stop. She pulls her head inside. Her foot is on the gas, she presses harder. It doesn't move; she hears the whizzing of the back wheels spinning. Is it quicksand or is she just stuck in wet ground? The engine dies. She opens the door and puts her left foot on the running board, pulls herself up holding onto the doorframe. The rain slows and there is a dim moon glow sprayed across the sky. She looks down, but knows it would be unsafe to step down. A shiver of fright chills her skin as she feels the truck sinking.

She looks quickly—the windows should be down to help it sink. Her knee on the seat, she reaches across to the passenger side to roll that window down. Pulling back, her jacket catches on the gearshift. She panics, twists her torso, but cannot free herself. Beads of sweat pop out on her forehead, alarmed that she may be doomed to suffocating at the bottom of a quicksand pit. She jerks hard, but is still caught. Reaching around with her hand, she pulls on the jacket. Moves forward and continues pulling, nearly hysterical, barely able to maintain use of her shaking hands. Suddenly the jacket releases and she falls forward. Her hip hits the horn and the sound blurts out like a foghorn echoing off the ocean. She is stunned. "Oh my God!" She is sure the sound can be heard for miles. She straightens up, little stamina left, her arms achingly tired.

Dorothea steps on the running board again; this time her foot feels wetness. She holds onto the doorframe with her left hand and, with her right, reaches for the rim of the truck bed. The foot on the running board is trapped in sludge; she feels the muck oozing up over her ankle. She pulls with her arms, holding onto the truck bed while pushing with her free leg against the floorboard. Her foot comes loose with a sucking sound, but her shoe is lost.

"Damn," she groans. She puts her wet foot beside her other foot. She can see that the truck is sinking. It is definitely quicksand or some type of muck that is swallowing the truck. Holding hard with her hands, she swings her dry foot over the edge of the truck bed. She reaches for the edge of the rear window; there is only a slight ledge that her fingers can pull against. They slip and she falls backwards into the door. She grabs with her left hand and stops her fall. Her leg aches from sliding over the truck bed's rim. She pulls herself up again, groaning, almost exhausted. She reaches for the window ledge and pushes her leg into the truck bed. Straining, she pulls her whole body up and into the back of the truck.

The truck stops sinking; she can feel it is stationary. She worries that she did not reach the quicksand; that the truck will stay here, partially sunken but visible. Maybe it will suddenly drop. She has to get off, there is nothing left for her to do. It's out of her control.

Knees bent, she holds her arms out like wings, fingers splayed and stiff, ready to grab the side of the truck bed if there is a sudden shift. She carefully slides her feet toward the tailgate; looks out, trying to determine where the quicksand or muck ends. There are no trees or bushes near to define safe ground. With only the palest light from the moon, she can't tell if there is any grass or weeds near.

She reaches to the front for the tailgate, locks her fingers over the smooth metal to brace her body. Lifts her shoed foot over the tailgate and lowers herself while her foot searches for the bumper. With her foot planted on the bumper, she lifts and lowers her other leg, turns and hangs knotted against the tailgate. Both hands holding desperately. Not taking time to think, she releases her grip, swings her arms to the front and uses her legs to spring forward, lunging with every ounce of energy she can muster. The thrust gives her more force than she was expecting. Her arms stretching forward, she lands face down into wet, cold slime, grabbing blindly for anything that is near. She realizes her body is not sinking. Surprised, she quickly draws her knees up under her and stands.

She runs forward, feeling pains in her stomach and legs. Her foot with no shoe feels cold and numb. Turning she watches the truck bed fill as it slides lower. As the window openings slowly sink, she hears a gush of bubbling, sucking air—the steel carriage sinking with a woeful groan, like some massive animal dying. It continues downward until just the cab roof sits like a submarine hatch on the surface. As she stares, she can't be sure if the cab has disappeared or if it is level with the surface.

Realizing that the gun has fallen out of her belt, she panics. She looks around and then drops on hands and knees to search. Her hand hits the hard metal; she picks it up and wipes her hand and the gun against her jacket. Her index finger curled around the trigger, she levels the gun to the front.

She walks toward Ezekiel's heap of tin and boards hoping he is not there, hoping he won't confront her. Looking for the shadowy figure to emerge—not sure what to expect, she walks past the hut. She sees nothing. Haggard and limping, she moves into the dark woods, stiff against the rain, chilled to the core of her body.

At Sorrows Road, she looks both ways. Overweary, dragging her feet step-by-step, she trudges through water and mud, unsure of the distance. Head hanging down, she strives to maintain an even pace. Sue Ellen should be parked at the corner, where Sandy Bottom meets with Sorrows Road.

It seems this long, grueling night will never end. She strains to see Sue Ellen's car, the rain clouding her eyes. Finally, an outline. She puts the pistol under her jacket and with both hands manages to secure the cold metal against her back.

Light rain continues falling. The car's windows are foggy and dark. Dorothea reaches for the door handle, abruptly stops, wondering if D.W. could have made it this far. She pulls to see Sue Ellen jump awake as the door opens. "You okay?" Sue Ellen asks with wide eyes.

Dorothea sees the form of James Earl's body curled across the back seat. She sits on the seat-edge, uses her bare foot to push off the remaining shoe and then places both feet on the floor mat. She lays her head back with a low moaning sound and mutters, "Thank you, Lord Jesus."

Sue Ellen's eyes stay focused on Dorothea. She can tell that she is exhausted and thoroughly soaked; her wet hair hangs like black plastic, her soggy jacket is molded to her torso.

"I think there's a blanket in the trunk," Sue Ellen says as she opens her door. After retrieving a blanket from the trunk, Sue Ellen opens the door on the passenger side of the car and drapes a dry, musty-smelling blanket over Dorothea. Carefully, she closes the door, pushes the trunk down slowly, hoping not to disturb James Earl and then gets back in the driver's seat.

"How's that?" Sue Ellen asks.

"Good. Feels good," Dorothea answers. Her left hand reaches over and touches Sue Ellen's arm. Water droplets or tears run down the sides of her face.

THIRTY

"How did it go?" Sue Ellen utters the words in hushed tones, a timid searching, even though she is eager to learn the results.

"It's done." Dorothea barely parts her lips, letting the words slip out.

Sue Ellen turns the key and the low hum of the motor is followed by the steady whirring of air from the defroster fan. She can see that Dorothea is totally exhausted; can't imagine what she has been through. Sue Ellen reaches for the dials, turning the temperature knob to a warmer setting.

Dorothea sits upright and turns to look behind her. She looks at James Earl, a large towel draped over him. Her hand grasps the top of the seat so she can get a better look at the boy sleeping.

"Fell asleep soon as it got dark. I think the rain tapping on the car may have helped some," Sue Ellen explains, "besides, I'm not that interesting." Big grin.

Dorothea turns back to the front, puts both hands up to cup her face and holds them there, over her eyes. Her fingertips move from the middle of her forehead to the sides, rubbing against the skin. Her hands move back and forth as her fingers continue massaging.

Sorrows Road

"Ready to head back?" Sue Ellen asks. She looks closely at the windshield, trying to gauge the effectiveness of the defroster. She wipes the back of her hand across the glass.

"I wonder if you'd mind going down Sorrows Road?" Dorothea asks. "It's a little farther that way, but the road might be better."

"Heck no, you know your way around these parts better'n me. Just go to the right here?"

"Yeah, take it kinda slow, I want to see if I can see anything."

Sue Ellen looks at her, momentarily, wondering what she wants to see. Dorothea is looking the other way, wiping the edge of the blanket back and forth across the window.

"You think somebody would be out there on a night like this?"

Dorothea doesn't answer; just keeps looking out the window.

After driving over here and waiting in the rain for a couple of hours, Sue Ellen is eager to talk, itching to know what happened.

"You talk to D.W. about the money?"

"Yeah, of course I did."

"And did you get it?"

"No." Dorothea's voice is almost too quiet to hear, with the windshield wipers flipping back and forth.

Sue Ellen looks at her again. She is driving slowly, cautiously. The road is straight, her only concern is an occasional mud puddle on the road. The rain has washed away some of the dirt, making the road bumpier than it was earlier in the day.

"No, I didn't get my money," Dorothea says in an even, relaxed voice, "but just the same, we came to an understanding."

Sue Ellen thinks about it for a minute. "What kind of understanding?"

"Well, he knows what he's done wrong," she hesitates, "and, and he agreed to make it right." Dorothea sits up, tugging at the blanket, pulling it back up around her shoulders.

Sue Ellen looks straight ahead, but notices the agitation.

Dorothea peers out the window again, into the darkness.

"Are we close to that road where you met him, yet?"

"Yeah, it's just up here," Dorothea replies without turning away from the window.

The rain seems to have ended. Sue Ellen, tired of the wipers slapping side to side, turns them off. Presses in the chrome lighter and pulls a pack of cigarettes off the dashboard. Jerking her hand, she coaxes a cigarette out of the pack and curls her lips over the filter tip. With the popping sound of the lighter, she reaches down, brings the orange glow to the end of her cigarette. Putting the lighter back, a feathery cloud of white smoke leaves her lips. Her left hand rolls the window down an inch and the trail of smoke bends and flows toward the opening.

"When you get down here where the street cuts off, go left. I want to drive by D.W.'s house again."

"You do? What . . . " Her voice halts abruptly. Sue Ellen starts to move her head toward Dorothea, but stops short. Puts the cigarette to her lips.

Since the rain stopped, crickets and frogs have elevated their chirping and croaking, creating a prickling chatter that vibrates in the heavy air—a continuous, penetrating static.

"This it?"

"Yeah, stay slow, but don't stop. Just keep moving."

At a distance, Dorothea can tell there is still no light at D.W.'s house. As they get nearer to the opening, she looks to see if the light is still on at Granny's.

"Who in the world?" Dorothea quickly rolls her window down.

"What? Who do you see?"

Dorothea swings her head sideways, toward Sue Ellen. "Keep going," she says, swinging her head back the other way.

Sue Ellen looks out the window on Dorothea's side and sees a car parked in the bushes, just off the road. "What is it?" she asks quietly, aware that James Earl has moved.

"That car parked there, by D.W.'s. Couldn't tell much about it, but I ain't ever seen it before."

"You don't know whose it could be?"

"Ain't got the slightest idea." Dorothea's voice shakes; she rolls the window up and sits with her mouth hanging slightly open. "Had a white top. Couldn't tell what kinda car it was."

"Looked like an older Ford," Sue Ellen says.

Sue Ellen keeps glancing at Dorothea and back at the road.

"Didn't you say he has a girlfriend? Could it be her car?"

"Don't know," Dorothea says, "could be. I think there was someone sitting in the car. Too damned dark to know for sure." She turns in her seat to look behind, wondering if the car will follow them.

"What do you think they might be doing?" Sue Ellen takes a quick glance at Dorothea. "Could it be something about us taking James Earl?" Her whispering voice has an anxious edginess.

"Damn," Dorothea throws the word out with her breath, as though they might have struck a tree in the middle of the road. She heaves heavily, nervously. "Go on a ways up and I'll show you where to turn around." Dorothea turns again to look through the back window.

Sue Ellen watches the road as far as the lights allow, in every other direction there is only blackness. Occasionally, tall trees near the road's edge are faintly etched into the misty darkness by the car's glowing beams of light.

"At least they ain't following us," Dorothea says.

Sue Ellen looks side to side, half-expecting something in the dark night to jump out. She has no idea where she is or what kind of danger they might be involved in.

Dorothea waits until they go around a bend in the road, a fair distance away from D.W.'s. "I think we've gone far enough. Stop here."

The brake lights glow as Sue Ellen stops.

"Okay, let me look." Dorothea rolls the window down again and stretches to see the road's edge. "Yeah, go ahead and back up. Take it easy though."

Dorothea lifts herself off the seat to get a better view. Turning her head, she calls, "Whoa. Don't go any farther." She slides back into her seat.

"That's good, I can make the turn. How's James Earl doing?"

Dorothea is thankful that the car rides more smoothly than Mac's truck. She looks over her shoulder. "Still asleep, thank goodness. He's sleeping good."

Sue Ellen drives at a slow, even pace. If there is someone in the car, he or she would have seen them go by. Now that they are passing again, surely it will look suspicious. She wonders what to expect.

As they approach the area of D.W.'s house, Sue Ellen rolls her window down and she and Dorothea both scan the area. The car is nowhere to be seen. Sue Ellen takes her foot off the gas.

"Pull over a minute," Dorothea taps her on the arm. "Turn the lights out."

"What are we gonna do?" Sue Ellen asks.

"Just sit here a minute, see if we see anything," Dorothea says as she rolls her window down half way. "Car was here, now it's gone. Wonder who it was." She continues looking all around.

Sue Ellen's head turns quickly, one direction then another.

Turning toward Sue Ellen, Dorothea shakes her head side to side. "Reckon we might as well go on."

Sue Ellen pulls the car out into the road. At Sorrows Road she turns left, and then after a short distance, she turns right onto the paved road toward Cuttsville. As she picks up speed, the tires sling mud against the fender panels, sounding like prattling thumps from a machine gun.

After a mile or so, the rain returns, light and persistent. Sue Ellen slows down.

Dorothea grabs Sue Ellen's shoulder. "Turn your lights off," she commands in a loud whisper. "Pull off the edge."

Frightened, Sue Ellen pushes in the knob, cutting the lights off.

"No brakes!" Dorothea squeezes her shoulder.

Sue Ellen lets the car slow on its own. No other cars on the highway. When she looks ahead, she sees what Dorothea sees: bouncing lights emerging from the woods. Sue Ellen eases the car to the edge of the road, cautiously testing the firmness of the berm. Gradually, it rolls gently to a stop. The lights in the woods, coming perpendicular to the highway, continue bouncing up and down, flickering through the trees.

Dorothea and Sue Ellen sit quietly. The lights are getting closer to the edge of the woods.

"Scrunch down so they can't see anyone in the car," Dorothea says. They both peer over the dashboard, watching.

The lights suddenly spring out of the woods, slicing though the rain. The car stops.

"Whoever it is," Dorothea whispers, "that's another road goes down to Paradise Lake. Must be looking at the car."

"Shit, what do we do if he comes toward us?"

"Start the car and take off outta here." Dorothea hears herself breathing rapidly.

"I hope I'm able to do it," Sue Ellen's voice modulates with fear. "It looks to me like there might be two men in the car."

"I can see the driver still looking this a way."

The lights move slowly forward. As the car reaches the highway, it turns right and charges forward, fishtailing on the slippery road.

"He's going like a bat outta hell," Sue Ellen says, as she pushes up in the seat. "Same damn car—a 56 Ford. Any idea who it is?"

"No. Don't know who it could be." Dorothea folds her arms across her chest, her eyes fixed on the taillights of the stranger's car, growing smaller and fading.

"I guess it could be a coincidence," Sue Ellen says.

"Yeah, maybe." Dorothea changes her mind almost immediately, thinking about the car being at D.W.'s house and now the same car coming out of the woods. She knows there must be some connection.

Sue Ellen pulls the Mustang back onto the road, pulls the knob and the lights snap on. She stares out at the road swashed with foggy white light. "You call that Sorrows Road back there?"

Dorothea turns her head in Sue Ellen's direction at the question. "Yeah. What makes you ask that?"

"Sorrow, like sad or crying-type sorrow?"

"Sorrows, with an s on the end."

"Why's it called that?"

"What made you think about that?"

"Just curious." She takes a quick glance at Dorothea. "It's unusual."

"Well, Miss college girl, durn if you didn't ask me something I know about." Dorothea smiles, her exhaustion has dissipated, the rush of seeing the strange car at the end of an unnerving day has left her wide awake, even jittery, the way she gets with too much coffee. "Least ways I think I know the answer, because a schoolteacher was talking about it one day when we were having recess. That's one thing I've never forgotten."

"So where does it come from?"

"Well, this teacher said . . . Well you don't know about it, but if we'd gone straight across on Sorrows Road, out a couple of miles, there's a place used to be Sauers Mill. Ole man Sauers had this grist mill out there where he used to grind corn and he sold it all around. I reckon like grits and corn meal and such. This was back in the 1930s or 40s, and he was an important person round these parts. Well he had lots of colored folks working for him. And from what this teacher said he treated em bad, beatin em, and probably even shot a few, is what she said.

"But no one was ever able to prove he did anything. Mostly, I think people didn't try hard to find out what was goin on. But this teacher . . . I know now, her name was Mrs. Padgett." Dorothea languishes on this childhood memory. "I liked her; she was a nice teacher. Anyway, Mrs. Padgett said they even sent some state lawmen in there to see what was taking place. People knew what kind of man Sauers was and nobody liked him. But anyway, that road was called Sauers Road cause it went to Sauers Mill. I don't know how long it was like that.

"But then at some time it just got so bad that these coloreds rose up and hung ole man Sauers. And people went out there and Mrs. Padgett said Sauers was hanging in a tree and there was eight or nine colored men shot to death and a couple of white men that worked for Sauers was strangled or beat to death. And then after that, she said they found graves and I don't think she knew just how many people was killed out there."

"Damn, sounds like a bloody war."

"Reckon it was. Lots of young people don't know about it anymore. It's kind of an old story now. But old folks knew it put a bad taint on the whole area. Mrs. Padgett said after that nobody wanted to call it Sauers Road no more, and people started calling it Sorrows Road because of the things that happen there." She pauses, pondering the gravity of it. "And it's been that way ever since."

"Wow, that's something," Sue Ellen interjects.

"I went out there once with a friend. Betsy was her name. Her boyfriend drove us out. There wasn't much there anymore, just some piles of old wood where the buildings fell down. A few small mounds grown over with weeds. Maybe they were sawdust piles."

"Sounds like an eerie place."

"It was kinda spooky. We just stayed on the side of the road. I wouldn't walk out in that field for nothing."

"Can't say I blame you."

"After that, Betsy and me weren't friends anymore."

"Really, why not?"

"She thought her boyfriend was paying too much attention to me, I think. I believe she was aggravated about that."

"You seem to attract men to you, Dorothea."

"Yeah," she smiles, "just never the right kind."

"Well, you're not alone in that department." They both laugh.

Gazing into the darkness outside, Dorothea thinks about Sauers Mill and the quickness of dying, how easy a life can end. Now there's only a partly remembered story hanging on by a thin thread, soon it'll be gone. In the distance a faint glow indicates Cuttsville's presence.

"You didn't tell me much about your meeting with D.W. What did he say about James Earl?"

Slumping in the seat, Dorothea can feel the pressing hardness of the gun. She sits up, leans against the door. "I made him see it was for the best. It's what Patsy wanted and he knows it. He wasn't happy about it, but he came around just the same."

"Damn." Sue Ellen glances sideways. "I can't believe he didn't raise hell with you."

"Well, he did at first, but I got him to change his mind. It wasn't as hard as I thought it would be."

Sue Ellen pushes in the lighter and reaches for her cigarettes on the dashboard.

The rain is a drizzle, the monotone hissing of the car's tires makes a restful song. Dorothea's damp clothes are uncomfortable, but at least it's warm inside the car. She thinks about Donna, Darlene, and about James Earl.

Still she remains edgy. Both the vision of D.W lunging at her and the loud bark of the pistol resound in her mind. Maybe tomorrow the rain will be gone. If the sun comes out, everything will look clearer and brighter. With a good night's sleep and a sunny day, she'll feel better able to handle whatever comes next.

THIRTY ONE

The phone rings, waking Roy. "Yeah, hello," his voice rasps into the mouthpiece.

"Are you asleep?" His sister's high-pitched voice tingles like a bell. "What did you do-o-o last night?"

"Ohh," he moans slowly, "you're too young. I can't tell you."

"We-e-l-l, sleepyhead, me and your mother are coming to Parksdale today."

"What for?"

"To go shopping. To do what we do best, just like you sleeping." She snickers at her cleverness.

Roy rolls his head on the pillow. He could easily lapse back into a deep sleep in seconds.

"Mom wants to know if you need any clothes. You can go shopping with us—won't that be fun?"

"Uummm, you're awfully cheerful this morning."

"I'm always cheerful." Her voice takes on a more serious tone, "Say, have you seen Dorothea lately?"

"No. Not for a month or two."

"Well, D.W. is gone. I wonder if she knows."

"Gone?" The fog in his head begins to clear.

"Yeah, they think he high-tailed it out of town because Clarice has never been found. Janice said the sheriff went to the store to ask D.W. some questions and his father said he hadn't seen him for a couple of days."

"Really?" Roy sits up on the edge of the bed. He runs his fingers through his hair, rubbing his scalp. "So they can't find him either?"

"Guess they haven't yet. Janice said she was worried that Clarence might have done something. One of his friends told her Clarence had asked a buddy to help him because he wanted to even the score with D.W."

"Was that before D.W. left town?"

"Yeah, about a week before. But, since D.W.'s boy and his truck are gone too, she doesn't think Clarence had anything to do with it."

"Boy, Cuttsville sure has its share of excitement."

"Yep, there's always something going on. Hey, are you going to go shopping with us or not?"

He scratches his head; his face displays a mild grimace. "Guess not this time. I need to take my car to the garage today." He hears her pass the message to their mother.

"Well, how about meeting us for something to eat, around four or five?"

He pauses to think about it. "Don't know if my car will be fixed by then. I was going to leave it and get a ride back to school. Where will you be?"

"How about that Johnny's place by Kmart? We know where it is; want to meet us there at four? I know I'll be hungry by then."

"Alright, if I can get my car by then I'll meet you there. But if you don't see me don't wait for me."

"Well, try to be there," she says.

Since they're coming over, he'll feel bad if he doesn't make an effort to see them. "Okay, I'll try."

The news makes him wonder about Dorothea. Is she still at the donut shop? Did she ever go to the sheriff or anyone to see if she could get her money back? He thinks about Henslowe; he seemed nice enough. Hard to believe he would lie about who came in with D.W. to get the money. He said she was blonde—must have been Clarice, sure as heck couldn't have been Dorothea.

Roy splashes water on his face, rinses out his mouth, dresses and leaves. He knows he should've gotten to the garage much earlier. He had new spark plugs put in at another shop and it still sputters. Not running right. He trusts Bob. You can tell the guy knows what he is talking about when it comes to cars.

When he arrives, the shop is busy.

"It could be the carburetor." Bob gives him a straight look. "It could take a while. I'll prob'ly need to keep it till Monday."

"Oh, Monday." Roy stuffs his hands in his pockets.

"Yeah, I got some others I got to get out today. I ain't sure I can even start on it today."

Sputtering like it does, it could quit running anytime, Roy thinks. He tilts his head back, hoping to find another answer.

"You might as well come back early Monday morning," Bob says, trying to be helpful. Tools bang on metal, something like a wrench bounces on the floor. A mechanic, sitting half way inside a car, is pumping the gas pedal, sending gray smoke into the air.

"Yeah, guess I'll do that," Roy says with disappointment.

Bob turns and moves quickly to the center of the garage.

Roy drives away, noting that for some reason the car performs better in the cool of the morning. Once it heats up the sputter seems to get worse.

He decides to stop at the donut shop. Maybe Dorothea will be there and, besides, he needs a cup of coffee and something to eat. He pulls into the crowded parking lot. As a Davis Plumbing truck pulls out he takes the empty space behind the building. Inside it is bustling. Why, he wonders, are so many people eating donuts at eleven o'clock. Isn't it too close to lunch to eat donuts? He moves toward an open stool at the counter, sits and thinks about himself eating donuts at eleven o'clock.

Roy watches as people pass back and forth to the back area where the donuts are cooking. Three or four women, but not Dorothea. He keeps looking. He noticed a young man at the cash register when he came in, so Mac's not here either. He waits, thinking about how good the coffee and donuts will taste.

"What'll yeh have?" the woman asks, laying a spoon and napkin on the counter.

"Coffee and two of the plain cake donuts," Roy replies. People are leaving; the place is thinning out. Roy decides to ask the waitress about Dorothea when she returns.

She sets the coffee and donuts on the counter with a clanky quickness.

"Miss, do you know Dorothea who works here?"

"Dorothea. She don't work here no more."

"Oh?" Roy's scrunched expression plies for more information.

"No. She left about a week ago. Her un Mac both is gone."

Roy's face relaxes, mouth widening as he takes in the message. The waitress spins away. Thoughts race through his head. Both Mac and Dorothea gone at the same time. What does this mean? Gone where?

He savors the first bite of the warm donut. The tartness of the hot coffee is a good complement. He stares at the glass cases and thinks about the first night he came in here and met Dorothea again. What a surprise. How down and destitute she looked in that poor fitting waitress apron and paper hat. Maybe she is on to something better. Maybe she found a way to get her money from D.W. and things are easier for her now.

He takes another bite of donut. It's Saturday morning, nothing urgent to do until four o'clock. Maybe he should drop by Dorothea's house? He has some reservations. What if Mac is there? Nevertheless, feeling some guilt, he is curious if she has heard about D.W. and whether she has made headway on reclaiming her money.

He finishes off the coffee and feels content that this will hold him until he meets with Melissa and his mother. He takes his ticket to the cash register and pulls his wallet out of his back pocket.

Outside, the sweet taste of donuts lingers in his mouth. The noonday sun has warmed the air. A few small cumulus clouds loom above, but otherwise the sky is clear. Inside, the car smells of heated upholstery. But he has learned not to leave windows down, too many showers popping up this time of the year.

Roy drives to Dorothea's house. The car stutters once, but keeps going. He pulls close to the curb, under the shade of a large, twisted oak. Looking around before opening the door, the neighborhood is quiet and peaceful.

As he walks up the sidewalk, it seems almost too quiet. The steps squeak under his weight. He knocks on the wood edge of the screen door. The loose door rattles against the doorframe. He glances along the porch from side to side, no sounds come from inside. Pulling the screen door open, he taps harder on the front door. A soft breeze sweeps across the porch and he hears the high-pitched squeal of a child off in the distance. He waits. No one answers. He continues to look in every direction and then steps away so the screen door can close. He doesn't want to give up, so he moves to the front window to take a quick look inside. Cupping his hands around his face to block out reflections, he peers inside. No furniture. His eyes move side to side, everything seems to be gone.

"Hello."

Startled at the sudden sound, Roy looks to the end of the porch.

"You looking for Dorothea?"

"Uh, yeah. You know where she is?"

"You're Roy, right?"

"Yes, I . . . Who are you?"

"I'm a friend of Dorothea's, live right above her." She motions up with her head. "My name's Sue Ellen." Her hair is light brown and frizzy, she offers a pleasant smile. She is wearing a large, slightly rumpled shirt that hangs to her thighs.

"Has Dorothea moved?"

"Yeah, she left a week ago. She left something for you. I wasn't sure how I would get it to you. You want to come up for a minute; I'll give it to you."

Roy walks toward her, watches her turn the corner. He wonders what it could be. Did he leave something behind the last time he was here? As he reaches the corner, she is walking up a stairway to the second floor. She has khaki shorts on under the shirt. He watches her hips sway. At the top of the stairs, he stands outside the open door.

She turns. "Come in if you like." She walks deeper into the interior, disappearing into another room.

Roy steps inside the doorway and turns to close the door, but then decides to only partly close it. He looks around the sparsely furnished room. He looks to see if there is any evidence of a husband or boyfriend. She comes back into the room walking toward him, the soft smile still in place.

"This is nice up here. You're up with the treetops."

"It is nice. This is a very quiet neighborhood." She holds her hand out with an envelope. "Dorothea left this for you."

He reaches out. The envelope is a little scuffed and wrinkled. On front 'ROY' is penciled in large printed letters. "Do you know where she has moved?" he asks, looking down at the white envelope.

"No. Not for sure. Go ahead and have a seat," she says pointing her arm in the direction of a straight-back chair. She moves sideways to a metal-frame chair with a blue plastic seat. "Said she was going to try to start out fresh in a new place."

Sue Ellen leans forward, her arms resting on top of her legs. She promised Dorothea not to tell anyone about Patsy's sister in Florida, and that her husband said he could get Mac a job there. Besides, she thinks it's unlikely that Roy wants to know all the details anyway.

"Said she just had to get away." Sue Ellen's face takes on a dreamy, far-away look. "Said she felt things were working against her here."

The smile is gone, her eyes cast down. "I'm gonna miss her and the girls. But I understand how it is. She's had a rough time, especially losing Patsy. That really hit her hard." She wraps her arms around the front of her waist. "Did you know about Patsy?"

"Yes. I heard she died. Dorothea told me how close they were." Roy focuses on Sue Ellen, trying to gauge what she is feeling about Dorothea.

"She said she would write to me as soon as she settles somewhere. I think she wants to keep her whereabouts secret; I think she worries about certain people, you know, people who could cause her problems."

Roy hears the dim patter of light rain falling softly on the leaves just beyond the door. There are also muted sounds of birds chirping, so he knows it can't be raining hard.

"But," Sue Ellen says, "she was feeling good about things when she left. She seemed real happy and hopeful about the future."

A faint smile makes her face pleasant. Roy feels very comfortable in her presence. She seems like a nice person, someone Dorothea could trust.

"You can open it if you want." She waves her hand at the envelope. Roy jerks his arm as though suddenly called into action.

She puts her hand forward again. "I mean, you don't have to." Her eyes widen apologetically.

"No. That's fine," Roy says, putting his finger under the back flap and pushing up. "Let's take a look." He has no idea how lengthy or what direction the message may take. He pulls the envelope apart at the top and reaches for the paper inside. At the same time, he thinks there is certainly no obligation to show it to Sue Ellen if he chooses not to. He sees that it is only one sheet from a lined writing tablet. Unfolding the page, Dorothea has printed only a few lines in pencil. He is surprised how short the note is.

> *I am leaven town with Mac. Don't tell no body. We want to start over somewhere else. Thanks for your kindnes. Good by*
>   *Dorothea*

Roy looks at the words carefully, wondering why she took the time to write him a goodbye note. He has the uncomfortable feeling that she has been much more gracious than he was. She was the one with problems and he didn't do much to help.

"Here." He holds the note out to Sue Ellen. "It's a note saying goodbye." His voice catches in his throat. He hopes his face is not flushed.

Sue Ellen holds the note tightly with both hands, reading through the lines. "Ahhh, that's sweet." She looks at him, a big smile, eyes glistening. "She really liked you. Mentioned your name several times, enough that I knew it was you when

I saw you downstairs. Said you all had been neighbors and played together as kids."

"Yeah." Roy smiles at the thought of their childhood days. "Well, I wish I could have done more to help her."

"I wouldn't worry too much about that. Dorothea's a wonderful person, but she's lived a lot of life in her 22 years. The things she's been through makes her tough as nails when she needs to be." Sue Ellen hands the note back.

Roy puts the paper back into the envelope. "Guess I better be going." He stands and holds out his hand. Sue Ellen responds. Her handshake is anything but vigorous. "It's been nice meeting you."

"You too, finally," her lips curve into a bigger smile. "I'm heading to work shortly or I'd offer you something to drink. If you want to come back some time, I can let you know if I hear anything from Dorothea."

"Yeah, I'll do that." He backs a few steps. "Bye." He smiles and turns to pass through the door.

Stepping outside, there is no sign of rain, just a pleasant stillness. So now he knows that Dorothea left with Mac. He hopes she will be happy. He feels good knowing that he did not create any unsolvable problems.

Roy holds onto the painted wood rail as he descends the steps, one step at a time. Doesn't seem he will ever learn what happened with D.W. and her money. Maybe she decided it was not worth the aggravation. Then again, that was a lot of money.

He takes a sidelong glance as he passes the front windows of Dorothea's apartment. Then he turns and walks down the creaking steps.

EPILOGUE

After several years, Roy does hear about Dorothea, in a roundabout way. He was on the phone with Melissa when she mentioned seeing Dorothea in town. Her grandmother Crawley had died and she came for the funeral. Melissa was in a new restaurant in town with a friend and somehow Dorothea found out who she was and came to her table. She introduced herself and asked Melissa if she was Roy's sister. So they chatted a few minutes.

Melissa said Dorothea asked about him; wanted to know how he was doing. She said to tell him 'Hello' for her. Melissa said she looked good and was nicely dressed.

Roy wondered if she made it through her ordeal with D.W. and got her money. But Melissa said if D.W. vanished, her money probably vanished with him.

A year after hearing about Dorothea and Mac leaving, Roy entered graduate school and later started dating a student from Columbia, South America. They lived together for two-and-a-half years and then she left to accept a teaching job in California. Roy has been teaching at the university in Parksdale for the past two years.

Roy has thought of Dorothea from time to time, especially when he drives by the donut shop or when he goes through downtown and is near the street where she lived. He hasn't forgotten her.

DOROTHEA AND MAC have lived in the same location since moving. They were married in June 1964 and live in a white, wood-frame house on a country road. Large live oak trees shade the back yard. Dorothea planted a magnolia tree in front the first year they lived there and it now stands twelve to fourteen feet tall. She delights in standing outside in the spring and breathing in the sweet smell of the magnolia blossoms.

Their house is about a half-mile from where Evelyn and Tom live. It is close enough that Dorothea often walks there rather than drive. Evelyn has been Dorothea's best friend ever since she and Mac arrived.

Tom got Mac a job working at the gas transmission station, which is part of a system that transports natural gas from Texas to Florida. Tom is a supervisor and often travels for the company.

James Earl continued to do well in school and then began attending college. He is a good student and has made the Dean's List twice. In less than two years he will graduate with a degree in engineering. Dorothea finds it a little unsettling that he is not called James Earl anymore, now it's just James. However, she knows that Patsy would be pleased and very proud of the son she loved so dearly.

Donna is pretty like her mother. She has lighter hair and is smaller in size, which Dorothea surmises is because of Billy's blondish hair and small build. She is the quieter of the two girls. Darlene is more outgoing and always busy with friends.

Dorothea and Mac also have two boys (Mac was at the hospital for both of their births). Jack was born the year after they left Parksdale. Dorothea named him after her father. Three years later she had her second son. She felt she and Mac had been together long enough that he would not be offended by her naming the boy Roy.

She thinks about Roy from time to time, usually when she sees a dark-haired man on television that in some way reminds her of him. She thinks about the time they kissed when she was in Parksdale. She daydreams briefly, but then she always reaches the same conclusion: It was never meant to be. She feels fortunate to be married to Mac. He has *helped her build a new life and he's a good and responsible father. Her love for him and her children continues to grow with every passing day.*

BACK IN CUTTSVILLE, nothing credible has ever come to light about the disappearance of Clarice . . . and no word about D.W. has ever surfaced.

3609559

Made in the USA